DRAGON'S REVENGE

DRAGON'S REVENGE

C.J. SHANE

Rope's End Publishing

Published by Rope's End Publishing
ISBNs:
978-0-9993874-4-3 paperback
978-0-9993874-7-4 hardcover
978-0-9993874-5-0 epub
978-0-9993874-6-7 mobi Kindle

Typesetting services by BOOKOW.COM

To my grandmother Albertina Césira Tomasone Arbrun who crossed the border at Ellis Island in 1912, and to all immigrants who seek a better life.

ACKNOWLEDGMENTS

Sincere thanks go to Diane C. Taylor (dianesfusedglass.com) for her excellent copyediting and proofreading, to Lynne East Itkin (lmeastdesign.com/) for excellent cover design; to Steve Passiouras at Bookow for making everything easier; and a special thanks to Dr. Tammy Euliano at https://teuliano.wordpress.com/ whose consultation transformed Dr. Ennis into a much better doctor.

Acknowledgment also goes to New Directions Publishing.

"Moonlit Night" By Tu Fu, translated by David Hinton, from THE SELECTED POEMS OF TU FU, copyright ©1988 by David Hinton. Reprinted by permission of New Directions Publishing Corp.

"A Farewell to a Southern Melody" by Huang O, translated by Kenneth Rexroth and Ling Chung, from WOMEN POETS OF CHINA, copyright ©1973 by Kenneth Rexroth and Ling Chung. Reprinted by permission of New Directions Publishing Corp.

CONTENTS

CHAPTER 1

Private investigator Letty Valdez had just unlocked her office door when her phone rang.

"Hi Letty, this is Seri."

"Seri! My favorite librarian! How are you?"

"Did you hear about the murder here at the Institute?"

"That was at the Institute? I saw a very brief news report this morning but it just said University of Arizona libraries," Letty responded. "One of your coworkers was found dead. Are you sure it was murder?"

"Yes, she was stabbed in the chest and lying in a pool of blood when we discovered her body. Her name is, *was* I mean, Stacey Frederick. The police set up a crime scene in the closed stacks of the Institute library, and they aren't letting much news out about this. They think they know who killed her. Her boyfriend. They questioned him not long after Stacey's body was found. He's on the run now. Stupid move on his part."

"Why are you calling me?"

"I just don't think that the boyfriend is the one who did this. Is there any chance you can come by the Institute this morning? I'd like to talk to you and share some info that the cops seem to be overlooking. You can consider this a potential job, too. I'll pay you for investigating this. I want this done right."

Letty would have offered to help out as a friend, but Seri knew her own mind. In fact, Seri had a reputation for being brilliant, a bit eccentric and someone who usually got her way. If Seri wanted to hire a private investigator, she would hire one. Nothing Letty might say would change that. The investigator might as well be Letty.

An image of Seri emerged in Letty's mind. Although they were about the same age – Seri was 31 to Letty's 29 – they were physical opposites. Letty was six feet tall, a Mexican American-Native American woman with dark brown eyes, rust brown skin and prominent cheekbones. A thick braid of black hair fell down her back. Seri was five feet one, blue-eyed with spiky blonde hair, and with what was typically referred to as "petite" features and bone structure. "Petite" was a word Seri despised so friends learned to never describe her that way. What Letty and Seri had in common was a high level of intelligence plus a love of solving mysteries. Their friend Jade sometimes teased them by calling them Sherlock and Mycroft.

"Inquiring minds," Seri liked to say. Seri was a professional librarian and the chief administrator of the new Sonoran Arts and Sciences Institute at the University of Arizona Library's Special Collections unit. Seri usually referred to it as "the Institute."

"Sure. I have to go downtown to the courthouse and serve some papers this morning. I'll come to your library after that. It will probably be early afternoon."

"Good." Seri ended the phone call abruptly. That was another thing about Seri. She was no-nonsense most of the time, and not much for social pleasantries.

There was nothing more to say to an ended phone conversation so Letty put the phone down and turned to her computer to start her work day.

***

Two hours later, Letty was standing near the entrance of the United States District Court on Congress Street in downtown Tucson. She found a place behind a large round pillar close to the entrance doors of the multi-story building. Not far away, she could see Jessica Cameron, the attorney with whom Letty often worked. Dressed in her regulation navy blue suit, white blouse, pearls, and heels, Jessica looked exactly like the high-powered attorney she was. Jessica made a slight waving gesture to Letty and smiled.

A black limousine pulled up at the corner. Two men dressed in dark suits got out first, looked around in every direction, then indicated to the man seated inside that it was safe to leave the limo. He was Tucson businessman Roy Lewis, a middle-aged man of average height and weight, with thinning dark hair. His eyes were hidden by dark sunglasses.

The man left the limo and began striding across the decorative concrete plaza toward the Courthouse steps. His two bodyguards were looking all around him, but failed to see Letty who was completely hidden now behind a thick concrete pillar near the glass main doors. Just as Lewis arrived at the short flight of steps that led to the entrance, Letty stepped from behind the pillar and pushed an envelope toward the man with the dark sunglasses.

"Mr. Lewis, consider yourself served with a subpoena to appear for a deposition in the case of Craig v. Lewis. If you have questions …"

Before she could get the final sentence out of her mouth, one of the bodyguards shoved his arm toward Letty with the intention of knocking her down. She sidestepped his attempt to push her by shifting her body sideways to the left. The bodyguard nearly lost his footing when his shove encountered only air. Letty took advantage of the opening. She thrust a big envelope with documents into the hands of Lewis. The man scowled at her with a look of fury on his face.

"You tell that bitch Cameron that she's got nothing on me," he growled. "And you better watch your back, Valdez. My boys will take care of you!"

Letty said nothing, just smiled. She stepped back as the three men pushed past her and made their way through the glass doors into the Courthouse. They disappeared inside.

Letty walked over to Jessica Cameron. "Lewis called you a bad name. He said you are a bitch," Letty smiled.

"I've been called worse," Jessica responded. "You are amazing, Letty. Six feet-tall and you somehow disappeared. They never saw you until too late. So now he's been served. Thank you so much."

"He threatened me with his goons."

"Well, let me know if they bother you. Or you can call your pal Zhou and he can beat them up." Jessica Cameron chuckled. She was referring to Zhou Liang Wei, a former Chinese Detective Inspector with whom Letty had worked on an earlier case, and who was now running a martial arts school in Tucson.

"Zhou is kind of tied up these days. He and his wife Jade are expecting their baby any minute now. If those boys bother me, I'll just have to use them as practice for all my new gong fu skills. I've been taking a class from Zhou. He says I'm his 'most advanced' student."

"Yeah, I heard he opened a school. And I'm not surprised you are his top student. Okay, call me in a few days. I'll have some more work for you."

Letty nodded, turned, and started the walk to her pickup which was parked across the street and down about a block. When she turned to wave goodbye, Jessica had disappeared.

***

Letty crossed the street. As she drew closer to her pickup, one of the thugs who had been guarding Roy Lewis lunged at her. Letty saw him just in time. She ran the rest of the way to her pickup and the man ran after her. She might have escaped but her pickup door was locked and that gave the thug time to catch up with her. Letty felt her heart pounding. The man was huge! She figured he was four or five inches taller than her and very muscular. He probably outweighed her by fifty pounds. She struggled with the key on the passenger side door.

The thug drew back his fist to hit her. She feinted to the side again and he missed her. But this time, his fist made contact with the frame of Letty's pickup. She heard a sickening thunk. He hit the frame around the passenger window so hard that a small dent appeared in the metal. The concussion shattered the door window.

The man pulled his fist back toward his body. Letty could see a fair amount of blood on his knuckles. His face and neck and even his shaven skull were now a deep red. He swung around toward Letty in a fury. Although Letty jumped away from him, his fist managed to make partial contact with her nose. She immediately felt blood dripping from a nostril.

The element of surprise was her only option now. Letty stretched out both her arms to the side, palms facing outward. She clapped her hands together then took a step forward. Her strange action confused the thug, and he hesitated. Letty's right leg went up in a rapid kick. It was a classic Zhèng Ti Tui move that she'd learned in Zhou's advanced gong fu class. Letty's right foot smashed into his jaw on the left side of his face. Before he could react, Letty took one step forward and kicked again, this time with her left leg and foot. Now the kick landed on his upper chest. The thug went down, stunned. He was on his knees. Letty jumped with both feet onto his knees which rested against the concrete. He groaned in pain. Letty knew he would be up again in a few seconds so she pulled away and looked for an escape route.

Across the street, she could hear Jessica calling, "Got him! Got him on video! He assaulted you! Definitely assault!"

Letty turned and could see Jessica jumping up and down in her heels, giggling and squealing. "Oops! Great! Oh, yippie! There's the cops."

She waved dramatically at a passing police car.

"Officer, officer! I just saw that man attack that woman. I have it all on video!"

By this time, the thug had risen to his feet and was gathering himself for another attack on Letty.

"Better not do that," Letty said quietly. The man hesitated again. He looked confused. "Look behind you."

Two cops were rapidly approaching them.

Sixty seconds later, the two cops had Lewis's bodyguard in handcuffs.

One police officer turned to Letty.

"What happened here?"

"I served some papers on his boss just a few minutes ago. I guess he decided to make an example of me. He sent this goon to beat me up."

"I have it all on video," Jessica said. She was at Letty's side now. She snapped a photo of Letty with the blood dripping from her nose. She handed Letty a tissue to wipe away the blood.

"Do you want to press charges?" the cop asked.

"I'm her attorney. Yes, we do. We'll get back to you on that. Meanwhile, I'd like to email you this video of the attack. It's a clear case of assault."

They exchanged contact information. The bodyguard was unceremoniously ushered into the back of the squad car.

"Damn," Letty said. "I'm so glad you were there. I don't know how long I could have held out. That guy was big!"

"Oh, I just wish your teacher had been here to see you. Well done, Letty!"

Letty smiled. The thug was lucky. He would have ended up in a lot worse shape if Zhou had been there. "Email the video. I'll show it to Zhou."

"Will do. Whew! Too much excitement!" Jessica paused. "Letty, I followed you because I had one more thing to talk to you about."

"Yeah? What's that?"

"There's this guy who has been talking to me. We met at a conference in connection with a client my firm is working for, and the guy asked me out. The first time I made an excuse and said I couldn't go. Now he's asked me again to go to dinner with him. I don't know why he's asking me out."

"Maybe because you are smart and successful and very pretty," Letty chuckled. "Maybe he just has good taste in women."

"Oh, whatever." She looked embarrassed. "I don't know him and none of my colleagues seem to know him either. I was wondering if you could do a background check on him. He's well-spoken and good-looking, too, but that doesn't mean he's a nice person."

"Is he an attorney? And does he have a relationship with any of your clients?"

"He told me that he had been an attorney in Seattle, but he changed careers several years ago and now he's an entrepreneur. He says he works in real estate. No, I don't know of any connections he has with our clients. His name is Bill West, and his company's name is West By Northwest, Inc."

"Okay. I'll check him out."

They parted for the second time. Letty drove away, wondering where she could get her passenger-side window replaced quickly and for a reasonable cost.

CHAPTER 2

LETTY found a reliable auto shop and dropped off her little pickup there. She took the city bus on Speedway Boulevard to the University of Arizona campus. The walk to the University's Main Library across the mall took about ten minutes. She entered the Special Collections Library, which was housed in a separate extension off the Main University Library. Instead of turning left and going into the Special Collections reading room, she ignored the elevator and climbed a short flight of stairs to the Sonoran Arts and Sciences Institute. She asked for Seri at the Institute's main desk.

Seri Durand appeared almost immediately and invited Letty back to her office, which was just off the public reading room of the Institute. The name plate on the door said, "Dr. Seri Durand, Director."

"Want anything? Coffee? Water?"

"No. Tell me what happened."

"Most of the staff, including me, arrived around eight a.m. yesterday morning. One of the other librarians, Amanda Flores, found Stacey. She was face up on the floor of the upper level of the Institute."

"What did you see?"

"Not much. Stacey was in a pool of blood. We could see what looked like stab wounds in her chest and maybe her stomach. I didn't see any weapon. We didn't touch her. It was obvious that she was dead and had been for a while. She was very pale. There was a lot of blood. I called the University police immediately. They came, and not long after, the Tucson police arrived, too."

"These rooms on both floors with all the books are off-limits to the public?"

"That's right. We call these rooms 'the stacks.' People can come into the main reading room which is public and sit at one of the tables to look at our documents, or they can use a study room or the conference room if they arrange for these in advance. They can come into the librarians' offices when invited. But only the library staff can go into the collection stacks. This level is large and mostly filled with shelving units for books, storage units for flat materials like maps, and storage units with drawers to hold smaller, unbound materials. We also have a smaller stacks area that's up one level on the third floor. That is where we keep the really rare materials. The stairs from this level to the third level are inside the stacks area. Both are off-limits to the public."

"People have to ask to look at library materials?"

"Right. They go to the desk in the reading room and give the librarian or library assistant a form with info about what they want to look at. Nothing can be taken out of the main reading room."

"Stacey was here before you opened?"

"Right. Stacey had been coming in early to make up for time she took off to take a class during regular office hours. She was working on a master's degree one course at a time. She was studying something in the business field. She was what we call a library assistant, not a professional librarian."

"Do you know how early she arrived?"

"In the past, Stacey typically arrived at 7:30 a.m. But it just so happens that she told one of the library pages that she was going to arrive at 7:00 a.m. and possibly even earlier. She said her boyfriend was giving her a ride."

"What do you know about the boyfriend?"

"Oh, he's kind of a dimwit," Seri waved her hand dismissively. "His name is Axel Something. Stacey said his parents named him after Axl Rose of the band Guns and Roses, but they didn't even spell it right."

"Why a dimwit?"

"I tried talking to him once when he was waiting to pick up Stacey. He was practically incoherent. He either started out slow or his brain was fried on drugs or something. Who knows? I hope the sex was good between them because the conversation must have been nonexistent."

"Why do you think she was with him?"

"Stacey was a sweet but submissive sort of person. Average intelligence. She did what was expected of her here but never took any initiative and never had any independent ideas. My guess is that she didn't require much in a relationship. She just wanted someone to be there and to show her some affection. She was like that with the folks on the staff, too. Seeking approval. Not demanding much. Not producing much, either."

Letty smiled to herself. Seri Durand had a reputation for being more than just bright. She was highly intelligent and had the arrogance to go along with it. Seri considered most people to be fools or borderline fools, and she didn't suffer fools gladly.

"Any sign that he abused her?"

"No. No bruises or anything. She didn't seem afraid of him at all or even intimidated."

"Why do the cops think Axel is the one who killed her?"

"I don't know, other than the fact that he dropped her off and he may have been the last one to see her alive. Usually he dropped her off outside the building at the corner. The cops aren't telling us much of anything. I did overhear them say that it looks like a stabbing but they didn't say with what. They took tons of photos, asked questions, took samples of blood and fingerprints and whatever. Then they took her body away. We got a call earlier this morning that we could request a clean-up team to get rid of the blood and clean up the scene. The team will be here this afternoon. However, the rumor mill is up and operating. One of the library pages has a friend who has a friend who has a friend. You know how that works. The rumor is that Tucson cops went to Stacey's house and questioned Axel. He denied knowing anything. Not long after the cops left, he disappeared. Did a runner. That was a mistake. It makes him look guilty."

"Who's handling the investigation?"

"Like I said, University police called in the Tucson Police Department, which is common in a murder case on campus. A TPD homicide detective showed up here. His name is De Luca, Tony De Luca. Apparently he thinks Axel was the last to see Stacey so De Luca may have concluded that Axel killed her. Or Axel is at minimum a suspect," Seri shook her head. "Then Axel ran."

"I don't know this guy De Luca. He must be new."

"He's not from here. He's got a strong New York accent. What about your friend Adelita García? Is she still a homicide detective? Could you call her?"

Seri referred to Letty's longtime friend going back to high school. She and Adelita had grown into adulthood together and had gone to high school and community college together. Then Adelita went to the police academy and Letty into the Army and to Iraq. They had a great working relationship when Letty returned from Iraq and became a private investigator. Adelita had to be careful what she revealed to Letty about ongoing investigations because of departmental regulations, but she had a gift for pointing Letty in the right direction in subtle ways. Letty returned the favor by sharing information when she could. She also had regulations to follow to maintain her professional license.

"Adelita is on her honeymoon in Mexico," said Letty. "I don't know if she'll be returning to homicide for a while. She's pregnant."

"Hmmm," Seri said. "Pregnancy can slow you down."

"Why do you think Axel is innocent?"

"I'll admit he could have killed Stacey. But they had no serious conflicts or problems as far as I can tell. And if he was going to kill her, why here at the library? Why not at home?" Seri paused and frowned. "Plus I have this feeling that someone else was here."

"Tell me more about that."

"Nothing firm. But I can tell you that there are some very subtle signs that someone was in the Institute's storage area upstairs when

Stacey arrived. I can see signs of a search. I know this place like the back of my hand. Someone was here and that someone was looking for something. I think Stacey surprised him or her."

"Anything missing?"

Seri shrugged. "Nothing obvious. But there are literally thousands of documents, video and audio tapes, CDs, maps, photos, you name it. It could take a long time to figure out what is missing and stolen."

"Have you had anyone asking for anything suspicious?"

"Our usual patrons are either professors from this university doing research, visiting professors doing research, independent authors working on a book, or students. It's usually quiet here so we always have students coming in to study. What do you mean by 'suspicious?'"

Letty looked out the window of Seri's office into the main reading room. She could see six individuals who looked like professors or independent authors. They were all a bit or a lot older than the students. They each had stacks of papers and books on their desks, and most of them were scribbling notes or typing notes into laptops. At least a dozen students were in the reading room as well. Some looked like they were studying, but several were interacting with their smartphones. She turned and gazed through Seri's window to the outside. She could see much of the campus mall one story below, some really tall palm trees, and a great view of the Santa Catalina Mountains to the north. She turned her attention back to Seri.

"Hmmm. Good question. I'm not sure. What are the entry points into Special Collections downstairs?"

"That double door into the main reading room is the main entry. There's also a door at the back of the big collections-storage room. It's always locked. Only librarians have a key. Go through that door and you'll find a staircase that goes up two levels. The main entrance door into Special Collections is locked when we're closed. The door at the back of the main collections-storage room is always locked. It's an emergency escape only. Windows don't open and it's a one-story drop if you break a window to get out."

"What about the Institute up on the third floor? Is there an exit there, too?"

"Only a fire escape door. It also is always locked. Loud alarms go off if you try to exit. But as I said, it's not easy getting into that room in the first place. We never use that exit. If, for some reason, one of the librarians wants to go out the back, he or she will use the exit from the large collections-storage room, not the upper level."

"Okay. Back to your feeling that someone was looking for something. What kind of subtle signs of a search?"

"Drawers slightly opened. Document storage containers tilted over on the shelves, not upright as they should be. A few books pulled slightly out on the shelf."

"Gosh. You must be super neat most of the time to notice small things like that."

"Makes it easier to find things if we keep everything in order," Seri said firmly.

"Or maybe you are really observant," Letty added. "So there wasn't any ransacking?"

"No. Definitely not. My view is that someone had something specific in mind but didn't know where exactly to look for it. The fact that the search involved so many different spots – shelves, drawers, storage boxes – indicates the intruder didn't know where to look. It may mean, too, that he or she was looking for more than one thing. I also think the person wasn't in a great hurry or else things would have been messier."

"Do you think he took anything?"

"It's very possible. We're going to do an inventory after the clean-up team is finished."

"So he was there for a while looking in several places and didn't expect anyone to come in at 7 a.m."

"Correct."

"Could you determine if there was any particular subject area he was searching?"

"Our collection is primarily southern Arizona and northern Sonora, including pre-colonial, colonial, and national periods of both Mexico and the U.S. I didn't see any sign of a particular interest in any particular time period or subject. But then, we haven't done an inventory."

"Do you have especially valuable materials?"

"Yes, of course. The entire collection is valuable. But if you mean solely in monetary terms, yes, we have some very valuable items. Maps, in particular. We have some original maps from the early colonial period that are worth thousands. You know this part of Arizona used to be part of Mexico and part of the Spanish Empire before that. So we have papers and documents from many of the early Spanish landholding families. We have documents from colonial government officials, and documents from Church missions, convents and monasteries."

Seri looked out the window, but it was clear her mind was somewhere other than the view. "We also have a lot of other stuff from the more modern era after the Anglo-Americans started coming in to this area and taking over. And, of course, after Arizona became a state, we have early and mid-twentieth century documents, too."

"Everything you've said so far suggests that theft is the most likely motivation for an intruder. Money is usually the motivation for theft."

"Yes, and I'm afraid when I start my inventory, I'm going to find some missing documents that are worth a lot of money. They will be hard to trace. This kind of theft is usually done by a professional with the intention of selling the documents on the black market to a collector. Too often the collector stashes them away in some basement vault where only he or she can look at them."

"Yes, I understand that's the case with art theft, too. The world never sees the painting again because it's hidden away in the climate-controlled basement gallery of some rich Japanese or German or American's mansion." Letty asked, "Any new materials that are especially attractive to a scholar?"

"We have new materials coming in all the time. There are boxes up on the third level in the Institute that I haven't even had a chance to open. They are mostly donations of family documents and memorabilia from a more recent era. Of the more modern stuff, some documents will be useful, but a lot is of interest only to the families involved. I have to sort out what's useful to scholars and what's not."

"Were the new boxes tampered with?"

"Yes, I noticed three boxes that had been opened and not closed properly."

"That means you saw signs of a search on both levels – the main collections-storage area and also up on the third level of the Institute."

"Right."

"Did you tell the cops this?"

"Yes, but not in the detail I just told you. They looked around and couldn't see signs of disturbance. I think they thought I was overreacting and fretting about my collection. That homicide detective De Luca made a note of what I said, but he didn't ask any questions."

"And no video cameras connected to security in here?"

Seri shook her head no. "Too expensive. There are some cameras in the Main Library, but they are in locations where students are most likely to shoot up drugs or screw each other or whatever students do when they aren't spacing out on their so-called 'smart' phones."

"Maybe they are studying?" Letty chuckled.

"Students? Studying?" Seri asked sarcastically.

"No idea what Stacey was stabbed with?"

"No. I did hear one cop say to the homicide detective that they couldn't find a weapon."

"The medical examiner will be able to help with that."

"As I said, forensics was here. They finished late and this morning told us we could get the place cleaned up."

"So it's no longer taped off?"

"No, but there's dried blood on the floor. As I mentioned, we have a team coming in this afternoon."

"Do you mind showing me even though there's a mess?"

"No, certainly not. Let's go."

As they left Seri's office, Letty looked around the reading room again. She noticed that several people were watching her follow Seri back into the collections-storage area. She made a note of their faces and general appearance, just in case she saw them again.

The main collections-storage room and the Institute's historical collections room one level up were exactly as Seri had described. Each had a locked emergency exit to the outside, large windows that could not be opened, no security camera, and multiple shelves, storage units and boxes full of documents.

Seri took Letty on a quick tour of both levels.

"Did the cops get fingerprints from the doors?"

"I don't know. They wouldn't let us in when they were working."

"How about this?" Letty leaned down and took a close look at a vent with a larger-than-average opening near the floor.

"That's the ventilation system. Air conditioning blows out much of the year and heating when needed."

Both women squatted down to look closely.

"Looks like the cover of the vent has been opened recently," Letty said. She pointed to flakes of paint on the floor and scratches on the surface of the pop-in-and-out vent cover.

Seri frowned. "You're right. Could someone get in this way by crawling through the ducts? The passage is pretty narrow but a small person could get through there."

"Right. But to know for sure, we'd have to take a look at a diagram of the ventilation system. Does the duct stay this big and where does the duct system go? The person would have to be thin for sure. Too chubby and you'd get stuck. You are small enough. You could do it, Seri."

"I'll try to get that diagram for you."

Letty stood. "Okay. I think I have enough to get started. I'll call this De Luca guy and see if he'll work with me. I'll check into Axel and see if I can find out more about him, too. I also think I should check out Stacey. She may have been involved in something on the side that you didn't know about. Maybe she had enemies. Let me know when this place is cleaned up and if you find anything missing. We'll go on the working hypothesis that this was a simple theft of valuable documents for the purpose of selling them to an unethical collector. But we'll have to keep our minds open. The motive could be something different," Letty paused, "and a diagram of the ventilation ducts would be really good, too."

"Okay. I'll do that."

Just as the two women were about to part, Seri said, "Oh, I forgot. I was going to call you about another matter when this happened. Remember I told you that we get boxes of family documents? I mentioned that we have some new boxes upstairs. Also, just a few days ago, I received an additional box of family documents from Maggie that came from her great-granduncle."

Maggie Graham was a friend of both Seri and Letty. She had been Letty's high school English teacher, and when Letty was threatened with becoming homeless as a fifteen-year-old, Maggie and her husband took Letty in as a foster child.

"There's some good stuff about Tucson in the 1890s and early 1900s. The old man wrote a memoir not long before he died in the late 1970s or around then. His name was Pete Arianos. What's interesting is that the old man's stepfather was a Chinese immigrant. The Chinese man is Maggie's biological great-great-grandfather. Historians reading this memoir will get some insight into the Chinese immigrant community in Tucson."

"Maggie has a Chinese ancestor? Wow! That's a surprise."

"Yes. I think it might be fun if Maggie and you and I and Zhou and Jade get together and read the first part of his memoir about the Chinese immigrant. It's a very romantic tale about Pete's mother Rosa and his Chinese stepfather."

"Was this one of the boxes that was disturbed?"

"No. I still have that box at my house. I haven't had a chance to bring it to the library yet."

"Any chance there's something valuable in the box that the intruder might have wanted to steal?"

"Not likely. I went through everything quickly just to see what's there. It's mostly family papers and a few photos. The memoir has the most historical value of anything in the box because it's a first-person account, but there are limits on the value of something that's so personal. Arianos was a respected attorney here, but he wasn't a political figure. I mean he wasn't a former governor or anything like that. He ran out of steam after writing about his experiences in World War I. I think he became too ill and couldn't continue. We'll make the memoir available to anyone to read as soon as it's classified and catalogued."

"So that means the theft is likely something valuable that is already in your collection."

"That's what I'm thinking. I just have to figure out what they were looking for, and if they found it."

"Okay. Let's get together and read the memoir. I bet Zhou will be interested for sure. And Maggie and Jade will love it, especially if there's a romance at the heart of the story."

"It's written from a kid's point of view, but the romance can't be missed. The father of Pete Arianos died when Pete was really young. Pete's parents were Italian immigrants. His mother, Rosa, and the Chinese man fell for each other, got married, and made a life for themselves in Tucson."

"Say when and where and I'll be there for the reading."

Seri nodded.

Letty waved goodbye to Seri and headed back to the city bus.

Seri stood at her office window and watched Letty walk away from the library. She was glad that she had called Letty. In the time that she'd known her, Seri had come to recognize and admire Letty's intelligence and competence. Today just proved this again to Seri. Letty asked good questions and she had noticed the vent misplacement. Seri had a lot more confidence in Letty's finding the murderer of Stacey Frederick, a lot more than in the police. In addition, Seri was deeply curious about what the intruder had been looking for. Letty would discover that, too. Seri was sure of that.

Letty picked up her truck, thanking the auto shop attendant for the quick service. Next stop would be the Tucson Police Department.

CHAPTER 3

SHE could have called ahead. That would have been the polite thing to do. But Letty had learned that the element of surprise often got her closer to her goal than handing out an advance notice. She was hoping that showing up at the front desk of the Tucson Police Department and asking for Tony De Luca would get her a quick meeting with the new homicide detective.

Letty was told to wait. She sat. Five minutes went by, then ten.

Suddenly a door at the far end of the waiting area was pushed open and a small, dark-haired man strode toward her. He wasn't smiling. Letty stood. She realized that she must be five or six inches taller than this man.

"Detective De Luca?"

"That's right. You are Letty Valdez, that Indian detective."

"Yes. Native American. Tohono O'odham to be exact. My mother's side of the family. My father is Mexican-American."

De Luca didn't extend his hand nor did Letty.

"Yeah, I've heard plenty about you."

"All good, I hope," Letty smiled.

De Luca frowned. "Come this way." He turned and walked away quickly. She followed him back through the doors he'd come through, down a hallway and into an office with a sign on the door that said, "Homicide Detective Anthony De Luca."

The detective gestured to a chair and Letty sat. He sat in the chair behind his desk and leaned toward her. His movements were quick, almost agitated, and his dark eyes were intense as he stared at her. He twiddled a ball point pen between his fingers.

"So 'Indian' is politically incorrect now?"

Letty smiled. Uh-oh. Off on the wrong foot. "Some prefer American Indian and I guess many of us who are younger like to be thought of as Native American. But this isn't a big deal."

"I'm short on time today, Miss Valdez. We had a home invasion on the southwest side last night with a couple of deaths. Just this morning, there was another homicide. Some guy with a gun and a bad case of road rage killed a motorist on Oracle Road."

"Okay," Letty said quietly. "I'll make this quick. I want to have a good working relationship with you. I know you cannot give me details of your investigations, but maybe you can point me in the right direction when possible. I'll return the favor. I had an excellent relationship with Adelita García, and I'm hoping to have the same with you."

De Luca sighed. "Okay. Maybe." He swiveled in his chair. "You're right, though. I can't tell you much of anything. Is there something you want to know right now?"

"I've been hired by Seri Durand, director of the Sonoran Arts and Sciences Institute. She's asked me to investigate the death of one of the Institute's employees, Stacey Frederick."

De Luca frowned again. "Why? She doesn't trust us?"

"I wouldn't say that, Detective. Seri Durand just likes to cover all the bases. She's familiar with my work. She's somewhat concerned now because she thinks that the police are dismissing this too quickly as a case of Stacey's boyfriend killing her. She thinks there may be more to it. Is it true that you think Axel Davies committed the murder?"

"Let's just say that taking off and disappearing shortly after we questioned him makes him a strong suspect."

Letty nodded.

"What makes Ms. Durand think there's more to this?"

Seri was right. The guy had a thick New York accent...or New Jersey. Letty was never sure which was which. In Iraq she got to know some fellow soldiers from the different New York City boroughs, and at least one soldier from New Jersey. They all sounded more or less the same to her Arizona ear. She had a sudden flash-back of watching some of them sitting around a camp table drinking illicit alcohol and arguing loudly about where to get the best pizza in New York City.

"Seri Durand said she has this feeling that someone was already there, probably when Stacey arrived early that morning."

"A feeling doesn't cut it."

"Okay. Let's put it this way. She saw some evidence of an intruder's having gone through the library's collection in the two areas where the public is not allowed. She said she told you this, but she thinks you may not have made note of her observations."

"Was anything stolen?"

"She just got the go-ahead today to get a team in there to clean up the blood. As soon as they can get the stacks area cleaned up, she is assigning her staff to do a thorough inventory."

"Okay," De Luca said dismissively. "She should inform me if any-thing turns up missing." He started shuffling some papers on his desk. Letty knew he was going to suggest that she leave.

"There's more."

He glanced up at her, his look penetrating.

"Dr. Durand says that you asked her about the keys to the emer-gency fire exit doors on both levels. The keys were not missing, and there was no sign that the doors had been opened. She said they make a big alarm noise if opened. Security would have noticed that."

"True. There's no sign of an intruder. That's why we are looking at Axel Davies. He admits that he gave her a ride to the library early that morning, and he admits that he went into the library with the victim. He claims he didn't stay. He says he only helped her carry in a box. But apparently he was the last person to see her alive."

"Yet there is sign of an intruder who may have been there when Stacey arrived. In addition to some of disturbed storage units, it appears that the vent for the AC/heating system near the floor had been opened and then closed again. Someone may have entered the Institute through the duct system."

"What makes you think that?" He frowned again.

Does this guy ever smile? Letty wondered.

"There are flecks of paint the color of the vent surface on the floor just beneath it. It looks like the missing paint came from around where the vent panel pops in and out. Since the library is regularly cleaned, those flecks are new. Seri, I mean Dr. Durand, said that she had not seen them before."

"And she goes around looking for bits of dried paint on the floor?" His tone was almost sarcastic.

"As she put it, she knows the library like the back of her hand. She's a very precise and exacting sort of person. She is very observant. She notices details. But in this case, I'm the one who saw the flecks of paint. I get paid to notice things like that."

De Luca's eyebrows went up. He picked up his pen and started scribbling on a notepad.

"Okay. That's worth considering. I'll definitely check that out." His face was more open now and he was no longer frowning. Apparently Detective De Luca needed some proof that Letty wasn't a total idiot. She had just given him that.

"Anything else?"

"No. But I am going to pursue this as well as attempt to learn more about Frederick and her boyfriend, just in case you are right about his murdering her."

"Note that I did not say Axel Davies murdered her. He's a suspect at this point. But I fully intend to follow every lead. You just gave me one. Thank you."

Letty stood. She wanted to leave on her own, not be asked to leave.

"I am always pleased to cooperate with and help out the Tucson police. As I said, I've had a great relationship with Detective García. I hope I'll have the same cooperative relationship with you."

Letty turned and walked out before Detective De Luca could say anything.

***

Letty wanted to finish up some paperwork so she went to her office. It was a small place: only two rooms, plus a tiny shelf-lined third room for storage and a tiny bathroom. The office was located in a nondescript strip mall on south Alvernon Way. The great advantage of the place was the view of the Santa Catalinas from her inner office. Letty loved starting and ending her work days watching the light change on the ridges and valleys of the Santa Catalina Mountains. Watching the light reminded her of serene time spent with her grandmother on the Tohono O'odham Reservation. She also liked that the light fell for a minute or two on her private investigator's license that was framed under glass and hanging on the wall. Leticia Fernanda Antone Valdez, Licensed Private Investigator, State of Arizona.

She shuffled the papers around and put a few sheets away in a filing cabinet. Then she turned on her computer. Quick searches turned up little of interest for either Stacey Frederick or Axel Davies. Stacey appeared to be everything she claimed to be and not much more. She had no record of interactions with the police, not even a traffic ticket. She graduated from one of the Tucson high schools, finished two years at Pima Community College, moved on to get her bachelor's degree in business administration at the University of Arizona. For a couple of semesters, she had been in a program to earn her MBA.

Social media posts were mainly from friends as far back as high school. There were trips to Mt. Lemmon, her volunteer work at the local animal shelter, links to favorite musicians, and similar posts. A little more than a year earlier, photos of Axel began to show up in her posts. Again, posts about him were primarily fun things they did together or relaxing together at home.

Letty learned from some of the photos that Axel was in an indie rock band called Marathon. She followed the comments to Axel's social media page, to his fellow band members and the band's page. Fairly quickly she was able to get a list of about fifteen young men and women who were Axel's "friends" and who commented regularly on his posts. Next she followed each of these far enough to get probable local locations and contact information.

She would start with Axel's friends. If he was on the run, it was likely that he'd go to the home of a friend. She made a note of which friends appeared the most often as commenters on his posts, and which of those were also band members.

It was late afternoon. Letty decided to do the background search for Jessica tomorrow. On her way home, she would take a step toward finding Axel. A few of the social media posts indicated that the band practiced in an old, run-down house south of 22nd Street. Photos were posted of the house along with an invitation to come by and jam with the band. Apparently at least one person in the band was renting the place, because if the house had been abandoned, the band would have had no electricity. They needed power for their electric guitars.

Letty turned off South Swan and made her way east through a working-class neighborhood, looking for the house she'd seen in the photo. Most of the houses were small and older. They had fenced yards and were fairly well kept. She could see at least one dog behind every fence. Not a few homes had an extra car or pickup truck parked out front, leaving the driveway open for the family's primary car.

As she drew closer to the address noted on the social media pages, the sidewalks became cracked, weeds made an appearance everywhere, and most of the houses took on a more forlorn and ill-kept appearance. She parked near the target house, walked to the front door and listened. She could hear heavy metal music starting and stopping. The band was practicing.

During one of the quiet moments, she knocked on the door. The house fell silent.

Letty knocked again, and called out, "Hey, Axel. Are you there?"

The door opened slightly, and a young man with tousled hair and a scruffy beard peered out. "Axel isn't here."

"I'm Letty. Can I come in and talk to you? I need to find him."

The door closed. Then it opened again after a brief moment.

"Uh. I guess so. Come on in."

Letty walked into the living room. It was pretty much what she expected. An ancient, worn-down couch with stuffing emerging from tears in the upholstery rested against one wall. The guy who opened the door sank onto the couch and picked up his guitar. Sitting next to him was another young man with a guitar. A drum set was in the corner and behind the drum set, another young man sat. He made no effort to make any sound. The place reeked of marijuana.

"I'm looking for Axel. Do you know where he is?"

"Who are you and why do you want Axel? Are you helping the cops?" the door-opener demanded.

"My name is Letty. I'm helping the librarian where Stacey worked. You know Stacey was murdered. The librarian asked me to help her find the killer. The cops think Axel did it, but the librarian doesn't agree."

All three nodded their heads.

"Do you know where he is?"

"He's on the run," said the drummer. "The cops came looking for him. They think he killed Stacey."

"Did he?"

"No way, man," the drummer answered. "Axel is too chill to do something like that. He loved Stacey."

"Do you know how I can find him?"

"No. Axel came by here and borrowed some money. Said he was taking off, but he didn't say where he was going. He's scared."

"He should be. The cops are after him. Running like this makes him look guilty." Letty paused. "Do you think you'll see him?"

"Don't know," the door-opener said. The drummer shrugged his shoulders.

"If you do, tell him he needs to turn himself in before the cops corner him somewhere. They might shoot first and ask questions later. He could end up dead for something he didn't do. If Axel is safe in custody, then we can go about the business of finding out who really killed Stacey. Then everyone will know Axel is innocent."

They all nodded again. She couldn't tell if they were agreeing, or just hoping she would disappear.

So Letty disappeared. She let herself out of the house and headed home.

***

Letty found little brother Will and his girlfriend Clarice already at home from their day of taking college classes. They were in the kitchen making some supper. Letty took a seat at the kitchen table.

She reached down and stroked Millie's back. The little pit bull had finished her dinner and was now leaning up against her beloved mistress.

"If I move, you're going to fall over," Letty said affectionately. Millie thumped her tail in response.

Will, all six feet three inches of him, slid his quiche into the oven. Clarice was teaching him to cook. Letty approved. Clarice knew how to make nutritious food taste good.

Will slumped into a seat opposite her at the kitchen table.

"What's up, Big Sister? What are you working on?"

"I served some papers today. Then I went to the University library to meet with Seri Durand. Earlier today, I received an email. I want to talk to both of you about this email."

Clarice joined them at the table.

"Remember that dog trainer from El Paso, Jack Gilliam, who used to be Millie's original owner?" Will and Clarice nodded.

"He emailed me and said he has a dog that he wants us to consider adopting."

Will sat up straighter.

Letty continued. "He's been out in California working with these groups that do search-and-rescue in case of earthquakes or other natural disasters like mud and rock slides. He's got a dog that was being trained to sniff out people in the debris. He thinks we might like the dog. It's a black lab. He says the dog is very friendly and good natured. I think Millie will like him, and I can take him on runs with me, too."

Letty had been hoping for some time to take a dog along with her on her morning runs. Millie the pit bull had never been able to run with Letty. Millie, her name was short for "milagro" – the Spanish word for "miracle," had an almost-useless front leg. Millie had been stolen from Jack Gilliam's home, brought to southern Arizona and used as bait in a dog-fighting ring. The tendons and ligaments of the small female pit bull's front leg had been severely damaged. When she was too injured to be used as bait anymore, the dog had been dumped out in the desert to die slowly in the hot sun. Letty had found and rescued Millie. After a stint at the vet's, Millie came home to live with Letty and Will.

"So if this dog is trained as a sniffer rescue dog, why does Gilliam want us to take him?" Will asked. He had a perplexed look on his face.

Letty smiled slightly. "Well, it turns out that this dog sort of flunked out of the program and now he needs a home."

Will grinned. "He flunked out of sniffer school?"

"Yes, Gilliam said he got too distracted. He'd start doing his job sniffing and looking for people under the debris. Then he'd get distracted by the rescue workers and by other dogs, especially female dogs."

Will guffawed. "He likes girls! I totally get that."

Clarice elbowed Will in the ribs. She grinned, too.

"What's the dog's name?" Clarice asked.

"Theodore Roosevelt."

Will hooted.

"I'm not even going to ask," Clarice giggled.

"But they call him Teddy," Letty added. "Gilliam says Teddy is a sweetheart, very friendly…"

"Especially friendly to the girls," Will broke in, a big grin still on his face.

"Gilliam says he doesn't want the dog to be adopted by just anybody. He thought of us first. So what do you think?"

"Yes!" Will and Clarice said at the same time. Will added, "Teddy will be a perfect fit here."

"Okay. That means you have to help take care of him. Agreed?"

They both nodded their heads.

"Millie will like him," Clarice said.

"And Teddy's going to like Millie for sure. She's definitely a girl!" Will added.

"Okay. I'll tell Gilliam to bring him to Tucson on his way home to El Paso."

CHAPTER 4

THE next morning, Letty sat on her back porch and nursed her first cup of coffee. She felt muddled and disoriented because of the dream that came to her in the night. It was another one of those Iraq dreams.

Jogging would help. Letty needed her three-mile run around her midtown Tucson neighborhood to clear her head. The Iraq dreams were fewer now, but they still appeared without warning and with no apparent connection to what was happening in her waking life.

Last night's dream, really a nightmare, had her out on convoy again, ready to stop spurting blood if her fellow soldiers' arteries were slashed open by shrapnel and bullets. There was the sound of an explosion, then flashing lights and a fire. She could hear the soldiers screaming, "Medic! Medic!" Her role as an Army medic seemed completely useless in these nightmares. She never seemed to get there in time, and she was never able to save any lives. She couldn't save one life in particular. Chava. She couldn't save Chava.

Letty woke up panting and fighting tears. Her hands shook when she went to the kitchen to make coffee. By the time the coffee was ready, she was a little calmer. She headed to the back porch with a cup to plan the day. The coffee and the run around her neighborhood would make life bearable.

An hour later, Letty was back home and feeling much better after the run. She gave Millie a bowl of dog kibble with a little bit of canned food mixed in. Millie gobbled it up, wagging her tail the entire time. Letty carried her second cup of coffee to the back porch.

Millie joined her. Letty reached down and stroked Millie's scarred head and neck. Letty would always be grateful to Millie because Millie had saved the life of Letty's little brother Will. Millie stopped a Hong Kong Triad gangster who was pointing his gun at Will's head. She clamped her jaws down on the Triad's wrist and put an end to his attempt to kill Will. The little pit bull became Letty's friend for life.

All was quiet on the street and in Letty's backyard. The house was quiet, too, because Will and Clarice were already gone for the day, off on their bicycles to attend their classes. Millie was snoozing in the morning sun in the backyard. Letty headed for the shower.

***

After showering, Letty drove to her office. She turned on her computer and started searching for Bill West, the man that attorney Jessica Cameron had asked her to check out. An hour later, she called Jessica.

"About this man Bill West, I couldn't find anything problematic. He has no arrest record and hasn't been sued for fraud or anything like that. Most of the information I found was in the newspaper, and that was mainly social."

"Social?" Jessica asked.

"Yes, I found that he was married when he was young. During his first year in law school, he married a fellow law student. They divorced after only one year. Other than that, the focus of the society-page news is that he has been considered one of Seattle's most eligible bachelors for several years. He's frequently included as an attendee at various high-class social events like fundraisers for the Seattle Opera. The newspaper stories praise him for his business success. Also I think the stories are a blatant attempt to titillate readers with his marriage eligibility. What I couldn't find much on were his business dealings. West By Northwest has been a partner, often behind the scenes, in a number of big real estate deals in Seattle, Portland, and Salt Lake City. News of his company's role often doesn't come out until the deal is done. It's possible, too, that he's involved in more deals, but his role is never revealed."

"Okay," Jessica said. "So I'm dealing with a guy who is considered very desirable by women, probably because of his money, and who made most of that from real estate dealings that are not fully disclosed. But just where he got his money to start in business and what exactly his company does behind the scenes are not really clear. Does that sum it up?"

"Pretty much. I'd have to access some restricted databases to find out more."

"Let's go with this for a while. I'll have to think about going out with him. I'm not sure. By the way, how are you? How badly did that thug hurt you yesterday?"

"I'm okay. My nose is a little sore. That's all."

"Okay. Let's connect later."

Letty had no sooner ended her call with Jessica when the phone rang again.

"Letty, this is Seri. One of my co-workers, our reference librarian Amanda Flores, had her apartment broken into last night."

"Is Amanda okay?"

"Yes, she's fine. She wasn't home. She spent the night at her boyfriend's place. She stopped by her place this morning on the way to work. That's when she discovered that the place had been ransacked."

"Has TPD been called?"

"Yes, Amanda came in late so she could meet with the cops first."

"So the place was a mess? Anything missing?"

"Yes, her laptop was gone, some jewelry, too, and she had about fifty dollars in a small wooden box. The box and the cash are gone. She says the place was turned upside down. All the drawers were open, furniture overturned, and even her mattress on her bed was displaced."

"They were looking for something."

"That's what I think. It's possible that the theft of her laptop and the other stuff was to deflect from what they were really looking for. What do you think?"

"Yes, very possible. That she works at the Institute is too much of a coincidence. Apparently the thief or thieves thought that she might have what they couldn't find in the library."

Seri sighed, "And you know what this means?"

"Yes. You're next."

"What should we do?"

"Call De Luca and see if he'll send a patrol car to your place to see if you've had a break-in."

"Okay. But he may just think it's an ordinary break-in and not connected to the Institute."

"He's an experienced detective. He should realize that the coincidence is too great. Meanwhile, I'm going to contact Marv and see if he wants to check out your place for me."

Seri sighed. "It would make me feel better if someone is watching."

"Do you want to stay at my house tonight?"

"No. I think whoever is doing this is a pro. They won't want to try a break-in while I'm at home. Too much trouble for them. Stacey was an accident, I think. They didn't expect her to be there. Also, I have a taser gun and a very good alarm system. It will be very difficult for anyone to break into my place."

"And you know how to use the taser?"

"Yes! No point in having one if you don't know how to use it."

"Okay, Seri. I'm going to want a meeting with you and Amanda. Before we meet, I'd like for both of you to do some serious thinking about all the interactions you've had with your library patrons recently."

"You want to know with whom we've interacted? That's a lot of people."

"Yes. I want to know as much as you can tell me about anyone who has expressed interest in any particular subject or collection of materials. We want to know especially if anyone has been asking about any new documents coming into the library. I hope you can remember the kinds of questions you've been asked. I'm thinking of something unusual or unique or maybe a pattern in the questions, so we might get a sense of what our murderer-thief was looking for. We have to start somewhere."

"Okay. I'll get together with Amanda. We'll talk and I'll make some notes."

"Meanwhile, I think we need to meet with Maggie and Zhou and Jade and start reading that memoir. There may be something in it relevant to this case. It's not much, but we don't have much to go on at this point."

"I'll call Maggie and Jade. Tomorrow is Saturday. Maybe we can meet at Jade and Zhou's house. Since she's so big and pregnant, it might be easier for her to be at home and not have to go anywhere.

"Good idea. Let me know what time. Talk to you later."

Letty called Marv next. Marv Iverson was Letty's former boss. Marv was a Vietnam vet who had been operating his own private investigation business for several years when he decided to hire an assistant. Letty applied. Marv favored her because she was a veteran, too. He trained her, encouraged her and led her through the process of becoming a licensed investigator. Later when Marv decided to retire, he turned the agency over to Letty. Marv found that watching football on TV day and night wasn't quite as exciting as he thought. He occasionally did jobs for Letty to relieve his boredom.

"Hey Marv, I could use some help now. Are you free?" Letty waited patiently. Marv didn't quite know how to work his smart-phone.

"Hi Letty, I figured out how to answer your calls. I'm going to learn how to text, too."

"That's good, Marv. But what I need today is for you to drive by a friend's house several times and make sure no one is loitering or trying to break in. It's not a real stakeout because we're not sure what's going on and we don't know if a stakeout is called for. I just need for you to check out the neighborhood and see if you see anyone hanging around my friend's place."

Letty gave Marv the details, he agreed to the job, and they signed off.

Letty spent the rest of the day doing the paperwork necessary to stay in business.

***

The drive to her small home in midtown Tucson only took about ten minutes. The days were shorter now, and the setting sun had turned the late afternoon sky a dusky magenta-pink. Letty pulled into her driveway and parked. To her surprise, there was a big black dog standing next to Millie at the fence. Both dogs were wagging their tails.

"So who are you?" Letty leaned over the fence and rubbed the black lab's head. "Millie, who's your friend?"

Letty's little brother Will came around from the back of the house.

"Hi, Big Sister. You just missed Jack Gilliam. This is Teddy!"

When he heard his name, the black lab turned toward Will and wagged his tail even harder.

Clarice appeared and stood alongside Will.

"He's a wonderful dog," Clarice said. "He and Millie took to each other right away. He submitted to her and let her sniff him all over. Then she let him sniff her."

"Smart move on his part," Will laughed. "Now Millie thinks she's the boss."

"Millie *is* the boss!" Clarice grinned.

Will turned to Clarice and whispered conspiratorially, "Go hide."

He turned and let Letty into the backyard. "You gotta see this. The dog is a genius. I can't believe he flunked out of sniffer school. He's really good at finding things."

"If you remember, it wasn't lack of sniffing skills that did him in."

"Yeah," Will laughed. "Girls are what ruined him."

"He seems happy to be here."

"Oh, he is! Millie loves him already, and he adores Millie. Go sit on the back porch and watch."

Will disappeared inside the house and came out again with a t-shirt belonging to Clarice. He called the dogs. He held Clarice's t-shirt out to Teddy and said, "Find Clarice, Teddy. Find Clarice."

Teddy sniffed. Then he began a circular search of the backyard. He was quick and systematic. Millie limped along behind him. Finally Teddy came to stand at the trunk of a large mesquite tree at the back of Letty's yard. His tail was wagging. He sat down and looked at Will.

Will said to Letty, "Sitting down and looking at you is his alert signal." Will ran over to the tree and looked up. "Found ya!"

Letty could hear Clarice giggling in the tree. She came down quickly. Both Will and Clarice made a fuss over Teddy and told him how brilliant he was. And Millie was reminded of her brilliance as well.

"I'm impressed. If I ever have to find someone in a tree, I'll know who to call."

"Very funny, Big Sister. He's a great dog. And you never know. You may need his superior sniffing skills sometime. Just don't let the oh-so-gorgeous Millie get him all hot and bothered."

Letty was happy and relieved to see them all so happy and so easily entertained. The new dog was working out well.

"Let's eat," Letty said. "I'm starving."

"Clarice made something for us. It's Korean food. Noodles and chicken and something called kimchi. I have no idea what it is, but it tastes good."

They sat at the kitchen table, and after a few minutes of slurping noodles and sampling kimchi, Clarice said, "Will and I want to talk to you about something, Letty."

"Oh, yeah. What's that?" She wiped sauce off her chin. The kimchi was indeed very good.

"Clarice and I think you should relax more and not work so hard. You need to have some fun."

"Fun?" Letty looked confused.

"I know it's an unfamiliar concept, but you should try it," Will wagged his finger at her.

Clarice asked seriously, "You've worked hard for several years, first in the Army and then getting your private investigator license. But what did you do before that? What did you do for fun when you were in high school?"

"Letty didn't have time for fun in high school. She was working then, too, to make money to help Grandma take care of me and my brother and sister," Will said.

Clarice turned to Letty. "Is that right?"

"I worked at a fast-food restaurant after school and on the weekends."

Will turned to Clarice. He gave her a brief summary of their childhoods. Will's father, also the father of Will's twin brother and sister Eduardo and Elena, died in a car wreck when they were very young.

"About six months after our dad was killed in a car wreck, our mom took off with that Navajo cowboy, and we went to live with our grandmother. Letty has a different dad than us. When she was little, she lived with us on the reservation. But later, our mom made her move into Tucson to live with her dad. She was living with him and his family in Tucson when our dad was killed. Then Letty's dad took off, too. So none of us had a dad. Or a mom." He shrugged his shoulders.

"But you told me that that Letty's teacher Maggie took her in as a foster child."

Will continued. "Yes, thank god for that because Letty was threatened with becoming homeless. She couldn't go back to the reservation because Grandma just didn't have enough to feed another person. Uncle Mando and Aunt Valerina helped us, but they were poor, too, and they had their own kids to feed. The family of Letty's dad didn't have the resources to take in another kid either. So Letty's going to live with Maggie was a good deal. Letty continued in school, had a home with a place to sleep and food to eat. She was able to work part-time to make sure that Eduardo and Elena and I had extras."

"What do you mean by 'extras'?"

"Shoes, for one thing. We were growing fast. Seems like all three of us needed new shoes every few months. Especially me because I got really big." Will was six feet three inches tall by age seventeen.

Letty noticed that Clarice's eyes had filled with tears.

"Shoes?" Clarice said softly. "Those are essentials, not extras."

"Well, yeah, you could say that. Also Letty's contribution made it possible for me to play basketball. I needed basketball shoes for that. That's an extra. Elena got to go to summer science camp because of Letty. Eduardo got the one thing he wanted most of all in the whole world, which was to keep that old mare he calls Bonita. Letty got to go to a good high school and stay with a family that could provide for her. Everything worked out."

Clarice was trying not to sob. "It's so unfair. Some of us have so much and others so little. It's so unfair."

Will put his arms around her. "It's okay. Don't cry. Look! We all made it through high school. Elena is at the university. Eduardo is studying to be an electrician. I go to college, too. Letty has a successful business as an investigator. We're all doing great."

Letty reached out and took Clarice's hand. "Don't worry. I lucked out getting to live with Maggie and Brian. I'll always be grateful to them. They were just out of college and in their first teaching positions. They didn't have much money, and still they took me in and made my life much easier. I was fifteen when I first moved in with them. I had regular meals and my own bedroom. They were very kind to me. I hope to repay them someday. So, do you see, Clarice? Everything is fine."

"No, it's not fine," Will shook his head seriously. "You need to have some fun, Big Sister. And, personally, I think you need a boyfriend."

Clarice's eyebrows went up at Will's audacity. She shook her head in agreement.

Letty's sharp intake of breath revealed her surprise, too.

"I'm too busy for a boyfriend."

"Okay. Let's start with some simple fun, and later, we'll work on finding you a boyfriend," Will insisted.

"I have fun! I'm taking Zhou's gong fu class. I go jogging." Letty sounded defensive even to herself.

Will shook his head no.

"Doesn't count. Gong fu is work-related, and jogging is health-related and work-related, too. I mean fun for fun's sake."

"Was there any free time at all in high school for fun?" Clarice asked. "Did you date?"

Letty frowned. "No dating. I was really very shy around boys. Occasionally I got to go on a hike with Maggie and Brian and some of their friends. Also I used to read when I had time. I really liked reading. It was like going to another world. I could forget this world for a while."

"What did you read?"

"Stuff for school, but I actually liked everything so it didn't seem like homework even though it was an assignment. Shakespeare, different poets, Charles Dickens…"

"Jane Austen?" Clarice asked.

"Yes, Jane Austen. And American authors, too, like Mark Twain and Poe and," she paused, "my favorites were *To Kill a Mockingbird* and *The Grapes of Wrath*. I also read a lot of history. I had a great history teacher."

"But you haven't had time to read since then?" Clarice prompted her.

"Not much. I read some novels when I was in Iraq, and I learned how to play cards. But most of my time was taken there trying to patch up the soldiers. That's what medics do. Someone was always bleeding."

"Letty, reading is a great place to start. I have a book for you now." Clarice disappeared.

"You need a boyfriend," Will said sanctimoniously. He looked down his nose at her and made a face.

"Shut up, Will!" Letty tried to suppress her laughter. He really shouldn't be talking to her like that. She was his Big Sister, after all.

Clarice returned with a couple of worn paperbacks. "These are science fiction books by a really super American author named Ursula Le Guin. She recently passed away. This one, *The Left-Hand of Darkness*, had a big influence on me. The other one, *The Dispossessed*, was also a big influence." She handed the paperbacks to Letty.

"Okay. I've never read any science fiction. So I'll be good and go try to have some fun. I'll start reading one of these tonight. Which one do you recommend first?"

Clarice frowned. "I can't decide. They are both great. Maybe *Left Hand*."

Letty got up from the table.

"Do you two mind taking care of the dishes? I had a run-in with a muscled-up moron and I haven't been sleeping well. I need to rest."

"No problem," Will said.

"I'll take Teddy with me tomorrow morning when I go jogging."

"Maybe he can sniff out a boyfriend in a tree somewhere," Will said with a grin.

"Oh, by the way, have either of you heard of a local band called Marathon?" Letty asked.

No, neither had heard of Axel's band.

Letty took the two paperback books and headed for her bedroom. She was followed by two dogs, both wagging their tails.

She tried reading but she was just too tired, and too worried about the break-in that had occurred at the apartment of Seri's library colleague. Letty called Seri.

"Everything is fine," Seri said. "De Luca said he would send some cops to cruise by my place. I've seen them go by at least four times."

"Marv's watching, too."

"Good old Marv. He's such a sweetheart. By the way, Jade says for all of us to come over to their house tomorrow morning. We'll start reading the memoir. That will be fun."

"That's good. Will and Clarice told me to have some fun. I'll see you tomorrow." Letty said goodnight.

Next Letty called Marv.

"So what's up? Did you see anything out of the ordinary?"

"Yeah, cops came by several times, much more than the usual neighborhood patrol. The last one was looking at me suspiciously." Marv laughed. "But no sign of any person lurking around your friend's place. Her neighborhood is very quiet."

"That's good to hear. I guess you can go on home and go back to watching football. Thanks so much, Marv."

They said their goodbyes. Letty felt somewhat relieved. Maybe the break-in at Amanda's apartment had nothing to do with the library intrusion and murder.

CHAPTER 5

LETTY was up early as usual. She found Clarice on the back porch drinking coffee.

"Clarice, will you distract Millie? I'm going to take Teddy for a run."

"Sure! Come on, Millie. Wanna play frisbee?"

The two went into the backyard with a frisbee. Letty attached a leash to Teddy and they went out the side gate. Teddy hit his stride with Letty immediately. He paced himself to run exactly at her speed. He didn't pull on the leash or stop to smell things.

When she arrived home, Letty found Clarice and Millie on the back porch.

Letty gave both dogs a dog biscuit. "He's great, Clarice. I think he's jogged with someone before me. No problems at all. I'm going to enjoy Mr. Theodore Roosevelt."

Teddy looked at Letty attentively.

"Okay, I'm off to shower and then I'm going over to Jade's. What are you and Will doing today?"

"El Tour de Tucson is coming up next month so we're going to start following the route to become more familiar with it. We'll be on bikes all day." El Tour was a big bicycling race that brought thousands of bicyclists to Tucson every year. Will and Clarice were enthusiastic participants.

Letty arrived at Jade and Zhou's house half an hour later carrying some honeydew melons and cantaloupe.

Jade showed Letty where to find a bowl, a cutting knife and a cutting board.

"Thanks for bringing the cantaloupe and melon. I don't have much energy for proper entertaining these days."

"I guess not," Letty smiled. "Are you sure you aren't carrying twins?"

Jade sighed. "I feel big enough for two babies! But the doctor says there's only one."

"How much longer?"

"I'm due on Wednesday."

"How's Zhou doing?"

"He's scared. He won't admit it, but he's way out of his league with this childbirth thing. He knows what to do when someone points a gun at him or tries to beat him up. But all that martial arts stuff won't help him a bit when he's in the delivery room with me," Jade laughed. "I hope he doesn't pass out. I've heard that some men do."

"Nah. He won't. But he will have a whole new respect for you."

Jade grinned. "I'm going to go sit with him on the back patio. Please open the door for Maggie and Seri when they arrive."

Letty nodded, and started the task of preparing the cantaloupe and melon. She watched Jade lumber out her back door and sink ungracefully onto the outdoor sofa next to Zhou. The window was open, and Letty could hear their conversation.

"Hello," Jade said to Zhou. "My name is Jade. What's your name?"

Zhou grinned. His wife, with her beautiful halo of red curls, was flirting with him. He would never tire of this woman.

"My name is Zhou."

"Your name sounds like Joe. J-O-E?"

"No, pinyin Zed-H-O-U. Chinese name."

"Ah," Jade smiled, "I heard you were a Chinese cop."

"Detective Inspector."

"Oh, that's so sexy."

Zhou laughed. "Really?"

"Then I heard you became a gong fu instructor here in Tucson."

"Yes, this is true."

"Oh my god. A gong fu instructor? Oh, that is even sexier! You make my heart flutter."

Zhou laughed again. "Miss Jade, you are a naughty girl." He brushed the red curls away from her eyes.

Letty was enjoying this. When Zhou first showed up in Tucson, sent at the request of Interpol, who would have thought that he and her friend, the elementary school teacher Jade Lopez, would develop such a torrid romance? But that's exactly what happened. Letty wondered if she would ever have this kind of relationship with a man. Maybe once would be all she got in this lifetime. And that once was gone now, lost in the sands of Iraq.

Letty heard the front doorbell ring. She wiped her hands and opened the door for Seri and Maggie. Seri carried a medium-sized cardboard box.

All three went to the back patio with the melon on a plate and the box.

"Okay," Seri said unceremoniously to everyone. "We'll start reading the memoir today. I know you'll really enjoy this and also learn a lot of Tucson history. The memoir was written by Pete Arianos. Pete was born in 1888 and died in 1976. He was the son of Maggie's great-great grandmother Rosa, an Italian immigrant to Tucson. Pete was also the stepson of Rosa's second husband, a Chinese immigrant that we'll come to know as Drago. That makes Maggie the fifth generation in the Italian-Chinese line."

"Maggie, did you know you had a Chinese ancestor?" Letty asked.

"Oh, I heard stories when I was a kid, but there was almost no information. It was thought to be a family story that maybe was just a myth. No one in my family kept good records or seemed to be very interested in genealogy. So this is all new to me. I'm very excited to learn about my ancestor. Does that make Zhou and me cousins?"

Zhou smiled and said, "Yes, of course."

Seri continued, "We think the Chinese man came to Tucson in 1896. He married Maggie's great-great grandmother, Rosa Arianos, and their first child – or children – because they were twins, were born in 1900. This memoir was written by Pete Arianos in 1974, six years before Maggie was born. Pete Arianos was an attorney for many years here in Tucson." Seri retrieved the memoir from the box.

The group fell silent, and Seri began to read.

***

Tucson, Arizona, July, 1974

Now in the 86th year of my life, I am forced to slow down and take stock, against my will I might add. I don't want to be this old. Nobody does. To get my mind off my aches and pains, I decided to write down as much as I can remember about my life and times for my family members and for any history-minded individuals who might be interested in what life was like late in the last century and early in this century. Memory is a funny thing. Sometimes what happened eighty years ago is more real to me than what happened yesterday.

I've had a good life.

There's so much to tell that I hardly know where to begin. I can't remember being born in Italy or the long voyage across the ocean and across the North American continent. Mama said my father was following the railroad and that's how we ended up in southern Arizona. I don't know why the two of them stopped in Arizona Territory. I was just a baby then.

The railroad went all the way to California. They could have gone out to San Diego and I would have grown up on the ocean. I can't really imagine living near so much water. I've been here in the Sonoran Desert so long that everything about it seems right to me, even the lack of water. I'm a desert rat.

Mama told me that she and Papa came from a valley in the Italian Alps not too far from Switzerland and France. That's where I was born. The valley was emerald green in the summer and there was always a lot of snow in the winter. That's what Mama told me.

Mama said that they left Italy because Papa had the wanderlust. She said he wanted to make something of himself. She never told me if she also had wanted to leave her homeland. I know there were times she missed Italy and her Italian family a lot.

My first memory is of my father's death and the funeral mass in the old cathedral. I remember Mama being dressed all in black and her crying. I remember the men from our barrio carrying his coffin to the cemetery and putting it in the ground. I had just turned four years old and I didn't understand a lot of what was happening. I just remember how sad Mama was. I was sad, too, because my papa wasn't there anymore and because Mama was crying. I didn't really understand death, the finality of it. I just knew that in that moment Papa was gone and Mama and I were alone.

My childhood memories are primarily of my life in the barrio in Tucson. It seems somehow appropriate that I begin with the story of Mama and Drago. My childhood was so influenced by both of them. So really this first part of my memoir is the story of Mama and Drago.

The first time I saw Drago, he was coming down our dusty street in late winter, leading a horse-drawn cart full of vegetables. This was maybe two or three years after my papa died. It's hard for me to remember for sure. To my young eyes, Drago was a man with a strange and exotic appearance. I had never seen anyone who looked quite like him.

Everything about him was different. The front half of his head was shaved bald. In the back, his black hair was in a very long braid that swung slightly from side to side against his back as he walked along. I found out later that the braid was called a queue. On his feet were these cotton shoes quite unlike the leather boots most men wore. He had on cotton pants and a shirt, if you'd call it that, which left most of his arms exposed. Those arms were very muscular and his skin was tanned golden by days spent working in the sun.

The man's horse was an old bay gelding. Though the horse was a little sway-backed and moved slowly, I could tell that the animal was well cared for. Behind the horse was a cart that held an enticing display of fresh produce.

I could see greens, spinach I think, peas, cabbage, carrots, and garlic, the kinds of vegetables one would expect early in the season before the real heat began. Sprigs of orange blossoms among the vegetables left a delicious scent floating behind him.

I didn't have enough sense as a kid to be afraid of anything or anyone and so I wasn't afraid of this strange-looking man. I was always a curious boy. I'd never seen anything like him. I couldn't help but stare. I really wanted to know more. Who could blame me? I'd never before *seen a Chinaman. Drago was smiling at me. His black eyes twinkled. I was just about to speak to him when Mama's voice interrupted.*

"Piero.....Piero…" I could hear her calling me from her kitchen. Mama was the only one who called me by my birth name. Everyone else in the world called me Pete.

"Mama, come and look at this," I called back to her.

I frequently spoke to her in English so she would learn. We had lived in America for several years by then but Mama still didn't have the confidence to speak English. Always it was Italian with me. To the neighbors in our barrio, almost all Mexican, Mama spoke a garbled tongue that was half Spanish and half Italian with some English thrown in for good luck. The neighbors seemed to understand her. And she always understood me, even later when I spoke only English to her. I realize now that she always knew more English than I gave her credit for. I think she spoke Italian so that I would not forget the language of my birthplace. Or maybe she spoke Italian so that she wouldn't forget it herself.

"Che cosa?" I could hear her calling from the kitchen where she was kneading bread dough at a big wooden table.

"Come and see, Mama. It's a man selling fresh vegetables."

That brought her quickly from the patio and out the front door to the street. Mama loved fresh vegetables. She said she needed them for the little restaurant that she operated out of our home. Even then, I knew that it was more than just for the restaurant. She loved the touch and color and smell and taste of vegetables. She liked to grow vegetables and flowers, too, but couldn't. She just didn't have the time to keep a big garden, not with all the other things she had to do to keep the two of us fed and with a roof over our heads.

My papa was killed not long after we moved into the adobe house in Tucson. Papa worked on the railroad and Mama baked her breads and cakes to sell. They'd saved some money and invested it all in that old house. Mama and Papa had big plans back then. They were going to fix up the old adobe to live in. They were going rent a place in El Centro and start a bakery and restaurant near the Old Presidio site.

They were going to make a little brother or sister for me. They were going to build a life for themselves in the new country.

But Papa's death changed all that. Things got a lot harder after Papa died. Mama might have considered going home to Italy but she had no money to pay for the passage. Everything she had was invested in that old adobe house. So Mama dried her tears and went to work.

I was glad we were forced to stay here. I couldn't remember the old country as home. I wanted to stay in the Arizona Territory. I didn't want to go home. I was already home.

Our adobe house on Convento Street was actually pretty big but only part of it was livable. It was in a big square shape typical of Mexican houses of the time. It had an open courtyard in the middle with the four wings of the house surrounding the courtyard. The front wing was flush up against the street with a door that opened to the street. We also had an empty lot next to the house. But a big part of the house was damaged and the roof leaked when it rained. So for a long time Mama and I lived in only part of the house. Papa was going to restore the rest of it but he died before he could even start. Drago was the one who ended up restoring the place and making it possible to use the entire house. But that was later.

Mama opened the restaurant at our house, lunches only. There would be no downtown bakery and restaurant. She couldn't afford a second place. She set up two long tables under the ramada in the large yard in the lot next to the house. It was cool there under the ramada in the hot seasons and warm enough in the winter. The outdoor ovens were also in the yard next to the house.

Our patio courtyard in the interior of the house was special because it had this big mesquite tree in it. The thick adobe walls and the shade from the mesquite made our little home cool even in the hottest summers. Mama made the patio off limits to her customers unless she invited them herself. On most days, she put me at a small round table under the shade of the big mesquite tree and gave me my lunch. When she'd finished with the customers, she joined me.

Mama worked day and night and in time after Papa died, she earned the loyalty of many customers. The Arianos restaurant was noted far and wide for its delicious meals and for the cakes and golden loaves of bread that you could purchase to take home after lunch. Few knew as I did that Mama was up at four every morning to make the hot buttered bread that she served every day. Mama worked all the time and so did I. We had to work hard or else we'd starve.

During the school year when I was gone during the day, Lupe came to help Mama serve lunch to customers and to clean up. Lupe worked for free for a long time. That's because Mama saved the life of Lupe's baby Dolores. Lupe was the daughter of Maria de los Angeles Gonzalez, who was Mama's best friend. Lupe married young. Her husband began to beat her even before the baby was born. One day in one of his rages, Lupe's husband picked up his newborn daughter and drew back to throw the infant against the wall. Lupe snatched the baby from his outstretched hand and ran for her life. She went home to Maria and never looked back.

A few days later the baby became very ill with a high fever. Susto, said Maria. Fright sickness. The baby is ill from fright because of what her father did.

Maria was sick then, too sick to care for the baby. Lupe was only 16 and didn't know how to care for a sick child so she went to my mama for help. Mama stayed up day and night for three days and worked to bring down the baby's fever. She taught Lupe how to bring forth the milk from her clogged breasts and how to feed the infant. Mama saved Dolly's life.

Lupe named the baby Dolores but we called her Dolly. "Dolores" translates as pain, grief, sadness or regrets. Never was a child more misnamed than was my Dolly. Dolly was happy all her whole life. She was always smiling. Dolly, my wife, my best friend, my partner, the mother of my five children. My mama saved my Dolly for me to love and live with for 55 years. And that's why Lupe came every day and worked for free until Mama eventually made enough to pay her.

I'm getting ahead of myself. I want to tell you now about the first time I saw Drago and his vegetable cart.

After I called her out to see the vegetables, Mama came up behind me whispering under her breath. She was wiping her flour-covered hands on an apron that was meant to protect her long skirts. Her eyes were wide and a smile grew on her face as she stared at the vegetables.

"Ah...che miraculo!" she said breathlessly.

What a miracle! Of course it was a miracle to have a selection of beautiful vegetables such as these. We live in a desert and it took a lot of work and a lot of water to coax this produce from the hot soil. Even at my tender age, I knew this. That's why I called her to come and see.

Mama barely glanced at the exotic-looking man. She turned her gaze to the vegetables. Drago watched Mama intently. The whole time there was a smile on his face.

There were many things I did not understand then. Now I can look back on those days and remember. I didn't know on that day I first saw Drago just how important this Chinaman would become to me.

***

At first Drago came every Monday morning. He attached a bell on his cart and Mama listened for it. When she heard him coming up the street, she wiped her hands and hurried out with her basket and a few coins to select the week's vegetables.

Drago watched her as she chose. He always had that same calm smile on his face. He noticed that she selected only the best pieces, the ones not over-ripe, the ones that would last the whole week, the ones that would taste the best in her dishes.

Later after he'd been coming for a while, Mama began to give Drago little gifts from her kitchen. Often she handed him one or two of her little fruit-filled pastries wrapped in brown paper. Drago always offered to pay her but she wouldn't have it.

Drago accepted the gift with a small bow. His little bows always made her smile widen. Often he would reach into the pile on the cart and select something to give her in return. More often than not, the gift was a bouquet of flowers. This never failed to delight Mama. She could not afford the luxury of flowers and would never buy them for herself. To receive them as a gift in exchange for her pastries was a very good deal, she thought.

Once I came upon them in those early days and I found Mama laughing. I think Drago must have been juggling three small melons just to amuse her. He stood there holding a melon in each hand with a clownish look of mock horror on his face. A third melon lay split open on the ground. Mama was laughing so hard tears fell down her face. Then Drago picked up the split melon, selected a clean chunk, and offered it to her. She took it and as she ate it, the juice ran down her chin. She bent forward to stop the juice from dripping on her clothing. Juice ran down Drago's chin, too. They both laughed harder. I grabbed the rest of the melon and ran off with it.

After Mama paid for her vegetables that first day and returned to her kitchen, I walked along the street and talked to this strange-looking man. Drago's English was really good. He spoke some Spanish, too.

"Where did you come from?" I asked.

"China. Jiangsu Province. My home town is Suzhou. You?" Even then he spoke to me as if I were a grown man.

"Italy. From the north in the mountains. I don't remember it at all. I was only a baby when Mama and Papa brought me here."

We walked a little ways without talking. I began again.

"What is your name?" I liked to ask questions but adults didn't always like to answer. This man didn't seem to mind my endless questions.

"Xia Yù Long."

"My name is Piero Dante Arianos. Dante is after my father. Piero is the same as Peter in English or Pedro in Spanish," I explained. "Everybody calls me Pete. What does your name mean?"

"Xia Yù Long. Jade Dragon. Long means 'dragon.' What is mother's name?"

"Rosa Arianos."

"Rosa," he repeated carefully. "This means 'rose.' Where is father?"

"Dead. My papa was killed in an accident when I was little."

Drago nodded sharply and fell silent.

Later when Mama asked me if I knew the Chinaman's name, I told her what he'd said.

"Dragon?...Drago, no?" she gave me the Italian word for dragon.

Ever after, she called him Signor Drago and I came to call him Drago as well.

That's how he got his name. Everyone called him Drago. He never complained. I guess he didn't mind being an Italian dragon.

Mama didn't fall in love with Drago right away although I think she secretly liked him from the very beginning. Who wouldn't like a man who brought her flowers and good things to eat and who could make her laugh? For a long time, Mama wouldn't let herself think about loving Drago. After all, he was a Chinaman, and we weren't supposed to even like, much less love, him because the Chinese were considered subhuman by many Anglos in those days.

But I think I know when Drago fell in love with Mama.

During my childhood the Catholics attended mass in a big cathedral close to our home. It's called St. Augustine's and you can find it still on Stone Avenue just south of downtown. The cathedral was rebuilt in 1897. Father Rodrigo asked Mama to sing at the rededication. Everyone knew that Mama had a wonderful voice. She could sing so well that she might have been famous had her life taken a different direction. When Mama sang, everyone stopped to listen.

Drago, too.

Mama agreed to sing at the rededication. She considered this a great honor and a spiritual responsibility. She wanted to do well to show her respect and devotion. Because of this, she began practicing every week as she had time, even though the rededication was six months away. She liked to climb a ladder up onto the flat roof of our adobe house and sing there, facing toward the south, toward the Santa Rita Mountains. The Santa Catalina Mountains were behind her, backing her up. I asked her once why she went up on the roof.

"It's the right place to talk to God and that's what I'm doing when I sing. Singing here helps me to be strong." Mama said. Mama was very religious. She talked to God a lot. She also talked to Jesus, the Virgin, and all the saints. Me, I never had much use for all that.

She was up on the roof one day when Drago came up the street with his cart. When Mama didn't appear at our front door, he entered the gate to the side yard hoping to find her at the outdoor ovens. It was then that she began singing. Drago moved into the yard and stepped away from the adobe wall so that he could see her on the roof. She was turned sideways to Drago and she never saw him there below her listening.

Mama stood straight upright, her long skirts moving slightly in the breeze. Her hands were clasped in front of her. She took another deep breath and out came that glorious mezzo-soprano, full and textured, subtle, rich with emotions I was too young to identify but would later know, emotions like passion and longing. She was singing the long Latin version of a sacred hymn, but somehow the music sounded like the yearning for a lost lover. Mama's voice dipped into seductive mystery and swelled into magnificent consummation. It seemed as if an entire world could be found in the sounds resonating from our roof. Tendrils of curly dark hair escaped from the knot on her neck. Her northern Italian skin, pale like a pearl, glowed in the sunlight, and her dark eyes sparkled. My mama was a beautiful woman and she sang like an angel.

Drago stood transfixed in our garden, his hands at his side, his head bent upward to watch her. He was utterly still, utterly silent. I know this because I was hiding high in the branches of a tall mesquite tree behind him where he couldn't see me. I was supposed to be doing my chores but I, too, liked to watch Mama when she was singing.

Drago stood for the longest time listening to Mama. I was watching Mama but when I looked at Drago, I saw that tears were running down his face.

I think that was the day that Drago fell in love with Mama, the day he first heard her sing.

***

A week or so after Drago first heard Mama sing, he appeared at our house with something really special, a box of ripe strawberries. Oh, so plump and juicy and sweet. And red. The strawberry plants on his little farm were just starting to produce. Only a few had become ripe, just enough to fill one box.

Drago was one of those Chinamen who had a little farm on the other side of the river beneath Sentinel Peak. They call it A Mountain now, but back then we called it Sentinel Peak because that's where we watched for Apache raiders. There were several Chinese men over there who had been farming for nearly twenty years. After they finished building the railroad, some of the Chinese stayed in Tucson. Several of them rented land together and began farming. We called their area the Chinese Gardens because mostly they grew garden produce, fruits and vegetables. Then they sold the produce in town.

Drago's Chinese garden was the first to produce strawberries.

When he came up our street that Monday morning, it was nearly midday, later than he usually came. About half of his produce was gone. He had a few good vegetables saved for Mama. And he had that single box of plump red strawberries displayed ostentatiously. There was no way Mama could miss it.

Sure enough, she pointed excitedly, "Fragole!"

"Strawberries, Mama," I said. "Speak English."

"Strawberries?" she repeated as a question, looking at Drago.

He shook his head sadly, "Very sorry. These are special, not for everyone."

"Ah, no?" asked Mama. Her voice was thick with disappointment.

"No," Drago said. His face was serious but his eyes twinkled. "These are only for una donna italiana."

Mama gasped. Then she smiled to hear what he was saying, and that he said the words in her native language. He was telling her that the strawberries were only for an Italian woman. She didn't know it but Drago asked me earlier how to say these words in our language. I was the one who taught him. I had to laugh, too, when I saw Mama's reaction.

Her eyes sparkled. "Ah, sì, Signor Drago," she asked seriously, playing along. "Do you know una donna italiana?"

He raised his eyebrows innocently. "Do I?"

"Sì, Signor Drago. Io sono una donna italiana. I am an Italian woman." Mama was blushing now and smiling still.

Drago told me later that he thought the Italian words coming from her lips sounded like music.

"Ah! What good fortune!" he grinned. With both hands extended, he bowed slightly and ceremoniously placed the box of strawberries in Mama's hands.

"Grazie, Signor Drago, grazie," Mama whispered. Thank you, she said. Her cheeks were very pink and I thought she looked even prettier than usual.

That box of strawberries won Drago his first invitation to lunch. Mama led him into the patio of our house to the place where the customers never went. She had a large round table there with chairs under a very large mesquite tree. That's where we ate our meals except on those few occasions that it was raining or too cold in the winter.

She and Lupe waited on the customers that day. Many of them were businessmen who worked in the center of town. In those days, El Centro was just a few blocks from our house. A few customers were ranchers who had come into town to buy feed and supplies. Some customers were Anglo and a few were Mexican. The Anglos had their table and the Mexicans had a different table under the ramada.

Whenever she had a break from serving, Mama would come and sit with Drago and me while we ate. She fed us handmade pasta noodles with her rich, thick, magnificently seasoned tomato sauce. Chunks of squash, peas, carrots, and onions with lots of fresh garlic from Drago's farm were tossed in and the whole thing was covered with a sprinkling of parmesan cheese. The cheese had come all the way on the train from San Francisco. The parmigiano was something the customers never saw. It was just for the Italians, Mama said, and for a certain Chinaman, too, as it turned out. She gave us pieces of baked chicken to go with the pasta and thick slices of fresh-baked bread covered with creamy butter.

That day Mama asked Lupe to handle the customers. After we finished the chicken and pasta, Mama washed the strawberries in a pan on the table in front of us while Drago and I watched. She made four servings, a bowl each for me, for Drago, for Lupe, and for herself. She cut the strawberries and crushed them a little so that the juice ran.

Then she spooned the strawberries gently over pieces of sweet cake she'd made only that morning. Mama poured thick, heavy cream on the cake and strawberries.

Drago ate everything with a pair of chopsticks that he produced from his jacket. Watching him pick up the bits of strawberry and cake with his chopsticks made Mama laugh. Somehow he even managed to sop up every drop of cream. Everything disappeared into his mouth.

"Good food. Good cook," Drago said when he finished. Contentment was all over his face.

"Grazie, Signor Drago," Mama answered with a satisfied smile. Mama liked her cooking to be appreciated.

Our Chinaman often came to lunch after that.

***

Drago began to come each Monday later and later in the day, more toward noon. Mama would always formally invite him to eat with us even though his presence came to be expected and, I think for Mama, eagerly anticipated. It's odd now to think of how people then thought the Chinese were so inferior. Fact is, Drago was the one who brought a little culture into poor Mama's life.

One day, after the first couple of lunches, he produced a small book from his jacket. We were sitting in the shade of the mesquite and relaxing after what had been an especially good and filling lunch. All the customers were gone, Lupe had gone home to her little Dolly, and I was lying in a hammock in the shade.

Mama looked at the little book with considerable curiosity. It was small, with pages so thin and fragile you could see light through them. They were covered with vertical lines of Chinese characters. The cover was brown and very tattered.

"You can read, Signor Drago?" Mama asked.

This may seem like a strange question now but at the time it wasn't at all. Most of the Chinese immigrants in Tucson were very poor and completely illiterate laborers who had come from southern China, hoping to make their fortune in America. They all hoped to return home eventually with some of their American-earned wealth.

Drago was different. He was far more educated than the other immigrants. And as we found out later, he had come to America to stay. He could not go home because of the political situation. Years later, when it was possible to return, he didn't want to go back anymore because of Mama.

"Yes, of course," Drago answered with a smile. "I read to you now in my childhood tongue - it is the Han language of China, not the same language as these Canton-speakers you know in Tucson. And then I translate to English."

He began to read and what he was reading was poetry, very old poetry from China. He would stand and announce the name of the poet, the dates he or she lived, and which dynasty ruled at the time. Then Drago read the poem, slowly and sonorously, first in Chinese and then in English.

Mama listened raptly. Hearing the beautiful lines was like feeding her soul, poor Mama, who worked night and day and lived only for me and the Church and her music. Now Drago brought her this poetry.

He started with one of the most famous poems by Li Bo.

"Xiao Rosa, Xiao Pete," Drago began. "Poem is called 'Drinking Alone in the Moonlight' by Li Bo. T'ang Dynasty."

'We promised to meet in the far Milky Way' was the final line of the Li Bo poem. When she heard this, Mama sighed.

"Oh, so beautiful, Signor Drago, che bello!" Her face was shining.

He grinned and read another. Drago went on like this for days, poem after poem.

I often fell asleep. There was something about his voice and the rhythmic recitation that just rocked me into a deep sleep. I missed a lot of Drago's poetry recitations because I was sleeping. As an adult, though, I came to understand what Drago was really doing with his poetry readings. I learned his intention because he left the poems among his papers. Each poem had been carefully chosen, as was the order in which he presented them to Mama. The order was very important. I could see it so clearly when I looked through his papers. Of course, as a child, I didn't understand that Drago was courting Mama. Food, flowers, kindness, laughter and poetry were the weapons in his battle to win her heart.

Some of the early poems in his collection were about the beauty of the landscape or perhaps a solitary person's struggle with loneliness. Later the poems turned to love, to conjugal contentment and sensual bliss.

When I discovered the poems in among his papers and figured out what he had been doing, I laughed out loud. How daring Drago was with my mama! I think the word "seduction" is not too strong really. Can you seduce a woman with strawberries and poems? I think our Drago did just that.

I'm getting ahead of myself again. I'll come back to Drago's poems later.

CHAPTER 6

"OH, this is so romantic!" Maggie and Jade said the same words at the same time.

Jade tried to get up from her seat. "Sorry. I need to go to the bathroom." Zhou helped her by pulling her up.

"What do you think of Drago?" Seri asked Zhou.

"I think he was from a mandarin family. The memoir mentions his papers. Are the papers in this box? I very much would like to read them."

Seri shook her head. "No, nothing in Chinese." She turned to the others. "Before the revolution, the educated intellectuals were called mandarins. They acted as civil servants for the emperor."

"How did Drago end up in America?" Letty asked although she guessed the answer. Life turns upside down sometimes. Something had turned Drago's life upside down.

"I think we'll find out in this memoir," Seri smiled.

Jade returned and Seri said, "Shall we continue?"

Maggie and Jade made tiny clapping motions with their hands. Seri began to read again.

***

In those days, I didn't think too much about what the adults were doing when I wasn't around. I had my own problems. I went to school every day. I helped Mama after school. In the evening after chores, Mama lit a kerosene lantern at the kitchen table and helped me with my homework.

"Remember, mi figlio, you come from an educated family. Both your parents were educated. Your grandfather was a teacher himself and your grandmother spoke five languages and taught piano. Study hard and do well." She placed her hand on my head as a blessing. Then she kissed and hugged me.

And there were Mama's prayers. On her knees by the light of a candle, she held the rosary in her hand and said her prayers. She prayed each night to the Virgin that I should be a good boy and a good student. She prayed that I would grow up to be a learned man and that I should find the way to make the world a better place for everyone.

Her admonitions and her prayers were not why I worked so hard in school. The real reason I worked so hard was so that I would grow up to make enough money to buy Mama a piano. It was Mama's dream to have a piano to play as she sang. I dreamed of buying her one and making her happy.

The truth is that school wasn't really all that hard. I did do quite well as a scholar. Later, when I was graduated from the university and became a lawyer, Mama told me that all her prayers had been answered on that day.

My biggest problems were outside of school. I was a small boy, slight of frame and never very tall as a child. It wasn't until late in high school that I gained my full growth. I was what you might call a runt. My skin was fair like Mama's, but my hair and eyes were dark like my Mexican friends in the barrio. I always played with the Mexican boys, especially my best friend José, who was Maria's grandson.

That I was small and dark and ran with the Mexicans made me a target. The Anglo boys picked on me constantly. They liked to shove me around. They took whatever coin or food that I might have in my pocket. Drago once gave me a sweet, juicy orange and they took that, too. I soon learned to carry nothing and to run when I saw them coming.

Not all of them were bad. My main tormentor was that Nate boy, Nate House. Nate's papa William House was rich. He had a ranch and a big mercantile store in El Centro. Mr. House was one of Mama's lunch customers. He didn't have a wife. Nate's mama died when he was a baby. You would think that not having a mama might make Nate more tender-hearted toward the less fortunate, but no. Nate was mean as a snake, pretty much like his dad. José and I became very good at finding new ways home from school so that Nate and his pals wouldn't see us and have a chance to harass us.

What I hated most about those boys was that they made fun of me for not having a father. At the time, I thought that their taunts didn't make sense. Some of them didn't have fathers, either, and like I said, Nate didn't have a mother. Even so, it hurt my feelings and made me angry when they yelled at me.

"Hey, runt," I heard them yelling after school. I hated being called a runt. It made me want to beat them all up and show them who was a runt. But if you think I had a hard time, you should have seen Wong the laundryman's son, Ping. That kid really was a runt. He didn't stand a chance. Ping got really good at running.

Also, they called me bad names, too, like "wop" and "dago."

Technically speaking, I was an Anglo just like them because I was born in Europe. But the Anglos saw me as an undesirable southern European or just another Mexican. Things were changing that way. The Mexicans once had ruled this country. Before them were the Papago Native Americans. But now more and more Anglos were coming. Some were on their way to California. Some came to stay forever in Arizona. Our land had once been part of a much larger Sonora, the northernmost state in Mexico. Then in 1854 Arizona was made part of the U.S. The Anglos were increasing in number. They had a lot of the money, too, and controlled most of the businesses and had the nicest houses. They started cheating and taking land from the Mexicans who had lived here for generations. They looked down on the Mexicans and, of course, they had always looked down on the Indians and the few blacks.

There were the Chinese immigrants in Arizona. Most were laborers who came to work on the railroad and in the copper mines. I found out later that a law was passed in 1882 called the Chinese Exclusion Act that barred Chinese immigration. But the Chinese in Tucson had been here for a while already. They were poor and illiterate. Anglos considered the Chinese to be down there on the bottom along with the Indians and the blacks, which was little better than slaves. There were a few Chinese who had some money but most of them didn't. If they escaped the mines or the railroad, they went to work as laundrymen, grocers or laborers. A few were lucky enough to become farmers in the gardens across the river.

Things were a little easier for the Chinese in Tucson compared to other places in the West, mainly because everyone in our little town had something bigger to worry about. We had a common enemy, the Apaches. We had to band together to protect ourselves from those wild raiders who regularly came down from the mountains to pillage the lowland settlements. Everyone, Anglos, Mexicans, Chinamen, even the Papagos, were scared to death of the Apaches. The Apaches were tough.

Drago was just another Chinaman to the Anglos. His real trouble started because of loving Mama. Nate House, you know that boy who treated me so mean? Nate's father William House used to come to lunch at our place just about every day. He usually brought two or three of his men with him. He called them hired hands but they were little better than thugs. Hired guns, really.

At first William House was polite to Mama. Then he got to be more and more familiar with her. I realize now when I think on it that he must have set his cap for her. Likely he had something less honorable than marriage in mind. I don't know. He was so rich and powerful. I guess he figured it was just inevitable that she'd see things his way.

I know for a fact that Mama didn't like him. She was always polite to him, but she never smiled at him. She never sang when he was around. She just took his money for the lunches and the loaves of bread he bought and his big tips, too. That's all. He asked to come calling and she always politely put him off, saying she was too busy to receive visitors. He just laughed. I guess he figured that she would give in to him eventually.

Then William House started touching Mama. He would pat her on the shoulder or grab her hand and even once tried to put his arm around her waist. Mama always twisted away gracefully. She started sending Lupe to wait on him and his men. That didn't work either. He started to seek out Mama. He was becoming a real annoyance.

It all came to a head one day when House stayed after all the other customers were gone. He watched Mama and Lupe clean up. House didn't know it but Drago was up on our roof making repairs before the monsoon rains began.

When Lupe disappeared into the kitchen with dirty dishes, House saw his chance. He rose to his feet as Mama was about to clear the dishes from his table. He grabbed my mama around the waist and said, "I think it's about time I got a little kiss from you, Miz Arianos."

Mama tried to twist away from him. Her arms were pushing at him but he was holding her so tight that she couldn't get away. House drew near and tried to press his lips against hers.

Mama cried out, "No! Mr. House! Please! No!"

I ran to see what was wrong. I got there just in time to see Drago descend the wooden ladder partly by leaping and partly by sliding down that ladder so quickly that he got there in no time. House released Mama and stepped back when he saw Drago coming to stand next to Mama.

The two men glared at each other. I could see a muscle twitching in Drago's jaw.

"This Chinaman bothering you?" asked House.

"No, no, of course not," Mama said. Mama was furious. Her face was red and her fists clenched. She always did have a temper. "You are bothering me, Mr. House. I think perhaps you best not come to lunch again." It was the longest speech in English I'd ever heard Mama make. And it was perfect English, too.

House's face turned crimson. He grabbed up his hat and stalked out of our yard.

Just as he got to the gate in the adobe wall, House turned, looked directly at Drago and pointing his finger angrily, he growled, "You stay away from her."

Mama and I watched in stunned silence as House stomped away. Drago had this look on his face that I will never forget. It was downright scary.

Mama started to cry. She pulled her apron up to hide her face and she stood there in the garden and sobbed loudly. Mama never did anything halfway, even crying.

Drago's face changed instantly from icy fury to tenderness as he turned to Mama, and said to her very gently, "Forget him, Xiao Rosa. Come with me. We read poetry now." Mama dried her tears and followed Drago into the patio. Soon enough I could hear her laughing again.

In all their long life together, Drago never could stand to see Mama cry, and he would do anything to make her laugh again. And usually he could.

House didn't come to lunch anymore and we thought maybe that was the end of it. Not so.

***

I told you that Mama and I lived in the barrio south of Tucson's central district which we called El Centro. Except for us, the barrio's inhabitants were all Mexicans. I grew up in that barrio, Barrio Libre we called it. That was my world and I was happy in it. My best friend was José Gonzalez, who was the grandson of Maria de los Angeles Gonzalez. José and I did everything together. We even got in trouble together.

It was no surprise then that José found Drago just as fascinating as I did. If we didn't have any chores to do, which wasn't often, José and I followed Drago around as he peddled his produce. We walked beside him and waited while he made a sale of vegetables or fruits. In between houses and the sales, we'd ask him questions about all sorts of things in the way children do.

We were deeply curious about him. We asked if we could go home with him. Drago said yes, but he told us that we had to ask permission from our parents. Both Mama and José's mother Sylvia Rodriguez de Gonzalez said maybe. Maybe someday if we were very good, and if Señor Drago wasn't too busy, perhaps we could go to his house for a little while on a Sunday afternoon.

Maybe.

Do you know how much a kid hates to be told 'maybe'? 'Maybe' is worse than 'no' because you still have a little hope but not much and you don't know when, if ever, you'll get what you want. 'Maybe' is agony to a child.

So José and I cooked up this plan to follow Drago home without him or our mothers knowing. After he finished his rounds, Drago took off walking with that cart and horse toward home. We waited behind a fence in Old Naco's backyard and finally we saw him pass us and go toward Sentinel Peak. Now days Sentinel Peak is called "A" Mountain because somebody got the idea of putting a big A on the side. In those days, though, we called it Sentinel Peak because that's where the lookouts went to watch for Apaches coming to raid us. The lookout watched for dust clouds raised by their horses as they came across the desert floor toward Tucson. If the lookout saw the dust, he would raise the alarm.

So José and I crept along in the twilight moving from tree to tree where Drago couldn't see us. Those of you who know Tucson now might wonder what the hell I'm talking about when I say we crept along from "tree to tree." There's nothing there now between downtown and Sentinel Peak but a wide flat stretch, the interstate highway, and that piss-poor excuse of a dry riverbed they call the Santa Cruz.

Back around 1897 and 1898, the land between the barrio and the Chinese Gardens beneath Sentinel Peak was really, really different than it is now. Back then there was a lot of water in the Santa Cruz River, a year-round flow. The river in the area I'm talking about sort of widened out and turned into a marshland with a small main channel and many small rivulets. All along the streams were tall cottonwoods and a bosque of really large mesquite trees. We called the marshland "la cienega." It was a paradise really. All that water in the river was full of turtles and fish and a million birds were in the trees. Early in the morning you could see their wings shining as they took flight. On the other side of la cienega was the old Convento of the San Agustín Mission.

That's all gone now. The Chinese were farming small plots over there on the other side in a place that had been farmed by the Papago for thousands of years and their ancestors, the Hohokam, before them. We called the Indians Papago back then but now they're talking about taking back their own tribal name. When they do that, we will call them Tohono O'Odham, not Papago. Now the Chinese gardens are all covered up with a trash dump. I refuse to go over there anymore.

When we got older, Jose and I went to the river often and fished the streams and climbed the trees and, in general, had a good time enjoying the Santa Cruz. It's all gone now. Everybody drained off a part of the river. Mainly it was the Anglo ranchers who wanted water for their cattle ranches and orange and grapefruit orchards, and there was the lake upstream. They drained off a lot of water to make that lake so that people could go swimming and boating. The lake is gone now, too, washed away in a big flood that changed the river channel. The Chinese took water for their gardens, and the Papago took water, too, just not as much as the Anglos and the Mexicans.

It makes me sick to look at the Santa Cruz now. It is nothing but a long straight dry ditch with ten-foot high concrete walls. Flood control they call it. Back then, when José and I were kids, the Santa Cruz River was a paradise.

So it was really possible for me and José to slip from tree to tree in the evening shadows and follow Drago to his little one-room adobe house. In time, we learned that he did the same thing every evening. He would feed and water his horse first. Then he'd wash himself down by stripping off his clothes under the ramada, wetting himself, soaping up and rinsing himself off by pouring water from the olla over his body. Then Drago went inside to eat something. He always drank this green tea, too. It was usually getting dark by then. José and I headed home by dark. If we arrived too late, we would definitely get in trouble.

Occasionally, especially in the early summer when the days were long, we could stay a little longer and spy on him. We did this off and on for several weeks and we thought we were getting away with it. Later, when I was grown up, Drago started a conversation once that went like this, "Remember those times when you and José followed me home?" That's how I found out that Drago knew all along we were out there. It makes me laugh to think about it now, but at the time I was embarrassed. We were just these little boys getting into trouble.

Once we went over during the midmorning when we knew he was selling his vegetables. We peeked into his window. There was a heavy padlock on his door. If there hadn't been a lock there, I don't know if we would have had enough nerve to go in or not. So we looked through the window.

Drago lived simply enough. He had only a bed, a table and chair, and some shelves with a few dishes and pots as well as a little cook stove. On the table were these long brushes, ink, and rolls of white paper. Hanging from the walls were long scrolls of that white paper with neat Chinese characters written on them. Drago wrote the scrolls himself. I don't know what the scrolls said. Drago told me once that they were poems.

José and I only went once during the day. We were too scared of being seen so we usually went back in the evening. We thought we were very clever spies to follow him like that. Really we were ornery little devils.

One evening not long after House and Drago had their little confrontation, José and I were surprised to discover that we were not the only ones following Drago home. Two men, both Mexicans, trailed after him. They were both on horseback and Drago was leading his old horse pulling the vegetable cart. I knew one of the men. His name was Francisco Guerra and he had a reputation for being a drunk. I knew he did odd jobs for William House because I saw House paying him some money once. Guerra immediately went and spent that money on a bottle of mescal. So Guerra and this other man were following Drago in the middle of the road, not even trying to hide. I reckon Drago knew they were there, just like he knew José and I were there, but Drago showed no fear.

About the time that Drago got really close to the river, the two men spurred their horses forward and cut Drago off. They both dismounted and exchanged some words with him. José and I couldn't hear anything, but the two Mexican men sounded angry.

What happened next still amazes me, even after all these years. The two men attacked Drago and Drago fought back. But he fought in a way the likes of which I'd never before seen.

The two went after him with punches and jabs. Drago gracefully stepped out of the way of their flailing fists. He used the momentum of their own bodies to throw each of them roughly to the ground. He blocked punches and when the chance came, he spun and kicked a man into submission as he himself agilely deflected or avoided all blows.

"Mira!" José whispered. "Look!"

"I see, I see," I whispered back. We were hiding behind a ten-foot-high cluster of nopal cactus in the growing gloom, both of us mesmerized by the sight of the three men going at it. Within three minutes, Drago had both of them on the ground licking their wounds. They glared murderously as Drago turned, took his horse's reins in his hands and walked away. He walked, I said. Not ran, but walked. Drago didn't even so much as look back.

I can't tell you how impressed José and I were at seeing Chinese martial arts for the first time. After that, we figured Drago was about the most macho man we'd ever known. I mean he could win a fight without even breaking a sweat.

We hid behind the nopales for a long time. We didn't want Guerra and the other man to see us. It wasn't until the two men picked themselves up and left that José and I started walking home. That was when I looked back and saw a man on horseback hiding in the shadows of a cottonwood tree. It was too dark for me to recognize him but it was clear to me that he'd been watching the fight and had never once revealed himself.

***

In those long summer days when José and I stayed longer to spy on Drago, we discovered that he had other things that he liked to do after he ate. Often Drago would leave the little house and start walking again but this time, instead of coming back to the barrio, he went in the opposite direction. He climbed Sentinel Peak to the west of his little farm, and sat down up there or crouched down like the Chinese do. He didn't do anything, just watched the sun set on the mountains.

I understand why he sat up there. The view of the mountains from that spot is great. The light moving across the Santa Catalinas is quite beautiful from Sentinel Peak because the mountains turn this magnificent copper color just before the sun disappears below the horizon. Hope I can see it one more time before I'm gone.

If he didn't go up on Sentinel Peak, Drago had another thing we saw him do frequently. On certain special nights, Drago left his little adobe house and headed back to El Centro. He always went to the same place, a big long adobe building on Pearl Street with a sign over the door that was written in those strange characters, just like on Drago's scrolls. He didn't come out for hours. José and I always gave up and had to go home before he reappeared again.

Our curiosity about the place was killing José and me, so one day I told Drago that I had seen some Chinese men going into the building. What exactly was that building? I asked. It was the truth, too. I did see some Chinamen going in there.

It's the Chee Kung Tong, he answered.

You can guess what my next question was.

"It is like a club or society for Chinese in Tucson," he said. "Because we are far from Chinese homeland, we meet together in this place."

"What do you do in there?"

"We talk a little and drink tea and sometimes we play a game called mah-jong. It's a game similar to your dominoes game."

That was enough to satisfy our little-boy curiosity. It sounded like boring adult stuff. The truth was much more interesting, but it would be a long time before I found out what really went on behind those doors.

***

"Okay, that's enough for today," Seri said. "Jade needs a siesta. We all need a siesta. Let's meet here again tomorrow for more about Drago and Rosa and Pete."

Letty turned to Zhou, smiling. "So Drago was another gong fu fella' like you."

Zhou grinned and nodded. "Chinese martial arts has a long history."

He pulled Jade to her feet. "Wife must rest now. See you tomorrow."

CHAPTER 7

THEY met the next day, again at Jade and Zhou's home. Not long after gathering together and sharing cups of coffee, Zhou's cell phone rang. He left the group and went into the house to answer the call.

When Letty entered the kitchen with empty cups a little later, she could hear Zhou speaking French in a low, growling voice. He was frowning.

A few minutes later, he returned to the patio.

"Letty, will you go with me later to the airport? We must meet Jean-Pierre Laurent."

"Laurent? Isn't he your Interpol colleague? He's coming to Tucson? Why is he coming here?"

"I explain later. We go in the afternoon. Okay?"

"Okay," said Letty. She was surprised at his behavior. Zhou was usually pretty cheerful, but now he seemed very annoyed.

"Gather 'round," Seri smiled. "Time for more of the adventures of Pete Arianos in nineteenth-century Tucson.

***

Although José had chores just as I did, he and I spent most of our free time together. When we could sneak away, we'd disappear together and play hide-and-seek with the other children in the barrio. Once José was given a ball for his birthday and we played with that until we accidentally kicked it into an arroyo just after a monsoon rain. The swirling waters carried it away. We both were sad at the loss but soon found other things to do.

Mancha was with us then. Mancha was my dog. He was the best dog in the world. Mancha and José were my best friends. Mancha liked to play hide-and-seek with us. He was good at seeking but not so good at hiding.

June is always the hottest month in southern Arizona. José and I would lie low during the middle of the afternoon. Everyone took a siesta after lunch, even Mama. It was too hot to do otherwise. Early in the morning, she did all her cooking and baking in an outdoor kitchen with outdoor ovens. The little adobe house stayed fairly cool that way. In the afternoon, Mama would close her bedroom door, take off her blouse and skirt and go lie on her bed dressed only in her camisole and pantaloons. She stayed in there in the middle of the afternoon for an hour or so. Then she'd rise and dress and begin work again. Later, after Drago and Mama married and they got electricity in our house, he bought her one of the first electric fans to come to Tucson. She loved that fan and she loved Drago for giving it to her.

July was our favorite month because that's when the monsoon rains began. The real name is 'tiempo de aguas,' which means time of waters, or 'chubasco,' which refers to a sudden violent rain storm. But the Anglos coming changed everything. They took to calling the summer storms "monsoon" and the arroyos are called 'washes' most often now.

We loved the monsoon because the storms were exciting. They were noisy and filled with crackling lightning. Also the rain cooled the hot summer air. But best of all during the monsoon, the arroyo west of our street would fill with water. The arroyo was a big gulch or dry creek bed that carried water to the Santa Cruz River in the rainy season. Sometimes we had to wait hours for the turbulent water to subside. It was too dangerous to go in the water too soon after the rains. We'd be swept away just like José's ball. After a while, though, the water would become still and settle into deep puddles at the bottom of the arroyo. José and I and all the other children in the barrio would jump into the puddles and splash around joyfully until the water dried up and we were left waiting for the next storm.

It was after one of these storms that Drago became a hero in our barrio. The arroyo west of the barrio was especially full and running with a muddy, raging torrent after a particularly big storm. No one went near the edge or even thought of trying to cross it. Drago was trapped on our side of the arroyo and was waiting patiently with his empty cart and his horse. He knew it might be hours before the water went down. He just hunkered down, squatting as Chinamen do, and waited. Or he stood up and leaned against the cart and looked at the water and the mountains in the distance and waited.

Mama told me to go fetch him and bring him to our house for supper. That's when I heard the screaming.

Upstream along the arroyo, one of the granddaughters of Maria de los Angeles Gonzalez, a granddaughter who was called Serafina and who was only three years old, wandered away from Maria's house and got too close to the edge. The sodden sandy bank gave way and Serafina slid into the turbulent waters.

Drago heard the women screaming. He followed their pointing fingers and saw Serafina rushing toward him in the torrent. Her little head bobbed up and down in the waves. Everyone could see that it was only a matter of time before she was pulled under. The arroyo emptied into the Santa Cruz River. The river also was way above its banks and flowing strong. Serafina would likely drown before she got to the river but if she did happen to make it there alive, the Santa Cruz would carry her away, perhaps never to be found.

She had only one chance of survival and that was Drago.

The women told us later that Drago didn't hesitate.

He jumped into the water just before Serafina's little body arrived at the crossing. It's hard for me to tell you just what this meant for him to do that. I mean the monsoon storms were like nothing you've ever seen. They were wild, violent, beautiful things. Still are. First the storms came as a heavy, dark blue cloud followed by winds that knocked over trees and blew the roofs off houses. Then rain. The storms were preceded by that wild and uncontrolled lightning that flashed from cloud to cloud across the dark sky like strands in an electric spider web. Mama would stand in the doorway that led to the yard and watch the sky and the wind ripping through the mesquite and palo verde trees. She loved it because it was so exciting. The monsoon was and is a wonderful and dangerous thing to behold.

So there was that baby taken away by the monsoon waters, carried along like José's ball to certain death by drowning. Drago jumped in after her.

Drago plucked baby Serafina's chubby little body from the rough waves and held her to his body as the water swept them both away. They were carried along for nearly a quarter of a mile before Drago managed to catch the roots of a palo verde tree that extended into the arroyo. By that time, the violent waters had bruised and banged him up pretty bad by knocking him into rocks and the walls of the arroyo. Somehow he managed to protect Serafina's little body with his own. She clung to his neck for dear life and he held onto her little body with one hand while he desperately reached out for something to grab. He finally found that palo verde root. That's what saved their lives.

Drago pulled himself and Serafina up the slippery, sandy walls of the arroyo and stumbled back toward Maria's house. He was met halfway by nearly the entire Gonzales family. They had been crying and screaming and begging the saints to help Drago.

The saints came through and helped our poor half-drowned, soaking wet and muddy Chinaman that day. I still don't know how he survived. Drago lifted his exhausted arms and handed Serafina to Maria. Serafina wasn't even crying when Drago handed her back. Can you believe that? She went from Drago's arms to Maria's, sucking her thumb and staring at everyone. Only then did she start crying, when she saw everyone else crying.

Drago collapsed on the ground and violently coughed up and vomited muddy flood waters. The men in Maria's family carried him back to Maria's house, stripped him down and washed him off with clean rain water, gave him some dry clothes and a small glass of tequila and lime to drink.

Our Chinaman fell asleep on a thick mat under the ramada in Maria's backyard. José and I watched him sleep and made sure the little children didn't wake him as they played around him. They took care of Drago's old horse, too. Later Maria fed him all the huevos and chorizo with frijoles and tortillas and salsa that he could eat. When the next day came, the waters had gone down enough for Drago to cross the arroyo and the Santa Cruz River and go home to his little farm.

In those times, there was a lot of anti-Chinese sentiment among the poor Mexicans in Arizona. The Mexicans blamed the Chinese for taking their jobs, first on the railroad and then in the mines. When the Chinese were banned from working in a lot of places, they opened up businesses in Tucson and in towns all over the West. They operated small grocery and supply stores, laundries, whatever to make a buck. The Mexicans resented them for that, too, resented them really for working hard, saving every last penny, and doing well.

Mexicans and Anglos even formed Anti-Chinese Leagues in several places in Arizona and around the West, including in Tucson. If the Mexicans and Chinese were at each other's throats then they wouldn't turn on the Anglos, who were the ones with the real power and most of the money.

None of this applied to Drago, though, after he saved Serafina. He became an instant hero. In case anyone forgot that he was a hero, Maria de los Angeles Gonzalez reminded them of that fact. Maria and her son Memo wouldn't let anybody in our barrio ever say anything against our Drago, even if he was a Chinaman.

***

Serafina's rescue was the talk of the barrio. The saints had answered everyone's prayers and she was spared. The Gonzalez family decided to hold a fiesta in honor of Serafina's salvation and in honor of Drago who was the one chosen to do the will of God. He was invited to come to the Gonzalez home on the next Saturday evening. He was told to bring his family.

Mama was invited, too. Everyone in the barrio was invited. Father Rodrigo didn't live in our barrio. He lived at the church. But he was everyone's priest so he was invited as well. Mama offered to bring some pan dulce and some loaves of her bread with butter. Most of the women brought something. There was so much food and drink that it could have fed an army. The Gonzalez boys filled the yard with luminarias so that when dusk fell, we could see our way around. The luminarias, little paper bags with sand in the bottom and a lighted candle upright in the sand, gave the entire Gonzalez yard a beautiful, magical look. Soon the house and yard filled with chattering neighbors.

José's father, Eusebio, and his brothers, Memo and Paco, began to play their guitars. They sang, too. I stood and watched Eusebio's fingers. Eusebio was teaching me how to play. He said I learned very quickly. This was a secret. Mama didn't know that I was learning. I wanted to surprise her someday. In my imagination, I would ask her to sing then I would whip out my guitar and accompany her.

Everyone was happy that night, laughing, chatting and singing along with the Gonzalez brothers. Then Drago arrived.

If I thought he looked strange before, I hardly knew what to think now. He was cleaned up and dressed up in his best Chinaman clothes. He wore a long ivory-colored silk jacket that extended almost down to his feet. The jacket had strange fastenings on the side of his chest and very long wide sleeves that came down to his fingertips. There were slits in the side of the jacket that revealed brown silk pants tied at the waist. On Drago's feet were elaborately embroidered silk slippers. And of course, he had that long, long braid hanging down his back.

The neighbors fell silent and stared. Finally Maria came forward and took Drago's hand and said warmly, "Bienvenido, mi amigo." Welcome my friend. "You no bring family?" she asked in English.

"No family," answered Drago. He looked a little nervous, even though he never stopped smiling. One by one, others came forward and shook Drago's hand and slapped him on the back. A drink was thrust into Drago's hand just as the Gonzalez boys began to play again.

Drago looked around until he found Mama. She was standing away from the others. Like me, she had been staring at Drago's unusual clothing and appearance. She continued to stare at him even when his eyes found hers. At the time, I thought Mama found Drago as strange *looking as I did. Now, I think she may have been thinking something altogether different.*

After a lot of eating and running around chasing each other, the children began to tire and were carried away one by one to bed. I was older and allowed to stay. The adults began to dance to the music of the Gonzalez brothers' guitars.

Drago found Mama in the crowd. He bowed low before her and said something to her. I couldn't hear him so I don't know what but I guess he asked her to dance. Drago was smiling when he extended his hand to her.

Mama accepted his hand and he led her to the center of the hard-packed dirt floor. Drago took Mama in his arms and they began to dance gracefully in circles to the sounds of a waltz. Mama's cheeks began to turn pink and she couldn't seem to stop smiling.

They were an exotic and beautiful pair, Drago in his Chinese silk clothes and Mama looking like an Italian Renaissance Madonna. I don't know where Drago learned to dance like that, maybe in Hong Kong, but he sure did make Mama happy that night.

I looked at Maria de los Angeles Gonzalez and Father Rodrigo. They had their heads together and were whispering. They stopped talking and watched Mama and Drago. I never knew what they were saying for sure, but thinking about it now, some seventy years later, I think I have a pretty good guess.

***

After the fiesta honoring Drago and Serafina's deliverance, Memo began to invite Drago to drink cerveza with him and the other men in the barrio. That meant that Drago had yet a third place he visited in the evenings. There was Sentinel Peak to watch the sun set, the Chee Kung Tong on Pearl Street, and more and more often, Drago went to Memo's house in the evenings. The men sat in the courtyard and drank beer and played cards and listened to Eusebio's guitar. Memo and Drago became close friends and stayed that way for years and years, just like me and José.

Now when I look back on what happened next, I think Drago must have made a decision that night of the fiesta. I think he decided that it was time to take a wife. He decided that he wanted Mama to be the one he would marry. I guess he figured he was going to have to give up being a Chinaman in order to win her hand.

A few days later, he appeared at lunch at our home dressed in American clothes. I mean to say, his Chinese clothes were gone forever. Instead, Drago wore denim trousers and a long-sleeve white cotton shirt rolled up at the wrists. Leather boots had replaced the cotton shoes. No one commented on his new clothes but I could tell that Mama and Lupe were dying of curiosity to know what was going on.

Drago lingered after lunch. Mama and Lupe were cleaning up and washing dishes in the kitchen when Drago motioned to me.

"I need your help, Xiao Pete," he said seriously. He pulled a long pair of scissors from his bag that normally was kept on the cart.

"The time has come for me to become an American man. I will not return to China. This is my home now. I have new life. I take new name also. Drago Shaw."

Shaw was an old Middle English name that sounded a lot like Drago's family name Xia which was pronounced "shah." So Mr. Drago Shaw he was from then on.

Drago handed me the scissors and said, "Please cut queue. Cut hair close to head, please."

My eyes went round with wonder. Even at my tender age, I knew this was a very significant moment in Drago's life. How significant I did not realize until later. My casual reading of Chinese history would inform me of the meaning of that long queue Drago had worn for all his life.

When the Manchu rulers overthrew the Han's Ming dynasty, the Manchus forced the queue braid on all men in China. After a time, the queue became a sign of respectability and honor. The only ones without the queue were identified as criminals and rebels, and rebels at the time were the same thing as criminals. For Drago to cut his queue literally meant that he couldn't go home because returning to China without a queue would brand him immediately as a criminal.

Of course, I didn't know it at the time but in fact, Drago really was a rebel, a real revolutionary, and therefore a criminal, too. Later, much later, when he was an old, old man, Drago told me how it was that he came to America, escaping in the middle of the night on a ship in Hong Kong harbor. I wish I knew more details. All I know was that Drago was the second son of an important mandarin family in China. As a young man, he'd gone to Hong Kong to study medicine and there he fell in with revolutionaries. Their group was called the Furen Literary Society. Later they joined forces with Dr. Sun Yat-Sen and his followers.

Drago's group advocated a coup against the Manchu's Q'ing dynasty. But the revolutionary movement failed and members were threatened with execution. Drago, or I should say Xia Yù Long, was forced to flee for his life. First, he hid in the ship that took him to Hawaii and from there to San Francisco. Eventually he came to Arizona where the Emperor's men couldn't find him.

At that time, the Chinese were still prohibited from entering the U.S. under the Chinese Exclusion Act. There weren't supposed to be any new Chinese immigrants coming into America at all. The white folk figured they'd had enough of the "yellow peril." And yet Drago had papers. He had papers that said he was born in America and that it was legal for him to be in the U.S. I don't know where he got those papers, San Francisco maybe. In other words, the papers said he was a natural-born American citizen. People like him were called Paper Sons. But I know for a fact that Drago was born in Jiangsu Province and came to America late in 1895. I know because Drago told me this himself.

All his life, Drago collected news stories about events in China. These clippings of his, and a few letters he exchanged with other expatriates, are included in a separate folder attached to this memoir. Drago knew about the eventual success of Sun Yat-Sen's revolution in 1911 and how the Q'ing dynasty was overthrown. By that time, of course, Drago had Mama, and me and eventually six more babies to think of. So he never seriously considered going back to his homeland.

Drago also knew about the civil war between the Maoists and the Kuomintang that came much later. And he knew about the Maoist government and all the changes that happened in China after that. Drago left the Celestial Kingdom forever in 1895. He was an American citizen by virtue of the fact that he had these forged documents saying he was born here. But I know that just as part of Mama's heart was forever in the Italian Alps, I believe part of Drago's heart stayed forever in China.

So cutting his queue that day on our patio meant that Drago was casting his fate in with all the rest of us who had immigrated to America. That day when he handed me the scissors, he was taking a big, big step. It meant much more than losing a long braid.

Drago removed his shirt and sat down on a bench. I looked at his muscled shoulders and chest and hoped that when I grew up and became a man, I could be just like Drago and look like him, too. I wanted to have muscles just like his.

I went to stand behind him and just as I was lifting the scissors to the nape of his neck, Mama came through the kitchen door and into the patio.

"Che cosa fai? What you are doing, Piero?"

Her eyes went wide when she saw the scissors.

"Dios mio," she said in Spanish. "My God" was something Mama said a lot and always in Spanish. I guess she figured that, since she was in Arizona Territory, she had to speak in Spanish for God to hear her.

"What are you...?" She moved around so that she stood in front of Drago and me. Her hands were on her hips as her eyes swept over Drago's bare chest and shoulders. She looked away, blushing. I saw her bite her lower lip. Then Mama turned toward us and bent over so that her face was on a level with Drago's face.

Smiling at him, Mama said, "Signor Drago, do you truly wish to cut long hair?" She shook her head and wagged her finger in front of his face in a teasing way. She never stopped smiling.

"Yes," Drago whispered. "I wish to be American."

"Va bene," Mama said. She looked at me. "Io lo farò." (I will do it.)

As for me, I didn't want to see. I was confused about what Drago was doing. The air seemed thick with emotions I didn't understand. I figured it was better for me to go off with Mancha and take a nap or find José or something. I handed her the scissors and ran. Mancha followed happily.

I didn't see what happened next. Drago told me that he lost his braid that day but really it was more than that.

Rosa came to stand behind Drago. She pulled a bit of yarn from her pocket and tied it tightly around his braid as close to the top as she could get it. She began to snip above the yarn very close against his head. She cut the queue away bit by bit until it rested heavy in her hands. She came to stand again in front of Drago, and laid the queue across his knees. She smiled.

"Now I cut hair very close and all grow out same and soon again I cut whole head." She gestured broadly with both hands. Rosa couldn't talk really without using her hands.

"Bene? Good? Yes, I mean, yes, you agree?" she asked.

"Yes. Please." Drago whispered.

Rosa moved around Drago now slowly snipping away at the hair remaining on the back and sides of his head. When it was very short all over and as close to the scalp as she could get it, she was satisfied. Later, as the shaved part of the front of his head began to grow out, she would clip his entire head until the hair was even all over.

"Finito," Rosa said. She handed the scissors to Drago and came to stand behind him. She brushed his shoulders with her towel and she blew away stray hairs. She rested her hands gently on his bare shoulders.

"Not be sad, Drago. All will be well," Rosa said in a soft voice.

***

After Mama cut off that long braid, Drago was often at our little home. So often that I wonder now how he was able to maintain his own place. He must have worked furiously when he wasn't with us. With Mama, he helped her to do things that she and I weren't strong enough to do on our own. He would climb or crawl to places she couldn't go, he repaired things, and carried heavy things, and in general, made himself very useful. And he continued to recite those Chinese poems to her.

There was one difference, though. Once she came to rely on the pleasure that the poems gave her and when Drago was certain that she wanted more, he asked her for a "trade."

"What is 'trade'?" Mama asked.

"I give you poems, you give me music. I want you to sing for me, Xiao Rosa."

Mama turned quite pink in the cheeks and murmured that her songs had no value compared to his beautiful poems. Drago gently insisted.

So sometimes after the poems were recited, Drago would sit back in the rocking chair in the patio and Mama would softly sing for him. Sometimes she sang religious songs from the Cathedral choir. Those were mostly in Latin. Often she sang Italian folk songs and occasionally an aria from an Italian opera. Those arias really moved Drago. Tears always leaked out of the corners of his eyes. Mama smiled at him tenderly when she saw the tears.

"Continue, please," he would say as he wiped his eyes with the back of his hands.

Once she sang him an old Italian lullaby, the same one she sang to me when I was a baby. And you know what? Drago went to sleep! Mama and I giggled to see him snoozing so peacefully so we tiptoed back into the kitchen to do the dishes. We left him there in the rocking chair to take his little nap, sung into slumber by Mama's lullaby.

Usually these poetry and music sessions started right after Mama cleared away the lunch dishes, wiped her hands on her apron, and sat down in a rocking chair under the tree. She waited contentedly for Drago to begin. This was her favorite time of day.

I remember how he made a show of shuffling papers as if he were trying to decide which poem to read first. I know now that he knew exactly which poem he would read. I was asleep during some of these recitations and sometimes I wasn't even present. That's because I was *off playing with Mancha and José. Yet I know all about the poems from finding them later in his papers after Drago was gone.*

Drago began with that famous Li Bo poem. I already told you about that one. The final line of a Ming dynasty poem by Yang Chi, "Five-Color," made Mama sigh and smile. "The butterflies might land on me!"

Later poems turned toward stories of parted lovers who suffered from longing for each other.

"'Moonlit Night' by Tu Fu," Drago announced, first in Chinese then in English.

"In Fuzhou, far away, my wife is watching
The moon alone tonight, and my thoughts fill
With sadness for my children, who can't think
Of me here in Changan; they're too young still.
Her cloud-soft hair is moist with fragrant mist.
In the clear light her white arms sense the chill.
When will we feel the moonlight dry our tears,
Leaning together on our windowsill?"

The day came that Drago recited a poem by Huang O.

"Xiao Rosa," Drago said softly as he seated himself on a little bench next to her, "This next poem is called 'A Farewell to a Southern Melody.' You will like." He smiled at her tenderly, and began to read first in Chinese then in English.

"The day will come when I will
Share once more the quilts
And pillows I am storing
Away. Once more I will shyly
Let you undress me and gently
Unlock my sealed jewel.
I can never describe the
Ten thousand beautiful sensual
Ways we will make love."

The silent space between Drago and Rosa became charged with electricity. Slowly, so slowly, Drago reached out and laid his hand on one of Rosa's. His eyes never left her face as his fingers clasped hers firmly. He could feel her warmth. She was trembling.

Rosa looked down at those two entwined hands. Her cheeks burned as the fingers of her other hand twisted the corner of her apron. She was silent but Drago could see a small, secretive smile forming on her lips. Seeing that, his smile widened.

Then Rosa's free hand released the apron corner and moved to cover Drago's larger hand.

Drago was certain that he had never been as happy in his life as in this moment.

CHAPTER 8

Now you might think that Mama and Drago had come to some sort of agreement. But Mama still had two problems that stood in the way.

The first problem was me. Mama wanted me to have a good father, one that I loved and respected. Having a good father for her son was very important to my mama. She believed that Drago cared about me and she thought I felt the same. But she had to be sure.

I was helping her wash dishes. She was very quiet, which was unusual for Mama because she sang all the time. She was so quiet that I was beginning to wonder if something was wrong when she finally spoke.

"Piero."

"Yes, Mama."

"Do you like Signor Drago?"

"Oh yes, Mama. He is a very good man. I really like him."

Of course, what I was thinking about at the moment was the birthday gift Drago had given me. Drago had come up our street that day with his horse and his cart and vegetables and something special for me.

Mama invited him to lunch. After we ate, Drago disappeared for a few minutes. He returned with a big box on his shoulder. I was too short to see but I could tell the box had no top. And it was moving and making sounds!

Drago was grinning from ear to ear and so was Mama. Apparently Drago had asked her permission first, because she seemed to know *exactly what was going on. Drago brought the box down where I could look into it.*

He said, "Xiao Pete, happy birthday to you. Here is your gift."

A puppy! My puppy Mancha was in that box. Mancha was squirming and jumping up trying to get out of the box. When Mancha saw me, he started wagging his tail furiously. I picked him up and Mancha licked me all over my face which made all three of us laugh.

Mancha was a beautiful puppy. He had spots all over him and one ear went down and one ear went up. He had one blue eye and one brown eye and a long tail that wagged a lot. Mancha was the best dog in the world. I loved Mancha instantly and I loved Drago for giving Mancha to me. Later, after we'd eaten some cake, I thanked Drago for my wonderful birthday gift.

Drago smiled and said, "Take good care of dog, Xiao Pete. Don't make your mother work more."

When Mama asked me if I liked Drago, what else would I say? The truth was that I thought that man hung the moon.

Then there was Mama's second problem.

Mama went over to Maria de los Angeles Gonzalez's house most every Sunday afternoon after siesta. They sat together in the shade on the portal behind Maria's house and did what they called "handwork." Often they were joined by Lupe and sometimes other women from the barrio. They would embroider pillowcases and sheets and tablecloths and all that stuff that women thought was so important to make a home.

What they were really doing was talking. They gossiped about everybody in the barrio. They talked about the work of the Church and the priest and all the Anglos who ran things in town. They talked about the weather and who was pregnant and who was sick and how the crops were doing and what new goods were in the mercantile and who had what they called "woman's trouble."

Lupe told Dolly who told me much, much later that on one of those Sunday afternoons, Mama was there with Lupe and Maria when Mama started talking about Drago.

Lupe said Mama was very hesitant at first. She spoke barely above a whisper and at first, Lupe couldn't figure out what was bothering Mama. I mean, she didn't talk about Drago directly but really she did. You know what I mean?

Lupe told Dolly that her mother Maria was so sweet and always kind but also she believed in being direct about things, especially matters of the heart. So Maria said outright to Mama,

"Rosa, I think it's time you marry again. Your Dante would want that."

"Sí?" said Mama, acting very curious but all those ladies knew that Mama was thinking the same thing.

"I know just the man for you," Maria continued.

"Sí?" asked Mama.

"Yes, I think that Señor Drago is the perfect husband for you."

"Sí?" asked Mama. Lupe said Mama turned really pink and started fanning herself with this fan that Drago had given her. The fan had come all the way from China and was made of ivory and white silk. Mama was fanning herself furiously. That's how Lupe knew that Mama was thinking just the same thing but couldn't say so.

"Yes, of course. He is perfect. He works hard, he is good with your son, he is honest, he is brave, he is handsome and kind. What more could you want?" asked Maria.

Then Mama said what was really on her mind. "But Maria, he is a heathen."

So that was the problem! Mama was so religious. I think she already loved Drago but it was really bothering her that he wasn't a Catholic. She couldn't help loving him. At the same time, she couldn't marry him as long as he remained what she called a "heathen."

Maria laughed. "That is a small matter. By the time the Padre and I get through with him, that Chinaman will be more Catholic than the Holy Father in Rome. A good man is hard to find, Rosa. Señor Drago is a good man. You better catch him before someone else does."

***

A few days later Drago didn't show up. He didn't come all day or in the evening. On the second day when he hadn't appeared for lunch, Mama was beside herself with anxiety.

"Something is wrong, Piero," she said. She made me go with her to find the priest. She told him about Drago's absence and expressed her fears that something bad had happened. Father Rodrigo took her seriously. The priest admired Drago greatly after Drago's rescue of little Serafina.

So the priest and I harnessed his horse to his wagon and we went to look for Drago. We followed the dusty road west out of town and toward the Santa Cruz River. In those days, the river widened out into the cienega with all those trees and birds. Several Chinese men had gardens at the foot of Sentinel Mountain on the other side of the main river channel and the marsh. The padre stopped to ask the Chinese men laboring in their fields. They pointed to a small acreage on higher ground toward the hill. I followed. I didn't want the padre to know I'd already been there.

There we found Drago in his tiny one-room adobe house. Really not in the house. He was lying on a raised pallet outside under the shady ramada. Mama was right. Something was really very wrong with Drago. He'd been beat up something awful. He had cuts and bruises all over his body. Both eyes were black and his lips were cut and swollen. He looked really bad. His eyes were closed when we arrived and I could hear him groaning.

Father Rodrigo sent me to get some water from the big olla inside the little house. The padre woke up Drago and helped him to sit up so that he could sip some water.

"What happened, Drago?" I cried. I could hardly bear to see how hurt Drago was. I was scared, too.

"Nothing, it's nothing," Drago whispered.

Drago was working in his field hoeing weeds when they came. He had been up for hours. His cart was loaded with fresh vegetables ready to take to town later. As he worked his way up and down the rows of peppers, then tomatoes on their wooden stakes, then a row of zucchini squash he'd planted just for Rosa, he thought about the poems he would read for her on this day.

The thought of his Italian beauty made Drago even warmer than the sun did. Of all his gardening tasks, he loved weeding. It gave him time to think. As he carefully hoed the rows, his thoughts were on Rosa, the way she called him to her table, "Va mangiare. Come to eat," she would say in that musical voice. He loved the sight of her fingers clasping the big blue bowl full of noodles, the swell of her breasts beneath her white blouse as she bent toward him, those tendrils of hair that escaped from her hairpins and brushed against her slender neck, the delicious scent of her as she walked by. What luminous skin, like lotus petals. And those dark eyes, so mysterious, so full of promises. How he longed to touch her, to pull her close.

Drago stopped in his reveries long enough to wipe the sweat from his face. That's when he saw them. There were five of them. They were coming for him.

He saw the men crossing the cienega where the Santa Cruz River widened out between Sentinel Peak and the town of Tucson. The Santa Catalina Mountains provided a beautiful backdrop to the scene: the desert, the wetlands with rivulets lined with tall cottonwoods and mesquite, the neat green fields tended by Chinese farmers, the little adobe town and presidio of Tucson east of the river.

Drago felt a coldness in his heart. He knew he was going to have to fight. He had no gun. All he had was his training in martial arts, his brains and his heart.

The five, led by House, rode their horses up the dusty road that led to his house and into his field. They trampled his vegetable plants. House looked down from his horse at Drago standing there holding the hoe like a lance and said, "I thought I told you to stay away from that woman."

Drago said nothing. What was there to say? They would have to kill him to keep him away from the woman he loved.

The men dismounted and formed a loose circle around him. Drago stood ready. One of the men began to move toward him. Drago spun suddenly whipping his leg around and up into the head of the approaching man. The man went crashing down, unconscious.

When he saw what Drago could do, House held back after that and let the other three men do the dirty work. Drago fought valiantly using the hoe at first and then his fists and feet. He was winning slowly, very slowly against them using his kung fu skills and brains to outwit them. When House saw that most of the blows and the hardest ones were going against his men, he entered the fray himself. Drago was tiring, the sun was hot, the three men fought dishonorably. More and more punches landed against Drago's face and chest until one finally brought him to his knees.

That was all it took. Once they had him down, House took over. He beat Drago nearly senseless. Then they left him there only half conscious in the hot sun and the broken plants of his garden.

After they were gone, Drago slowly dragged himself out of the field and under the ramada next to his house. It took him nearly an hour to move only a few yards. His ribs were broken where they'd kicked him as he lay in the dirt, already defeated. The cuts were full of dirt and bled when he moved. The bruises were already starting to show on his bronzed skin.

He pulled himself onto the pallet where he slept under the ramada on hot summer nights. There was a half a cup of tepid green tea left over from breakfast. Drago drank it and collapsed onto the pallet. He groaned in pain.

More than twenty-four hours later, Padre Rodrigo and I found him there.

Padre Rodrigo told me to tether Drago's horse behind our wagon. Father helped Drago to the wagon. The padre supported Drago with his shoulders. That was hard because Drago was tall for a Chinaman and the priest wasn't a very big man himself. I helped, too.

Padre gently assisted Drago into the back of the wagon where he lay down. Getting him into the wagon was hard. Drago's broken ribs caused him to turn white and groan. But he never cried out, never said a word. He gritted his teeth and took the pain. Father and I took Drago back to the Church and Father Rodrigo put Drago into his own *bed. Father sent me to fetch the doctor. Later, I took Drago's horse to Memo and Memo took care of the horse.*

The priest and I tended Drago's wounds after the doctor left. We made sure Drago got enough water because he'd gone so long without it. When Drago began to feel a little better the next day, we got him to eating again. That's when the priest allowed Mama to come and visit Drago. She came twice a day with warm soup and bread. Father Rodrigo was always present. It was the custom in those days, you know, not to leave an unmarried man and a woman alone together. Father Rodrigo didn't know about the poetry readings.

Mama brought Drago good things to eat for many days. She fed him her thick minestrone soup herself, spoonful by spoonful. Tears rolled down her cheeks. Drago just watched her through his black and swollen eyes as he accepted her spoon through his split lips. His own face was mournful, sorry not for himself but for Mama in her misery.

"Please do not cry, Xiao Rosa," he spoke gently to her. He could not bear her tears.

"Mia colpa, mia colpa," Mama whispered. My fault. My fault. She suffered to see Drago so hurt. She suffered because she believed that she was responsible for Drago's injuries.

***

Drago's getting beat up turned into an opportunity for Father Rodrigo to start turning him into a Catholic. Maria hovered in the background like a mother hen and encouraged both Drago and the priest. Father Rodrigo started by saying, "It is time for you to take a wife, don't you think, Drago?"

Notice that everyone, even the priest, called him Drago. None of us could even remember Drago's real name. We were all calling him "dragon" in the Italian language.

"Yes," Drago answered thoughtfully, "I think of this often."

The priest continued, encouraged by Drago's response. "You are here in America now, starting a new life. Yes, it's time to marry and have a family."

"*I want family very much*" *said Drago.*

Father Rodrigo was encouraged to hear Drago's words.

"*There's only one thing standing between you and marriage, I would say*," *said the priest. He looked at Drago, who was still lying in bed. Drago had been hurt so badly that it took him nearly ten days before he even had the strength to get up and walk around.*

Drago was surprised at these words. "*What is that thing?*" *he asked. He had an almost alarmed tone to his voice.*

"*Well..*," *said the priest.* "*Let's say there's a certain woman you had your eye on.*" *He glanced at Drago to see how his words were being received. Drago was looking at Father Rodrigo intently, realizing now that there was something he'd overlooked in his plan to win Mama's hand. He desperately wanted to fill in the gaps and discover what final obstacle stood between him and union with the woman he adored.*

Father continued. "*Let's say you fall in love with a woman who is very religious, a very sincere and devoted daughter of the Church. She might love you, Drago, but she could never marry you if you hadn't been converted and baptized in the faith.*"

Drago's eyebrows went up. "*Ah*" *he said. He understood exactly what the priest was telling him.*

"*You might want to consider taking instruction and converting to Christianity. Your conversion must be sincere, of course,*" *the priest finished. Things must be just as Maria described them, thought the priest.*

For a couple of days, Drago said nothing to the priest or anyone else about the matter. Then he took the priest aside and asked Father Rodrigo if he could receive instruction in preparation for converting and becoming a member of the St. Augustine parish.

Drago considered that now was his only chance. If he didn't marry Rosa and soon, House would continue to harass her. House would go after Drago, too, if he ever saw Drago at Rosa's house again. The next time, Drago knew, House would try even harder to kill him. But if Drago married Rosa, he reasoned, House could do nothing. The marriage would be legal and church-sanctioned, and House would have to respect that.

Already there was talk in the Territory of making illegal all marriages between Chinamen and either Anglos or Mexican women. If that happened, Drago wouldn't be able to legally marry his beloved Rosa. He didn't have much time. Converting to her religion seemed like a very small sacrifice to win such a great prize. Drago was right to hurry. The law making marriages like theirs illegal was passed in 1902 and not rescinded until 1967. Of course, by then neither of them cared because they'd been married by the priest in the eyes of God and the Church and soon enough, Mama was big and pregnant.

Drago began his instruction in the catechism of the Holy Church. Later, when Drago was better and had gone back to live at his little farm again, he continued to come into the barrio a couple of evenings a week to see the priest. No one knew about this except Father Rodrigo and Maria de los Angeles Gonzalez, who always knew everything. No one told Mama.

An interesting thing happened. Later, many years later, Drago told me himself that at first he sought instruction with the sole intention of winning Mama. Much to his surprise though, he found midway through the process that his conversion became sincere.

Father Rodrigo taught Drago about the scriptures, the Gospel, the Sermon on the Mount, and a lot of the parables recounted by Jesus in the Bible. Father Rodrigo said that Drago asked good questions and he made the priest understand his own faith better.

As for Drago, he decided that Jesus of Nazareth was a fully Enlightened Being just as Gautama Buddha had been. Jesus taught his followers to practice the spiritual discipline of loving kindness just as the Buddha had done. Based on this understanding, Drago decided that he could sincerely become a Christian and follow the teachings of the Buddha called Jesus.

So there he was, that Chinaman, learning to be a Catholic, and just in time for the consecration and dedication of St. Augustine Church.

Remember me telling you about how Mama was asked to sing for the dedication?

A few days before the event, Drago was back reading poetry to Mama after lunch. On this day, he sat back down next to Mama in her rocking chair under the mesquite tree.

"*Xiao Rosa, I want to go to church and hear you sing for dedication. May I, please?*"

"*Of course, Drago.*" Mama was pleased. His coming to church with us fit in with her plan of converting him from being a heathen and thus fit for marriage. Mama had no idea, of course, that Drago was way ahead of her. He'd almost finished his instruction with Father Rodrigo.

The new church was full that day. The Holy Mass went without a hitch as far as I could tell. I wasn't paying much attention. I was bored as usual and through most of the mass, I was daydreaming about playing with José and Mancha when it was over. José was a few pews away from me. He turned around every now and then and made faces at me, and I did the same until Maria saw us and made us quit.

Everything got better when it was time for Mama to sing. She was dressed in her very best dress of dark indigo silk. She stepped forth from the choir and after everyone fell silent, the organ began to play and Mama sang. Her wonderful voice penetrated every inch of the vast interior of the church. Everyone sighed and listened raptly to her rich and vibrant sound, so full of devotion and love and spirituality.

Drago was sitting beside me. He had on his best clothes, too, not those Chinaman best clothes but a dark suit and a starched and ironed shirt. He looked uncomfortable until Mama began to sing. Then he was, like all the rest of us, caught up in the magic of her music. When she finished, more than a few of the ladies were crying and I actually saw tears in the eyes of some of the men, Drago among them.

At the close of the service, everyone filed out. Drago stayed in his place, though, and when I started to move, Drago reached out and put his hand on my knee and said, "*Wait, Xiao Pete.*"

So we waited until Mama joined us. Then Father Rodrigo came.

"*Come now to the chapel,*" the priest said.

The four of us went into a small chapel off the main sanctuary and there we met Maria and Lupe and Maria's sons, Eusebio and Memo, who had become Drago's friends.

Father Rodrigo said simply, "*Thank you for coming. We are here to welcome into our midst a new soul into the Holy Church.*"

He directed Drago to kneel in front of a small altar. He and Drago exchanged some whispered words. Father took holy water and sprinkled it on Drago's head and made the sign of the cross over Drago. He said a bunch of things in Latin. He gave Drago his first communion. He made Drago into a Roman Catholic that day, a Roman Catholic Buddhist, I mean, though no one except Drago knew about the Buddhist part.

Mama stood by, stunned at first. Then she began to cry. Drago had to turn from the priest and hand her his handkerchief. He had a sheepish look on his face but I knew he was pleased at her reaction.

After the ceremony was over, everyone shook Drago's hand and Maria kissed him on the cheek. "Welcome, Señor Drago. Good luck to you." She glanced meaningfully at Mama then back to Drago. She wasn't talking about good luck being a Christian. She was talking about good luck with Mama.

Everyone left, even me, because the priest took me by the hand and said, "Now come with me, boy. We need to leave Drago and your mother to talk."

I guess Drago had it all worked out beforehand. What he had not anticipated was his own reaction.

Rosa and Drago stayed behind, alone in the little chapel. Rosa dried her tears and smiled sweetly at Drago.

Drago stared at her intently. He dropped down on one knee in front of Rosa and took one of her hands in his. Father Rodrigo had explained to him that this was how you proposed marriage to a woman in America. Drago looked up at Rosa. He froze. He just flat out became paralyzed with fear. He hadn't figured on getting so scared that he couldn't talk.

Xia Yù Long who had traveled across the vast Pacific Ocean from the other side of the earth, the exiled revolutionary who had cut off his queue and put away his silk tunic, who had taken up a new faith and a new life in a new world, who for months had wooed with food and poetry and gentleness this beautiful woman standing expectantly before him, this Xia Yù Long who was courageous and brave and smart and articulate, who was all those things and more, was suddenly struck dumb with overwhelming emotion.

Drago breathed raggedly and opened his mouth but no sound came out.

Rosa said softly, "You want to ask me something, Drago?"

Drago nodded dumbly. Still no words.

Rosa waited and when no sound came, she said sweetly with her most beautiful Italian Madonna smile,

"You want to ask me if I will marry you and be your wife?"

Drago nodded yes. His eyes filled with tears.

"Is that because you love me?"

Yes, he nodded. He brought her hand to his lips and held it against his cheek. He closed his eyes. Rosa could feel his tears on her fingertips.

"Drago," she commanded him to look into her eyes.

"I love you, too, Drago, and I will marry you."

Rosa bent forward and kissed Drago softly on his cheek.

Drago stood upright and took Rosa into his arms. Pulling her close, he pressed his mouth to hers and kissed her deeply, a long, tender and very passionate kiss that left Rosa blushing and breathless.

They drew apart just as I came back into the room.

"Piero, Drago and I have something to tell you," Mama said.

I looked into their faces expectantly.

Finally Drago found his voice.

"Your mama and I are going to marry," he said softly.

I whooped with joy so loud that it made Father Rodrigo come running.

CHAPTER 9

*A*UTUMN *came to the Old Pueblo and José and I returned to school. We didn't mind it too much. It's not that we were tired of summer. It was more like we were ready for something different.*

Mancha went with us to school every day. He sat outside the school door and waited. I liked to look out the window and see him lying there with his head down on his paws. Sometimes his eyes were closed and sometimes they were open watching for me. Once in a while, especially after he got a little older, Mancha would disappear. I think he had friends he visited in the neighborhood. He was always there, though, when the last bell rang. When I came out the school door, Mancha would jump up and come running with his tail wagging and a big smile on his doggy face.

José and I walked home and oftentimes Ping the laundryman's son came with us. The three of us figured that we were stronger together than just one alone. Those other boys led by Nate House still liked to pick on us. One time a boy that was always with Nate ran past me and José and Ping. The boy's name was Al. He reached out and grabbed my lunch box and knocked it on the ground. Usually there wasn't anything in it after school but once there was an orange I was saving. Drago gave it to me. The orange rolled on the ground and Al caught it and took off with it.

Later I saw Nate House eating the orange. Made me really mad. Al did that just to impress Nate. Actually I forgave Al for doing that. Everybody was scared of Nate because he was such a bully. Al was just trying to survive and he used my orange to smooth his way with Nate House.

After Mama and Drago decided to get married that day at the church, they set a date a few months in the future. Mama met with Maria on Sunday afternoons to make a beautiful wedding dress for Mama.

I came upon Drago and Mama once going around our house and grounds and talking excitedly to each other. Mama had a notebook in her hand and a pencil, and she was writing down what Drago said. He pointed to this part of the house and then that part and gestured grandly with his hands and laughed and talked some more.

They were planning to renovate the crumbling parts of the old adobe building on the far side of the patio and convert it into our new living quarters. Drago wanted extra bedrooms so I could have brothers and sisters, he said. The part of the house we were living in at the time, the front part that faced the street, was to become the new store Drago planned to open. The main door of the store would open onto the street. Customers could enter there and do their shopping. The patio and living quarters would be private space for our new family.

"We will do well, Xiao Rosa," Drago said. "We will make a good living for our family," he said softly to her. "I will be a good husband for you."

He took Mama's hands in his and she just looked at him and smiled and glowed. I think she admired Drago a lot as well as loved him. He kept his promise, too. He was a good husband. And he was a good father to all of us kids. He loved me every bit as much as he did my brothers Tony and Leo and our sisters and baby brother.

I guess it was because I was going to be his son that Drago started taking me places with him. Sometimes I would go help him in his big garden on the other side of the river. It was hard work but I liked it because I knew it would make me into a man like Drago.

While we worked, Drago told me that he was planning on opening a grocery and supply store in town but that he would always keep his farm.

"I came from landowner family in China, Pete. For many long generations we keep big farm. Many peasants work for my family."

He paused to look around and I realized that he was thinking out loud. He almost never talked about his life in China and I didn't want to interrupt him.

"I do the same in America. Someday I will own much land. I start with this small land. Yes. Land is precious. We will keep this land. Soon I will build house here for Rosa. It will be cooler here for her and she can have her flower garden. We will make the house on Convento Street into a big store. Later. Later....in a few years."

"Now all my learning in China is no good in America," Drago laughed ruefully. "Americans not so interested in T'ang poetry and fine calligraphy or understanding of Kong Fu Zhu philosophy. I am American now. So I will become merchant and farmer." He nodded sharply downward.

"You, Xiao Pete, are smart boy. You will become scholar. You will do well. Bring honor on our family."

For a boy to hear this kind of confidence and affection expressed toward me meant everything. I vowed right then to make him proud of me or die trying.

I asked him, "How do you say 'father' in China?"

Drago grinned and said, "Ba. Little children say 'Ba ba.'"

I wanted to call him Ba but I was too shy.

On Sunday afternoons when Mama was sewing, Drago took me along with him to other places, too. Mancha went with us everywhere. We climbed Sentinel Peak and watched the sun set. José was often with us on our climbs.

As autumn turned to winter and the days mellowed and became cooler, Drago took me with him on Saturdays to sell his fall produce in town: squashes, tomatoes, melons, and later greens like spinach. On his cart he carried an abacus. That's this Chinese thing with polished wooden beads on spindles that Drago used to calculate the cost of his sales. He could use it very fast, pushing the beads back and forth along the spindles with a clicking sound. He taught me how to use it. I got pretty good at it but never as fast as Drago.

Christmas came and luminarias lit up the neighborhood. We had a procession at the Church and Mama sang. Drago and I sat in the congregation and Drago beamed when she stepped forward to fill the church with her magnificent voice.

One day in the new year, Drago said, "Come with me, Pete. We go to tong now and help prepare for celebration."

"What celebration?" I immediately asked. Thanksgiving and Christmas were over and it was a long time until the next holiday. And the tong! He was taking me to the tong!

"Yes," he said with a smile as we walked toward Pearl Street. "Coming next week is Chinese New Year. New Year Spring Festival and Mid-Autumn Festival are the two big Chinese holidays."

He looked down at me and grinned when I asked, "Will there be mooncakes?"

Drago had introduced me to mooncakes in the autumn. I loved mooncakes. I especially liked the ones filled with sweet apricots and other kinds of fruit. Mooncakes are really great.

"No. Not mooncakes. But there will be other good things to eat. And firecrackers."

"Firecrackers!" I loved firecrackers and the Fourth of July only came once a year. Firecrackers in January was a dream come true.

Not long after, we were standing in front of the Chee Kung Tong door on Pearl Street. Drago knocked and a minute later, the door opened.

Standing there at the open door was Ah Lo, who worked for Wong the laundryman.

"Dai Goh! Please come in. Have you eaten?" Now this was all in Chinese and I didn't understand a word, but Drago told me later.

Drago answered in Chinese and then switched to English for my benefit.

"Pete, follow me."

My eyes were about to pop out of my head. I felt as though I had stepped into another world. Everything was different from the world I knew. There were red cloth banners with that odd-looking Chinese script on it hanging everywhere. The furniture in the rooms and hallway was made of wood and carved into interesting shapes.

I peeked into one large room. It reminded me of the inside of a church but all topsy-turvy, not at all like St. Augustine. It reminded me of a church because there was an altar with candles and a big cloth hanging down that had a huge gold dragon on it. The dragon's eyes were flashing red. On the opposite wall was another banner with a triangular shape and a Chinese character in the middle of the banner.

And the smell. A strange fragrance filled the air. It was exotic, pungent, not sweet exactly, just different. Incense, Drago told me.

We walked down a dark hallway and passed doors on both sides, some open and some closed. Just as we passed one, a dark wooden door was flung open. Standing there was a young Chinaman in rough work clothes. He stared at us with a dreamy half-smile on his face. His eyes were unfocused and it seemed he was a little unsteady on his feet.

I looked beyond him into the smoke-filled room. There were benches and wide wooden shelves with pillows and everywhere there were men lying or sitting. Most of the men were smoking very long, thin-stemmed pipes with small bowls. With one exception, they all looked very like the man at the door. They were young, hardworking Chinese laborers, dreamy-eyed, not quite present, laughing softly to themselves.

The one exception was a young Anglo man dressed in nice clothing. His shoes were off and his collar undone. He, too, was reclining against the wall and was smoking from the unusual pipes. His eyes were half-closed and he never looked our way.

The fragrance coming from that room was different than the incense, heavier, sweet, almost cloying. The scent lingered and permeated everything.

"What are they doing, Drago?" I asked. I'd never seen anything like the men in that room. They seemed almost to be drunk.

"They are smoking opium. The smoke makes them forget their pain."

"Did they get hurt?"

"Yes. They came to America. They work very hard all day for little money. They have no family, no wife, no children. They are poor and lonely. They miss China, their home. They smoke to forget loneliness and sadness."

I looked up at him. I must have had a confused look on my face.

"You must stay away from the pipes, Xiao Pete. Opium is a bad dream, a fog that fills the mind and takes over the body. It destroys people. Opium is the way that China was weakened and destroyed by the foreigners."

I had no idea what Drago was talking about but I got his message. I would do his bidding.

We continued down the hallway and now we could hear voices and laughter. Drago stopped at another door and knocked. It was flung open and I could hear a chorus of male voices rising in recognition of his presence.

"Dai Goh, Dai Goh," they called to him, "Join us in mah-jong."

I looked into the room. Five men had risen from a table covered with a felt cloth and were standing back respectfully to make room for Drago. I could see small ivory pieces with written characters on them scattered across the felt. I thought perhaps it was a game like dominoes and later Drago told me that I was correct.

Mr. Wong the laundryman came forward from the group of men. He was smiling but there was something wrong. Children often can perceive things that adults cannot see. And I could see that the smile was on Wong's face but not in his eyes. I'd never been this close to Wong, and I could see now that he wasn't very friendly.

Wong and Drago went out into the tong courtyard. I ran to catch up and watch.

Drago was seating himself at a long wooden table. Spread out before him were very long, narrow red sheets of paper, some brushes, a block of that very black ink he liked to use, and a flat stone block. He poured a little water on stone, put some ink there, and begin mixing it with a brush.

Wong made a few comments in his sing-song language. Then he stood back.

When Drago got the ink like he wanted it and when the brush was loaded with the black pigment, he began to write in large characters onto the red sheets. His movements were graceful, grand and sweeping, and ending with quick flourishes. Of course, I could not read what he wrote but I thought the black ink against the red paper was very beautiful. I wished Mama could see the calligraphy.

As he finished the first sheet, Wong gestured to a servant who quickly removed the paper. I watched him as he carried it across the courtyard and placed it carefully to dry in a little patch of sun against the other wall.

Drago continued painting on the papers for over an hour. I sat quietly and watched and wished that I could try. Drago was very quiet. After a while Wong disappeared. An old woman came with tea. When she offered it to Drago, she grinned at him and winked. He grinned back and said something in a low voice. The old woman giggled and answered in that incomprehensible language. For me, she had a cup of cold lemonade.

When he had finished the last of the red banners, Drago pulled out a smaller sheet of delicate thin white paper.

"Come, Pete. I show you how to write."

I jumped up and came quickly to the table. How did he know I wanted to learn?

Drago pulled me to stand in front of him. He put the ink brush in my hand and guided it as we made two characters.

It was beautiful. The characters stood one atop the other, almost intertwined, dancing elegantly and intimately with each other.

"What does it say?" I whispered. I felt as if I were engaging in a very ancient and secret rite.

"Feng and Long. Phoenix and Dragon. The two lovers."

Drago stood back and smiled at me. "We will give to your mother."

I grinned. When Drago turned to clean the brushes, I looked beyond him and saw Wong in the doorway. He was scowling.

Walking down the dusty street later toward Maria's house, I asked Drago, "What are the red banners?" It did not escape my notice that he had a couple of the red banners rolled up and under his arm. My phoenix and dragon calligraphy was inside the roll.

"The words are the poetic couplets we Chinese put over the door at New Year's celebration. We hang the banners next to the door. The poems wish good luck and prosperity for each household."

"You are writing them for other people, too?"

"Yes. For everyone. All Chinese in Tucson."

"Why you?"

Drago smiled and put his hand affectionately on my shoulder as we walked.

"I am the best educated man here. My calligraphy is considered beautiful. Most of the men cannot write at all. Wong can write but not well. I was a scholar in China."

I was quiet for a while and thought about what it meant that his life had changed so much.

"Drago, why did you come here?"

His mouth tensed into a thin line. He sighed.

"Long story. I tell you later."

"Is Dai Goh your Chinese name?"

"No," he laughed. "You know my Chinese name. Xia Yù Long. Remember?"

"Why do they all call you Dai Goh?"

"It is a term of respect. They recognize my ...." He paused. "I am American man now. Not the same. This is not China."

We walked on in silence until we arrived at Maria's to fetch Mama.

Later I learned why Wong was scowling at Drago. I was talking with Ping and José about the upcoming Chinese New Year's festivities. I couldn't wait to see all the fireworks.

"I want to come, too," José said.

"I have to come with Drago and Mama at first but I can meet you later."

Ping frowned. "Drago?"

"Yes. You know. His name is...." I hesitated, "Xia Yù Long." I wasn't sure I had the words correct.

"Xia Yù Long?" Ping frowned again. "Xia Yù Long is coming to Chinese New Year's with your mother?"

"Yes. They are going to get married. Drago will be my new dad." I must have said this with some pride in my voice.

"No. Not possible," Ping said firmly.

"What are you talking about?"

"Xia Yù Long cannot marry your mother because she is not....." he hesitated, not sure if he should say what he was thinking.

"Xia Yù Long is going to marry my sister," Ping finished.

I thought we were going to get into a fight. We yelled at each other and pushed each other a couple of times. One of the men told us to shut up and go home. Later I spoke with Drago about this at his little vegetable farm.

"What does Ping mean you can't marry my mama?" I asked. I was offended.

"Some Chinese people do not approve of Chinese man marrying a woman who is not Chinese. Not to worry, Pete. Not important."

"Why does Ping think you will marry his sister?"

Drago's mouth went again into that thin line when he was thinking about something serious. "Wong sent a man to speak to me and offer this match between me and his daughter. I considered it. Wong wants this because of 'guanxi.' "

He knew that I didn't understand this so he sat his tool down and crouched next to me in between two rows of spinach.

"In China, people marry to join families, to create something like a fishing net, a net to hold people together. We call this 'guanxi.' Wong wants me in his family net. He believes we create new family together and build our wealth here."

I listened carefully because he so rarely talked about China and the Chinese.

"Wong has a daughter. She is very young. Fifteen years. I said no. Now Wong is angry."

"You said no because of Mama?"

Drago nodded and smiled.

***

The fireworks were fabulous. I'd never seen anything like them. The night sky was filled with flashing explosions of light and smoke lingered everywhere. Mancha was scared so I made him stay at home. Mancha hid under my bed.

Chinese New Year was the best thing ever. It was even better than Mama and Drago's wedding which happened soon after. The wedding *started with a long mass in the cathedral. The place was full of people. The priest went on and on with all these prayers in Latin. I fell asleep so I didn't actually see what happened when they were married.*

The party after the wedding was a great one with lots of good food and drinks, plus music and dancing that went on into the night.

That night I slept over at José's house at his mama's invitation. I went home the next morning after breakfast. I was too young then to understand much about what went on between a man and a woman when they were alone. I only remember going into the kitchen and finding Drago leaning against the door post, a cup of coffee in his hand. He was watching Mama with a satisfied smile on his face.

Mama was kneading bread dough. She looked up at Drago every now and then. She smiled and blushed. Then she blushed even more. And smiled again.

Yes, the wedding was nice and going home and finding Drago and Mama so happy was nice, too. But the fireworks at Chinese New Year were the best ever. Chinese New Year is still my favorite holiday.

Chapter 10

As soon as Seri paused in her reading, Zhou stood.
"Sorry. Sorry. Letty and I go to the airport now."

"No problem," Seri responded. "We read a lot today. We'll meet again next weekend and find out what happens to Drago and Rosa. Actually we're getting close to the end."

"I think we know what's going to happen," Maggie grinned.

"Rosa found an irresistible Chinese man and she's not going to let him go. I know exactly how she felt," Jade said, glancing at Zhou and smiling.

He nodded affectionately toward her, but he was obviously preoccupied.

"Meet you at the car, Letty," Zhou said.

"Bye, everybody," Letty waved.

"Jefe!" Jade called to Zhou. "Invite your colleague to dinner here. I'll fix some Sonoran cuisine for him. Bet he can't get that in France."

As they were driving away, Letty asked Zhou, "Does Jade always call you 'jefe?' You know, don't you, that 'jefe' means 'boss?'"

"Yes, she often calls me this. Jade knows she is the center of my life. She knows she is the real boss because I will do anything to make her happy."

"I think you underestimate your role. I believe she actually thinks of you as the boss of your family."

Zhou nodded. "I will care for her to the end of my life."

"And why exactly are you so grumpy about Laurent coming here?"

Zhou glanced at her. "You know me well, Letty."

He sighed. "Laurent says he has information about a professional criminal well known in Europe who has relocated to Tucson. As you know, Letty, Laurent is a high official in Interpol, the International Criminal Police Organization based in Lyon, France. Interpol facilitates cooperation among police in the 192 member nations. He was very important in removing those false charges of bribery against me, and obtaining my release from jail in Beijing. I am very grateful to him. Laurent almost never travels on-site simply to inform local operatives about a criminal, unless perhaps there is a serious and immediate threat of terrorism."

"Really? That's interesting. So why did he come here now? What do you know about this criminal? Is it someone involved in terrorist activities?"

"No. The criminal is involved in theft. Usually jewels."

"Hmmm..." Letty's mind began to spin. Could this have something to do with the theft of something from the library that led to the murder of Stacey Frederick? But no theft had been established at this point. And it was highly unlikely that there were any jewels in the library's collection. Perhaps the thief had been hired to find something quite different. But what? Too little was known and Letty felt the frustration. Even so, learning that an international jewel thief was living in Tucson was very interesting.

"But this doesn't explain why you are so annoyed at his coming here. So there's another reason why he decided to come to Tucson?"

"Two additional reasons, I think."

Letty waited patiently.

"I think he wants me to return with him to Lyon and continue my work with Interpol. It is not easy to replace an experienced agent, and he does not want to lose me."

"Are you considering this?"

"No! I told him this already. I was strong and firm. But Laurent is persistent. He is accustomed to getting what he wants. He *must* understand. I will not leave Jade. I will not return to that life. I have a new life now. I am going to be a father."

"What's the other reason?"

"He's interested in you."

"Me!" Letty was incredulous. "I don't even know this guy. I just talked to him on the phone when you were in jail. I'm grateful to him for getting you released but that's it. I don't know him."

"He thinks you will be a good Interpol agent."

Letty's mouth dropped open. Interpol? Never in her life had she considered such work.

"Do you want to live that life?"

"Live in France and help cops chase international criminals around? No way! It sounds romantic but I think really it's a lot of hard work and very dangerous."

"You are correct."

"I had enough of all that violence in Iraq."

"True."

"I don't want to leave my brothers and my sister. And I have two dogs now!"

Zhou nodded.

"I can't leave the desert. I was born in the desert, and I've always lived in the desert. Europe has water. A lot of water. I can't live around all that water!"

That last comment made Zhou laugh.

They fell quiet for a while.

"There is another reason that Laurent is interested in you. He did not say this but I think I understand him."

"What's the other reason?"

"He is interested in you as a woman."

"What!" Letty fell silent, dumbfounded.

"Laurent has a reputation as…..I don't know the word. But he likes women."

"Jeez. He sounds like my new dog Teddy."

Zhou looked her and shrugged.

"The Europeans have a fascination with Native Americans. The Germans, especially, make a fetish of Native Americans. The French also are very interested. Laurent saw your photo. He told me that he thought you were exotic and beautiful."

"Exotic and beautiful? Good lord. He must be desperate."

"You are very humble, Letty. I think that a brief dalliance is okay if you wish this, but be careful. Mind your heart. Laurent is very charming. Do not fall in love with Laurent."

"Zhou, you are so sweet to watch out for me. You are like a big brother."

Zhou grinned. "I am honored. You may call me Dàgē."

Letty tried to say the word for Big Brother but the Mandarin tones didn't come easily.

Zhou laughed. "No problem. You call me Zhou."

***

By now they had arrived at the airport. They parked in the airport parking lot and went into the terminal.

"We are late. I look for Laurent in the baggage claim," Zhou said.

Zhou disappeared and Letty sat down to wait in front of a floor-to-ceiling window. She could see the Santa Catalina Mountains covered in sunshine off to the north. The sky was an intense blue.

Her thoughts returned to the murder in the library. Seri hadn't mentioned finding anything important missing when doing the inventory. She had been especially concerned about colonial-era maps and documents because of their value. But so far nothing had been found missing.

Letty felt really stumped. She agreed with Seri. It was unlikely that Axel had killed Stacey in the library. If there had been an intruder there, what the hell was he, or she, looking for? Nothing appeared to have been stolen. Perhaps there was something that the intruder thought should be in the library but wasn't. She'd have to ask Seri about that.

Five minutes passed. Letty noticed a reflection in the window in front of her. There was a man behind her. He had been there for a while. He was leaning against a post. He didn't move. He seemed to be watching her.

She stood up and came around to stand in front of him, her hands on her hips.

"What?" she said, frowning.

"Ah, Mademoiselle Valdez. I am so sorry. Please forgive me."

The man's French accent was very strong. Letty cocked her head and took a good look. Tall, longish dark hair, a hawkish, aquiline nose so prominent in the French, intense gray-blue eyes. Definitely an attractive man.

"Laurent?" Letty asked, unsure.

The man bowed slightly and reached for her hand. Letty let him take it.

He bent again and kissed her hand.

Letty couldn't help herself. She smiled despite her best effort to be serious. She found him rather amusing and certainly charming.

"You should have introduced yourself!"

"Yes, yes, of course. I was struck with your elegance and beauty and I could not move."

Letty laughed. Charming? This dude invented charming.

"Okay. I forgive you for being so rude."

He smiled seductively.

"Stop already. Zhou is going to have a fit if he sees you behaving this way."

She glanced to her right and she could see Zhou coming. His mouth was in a thin, tight smile.

"Ah, Zhou," Laurent whispered. "So conservative. So Chinese."

Letty hadn't thought about Zhou that way, but she could see how he might be thought of as personally conservative.

Zhou and Laurent exchanged a typical French greeting, a brief embrace and air kisses on both cheeks.

"So you have met my colleague, Letty Valdez?"

"Yes. And what a great pleasure," Laurent said, his gaze on Letty just a bit too lingering to be understood in any way other than seductive.

"Where are you staying, Mr. Laurent?" Letty asked.

"At the Arizona Inn."

"Do you want to go there first or shall we go to my office? I'd like to learn more about this jewel thief."

"Then let's go to your office," Laurent said.

The drive to Letty's office took about twenty minutes. She ushered them through the almost-empty front room into her personal office space. She arranged chairs for Laurent and Zhou. Letty sat behind her desk.

"So, Mr. Laurent…."

"Please call me Jean-Pierre."

Letty glanced at Zhou. He was frowning again.

"Okay. Jean-Pierre. Why are you here? Zhou tells me you don't usually travel so far unless there's a serious threat."

"True. I do want to tell you about the thief. Also to be frank, I am hoping to persuade Zhou to return with me to Lyon. We desperately need him now."

Zhou looked at Laurent with annoyance.

"Laurent!" he growled. "How many times must I say 'no'!"

Laurent shrugged his shoulders. Clearly Laurent was a man who refused to accept the word 'no,' Letty thought to herself.

"My wife Jade has invited you to dinner. Perhaps she can convince you," Zhou said.

"How lovely," Laurent said with a smile.

"But you must not persist. I do not want my wife to become disturbed by you."

Laurent sighed, "Very well."

"What about the jewel thief, Jean-Pierre?" Letty asked. "You know, really, you should be talking to the local cops. I can set up an appointment for tomorrow." Letty thought maybe she would get some brownie points with the taciturn Detective De Luca if she set up a meeting between him and an Interpol official.

Laurent looked past her to the late-afternoon bands of sunlight moving across the Santa Catalina Mountains. The sky was beginning to turn into the shimmering gold and magenta colors of early evening.

"You live in a beautiful place, Mademoiselle Valdez."

Letty figured at this point that inviting him to call her Letty would be moving the momentum in his direction. She was a self-aware person and she was aware at this moment that he was the first man she had felt any attraction to at all since Iraq. She hadn't thought about a man for a long time, not since Chava had been blown to smithereens by an IED. The nightmare of Chava's violent death was still with Letty. What she felt toward Laurent was new and, much to her surprise, quite pleasant.

"Yes, I agree. The Sonoran Desert is beautiful. I was born and grew up here and I will never leave."

Laurent's eyebrows went up. "So you have no interest in joining Interpol."

"No. None at all."

"Perhaps before I leave here, I can convince you otherwise," Laurent continued. "Meanwhile, allow me to inform you about Audrey Parker. Ms. Parker is an American who has lived in Europe most of her adult life. She only returned to the U.S. a few months ago. We have followed her career as a jewel thief for nearly twenty years. This is a case of strongly suspecting that she committed the thefts, but we have never been able to prove her role."

"Where does she steal the jewels and what happens to them?"

"She has worked in several countries but primarily in France, Germany, Italy and the U.K. We also think she may have stolen jewels in Japan as well. She is a master thief who works for hire. By that, I mean she does not steal to keep the jewels or sell them herself. She is hired by unscrupulous collectors or their intermediaries. She targets specific items requested by these collectors."

"Why haven't you been able to tie her to the thefts?"

"If I knew that, Mademoiselle Valdez, she would be in prison now," Laurent smiled.

Letty sighed, feeling a bit foolish. What did she know about international jewel thieves?

"One time we came very close. We identified and then apprehended her based on some CCTV footage. However, the jewel in question, a very large-carat diamond ring, was nowhere to be found. We couldn't prove that she had taken something that she was not in possession of."

"Do you have an idea why she's in Tucson? Is there any indication she is still working as a thief?"

"She was born and grew up in Arizona, and now she has returned to the land of her birth. It appears that she has retired. She lives well in a gated community in the north of the city of Tucson. We only know that before returning to the U.S., she transferred several million dollars into a Tucson bank. There is no need for her to work again."

"I haven't heard of any big thefts recently. Of course, the police don't advertise everything they are working on. I'll definitely arrange a meeting for tomorrow with a detective I know."

"Very well," Laurent said pleasantly.

"Letty, I'll drop you at your home. You come to our house for dinner. Okay?" Zhou asked.

Letty nodded her assent. All three rose, Letty locked up her office and they headed for Zhou's car.

***

At home, Letty made a quick call to Detective De Luca. She knew he worked in homicide, and the jewel thief wasn't a killer as far as she knew. Yet he was the cop she'd most recently talked to and she still had hopes of developing a relationship with him. De Luca responded positively and told her to bring Laurent and Zhou into his office at nine the following morning.

Next Letty fed Millie and Teddy and made sure they had enough water. Clarice and Will were studying together. She didn't want to interrupt them.

Clarice had other ideas. She followed Letty outside with the dogs. Much to Letty's pleased surprise, Clarice informed Letty that Jade had texted her and invited Clarice and Will to eat with them, too. That was very kind of Jade, Letty thought. Letty always felt that she didn't get to see enough of Will and Clarice because she worked such long hours and because they were both busy college students.

"I have a test tomorrow, Letty," Will said seriously when he joined them later. "It's math. I don't get the point of math. But I have to pass this class. So we can't stay out late."

"The point of math?" Clarice sounded dismayed. "The point is to figure out things like how many calories you need to take in to have enough energy to make it to the end of the bicycle race; or how many miles you have to go when the race is described in kilometers, not miles; or how many milligrams of pain killer you must take when your muscles are aching. Or how many kisses you have to give me in order to get help with your math assignments."

Will grinned. "Okay. Okay. I get it."

Clarice was referring to Will's passion for long-distance bicycling and also to their deeply affectionate relationship. Letty was happy for Will. He'd been such an undisciplined teenager until Clarice came along. She was a mature, level-headed girl who kept Will in line much better than his Big Sister Letty ever could. Those Clarice kisses were a big motivator for Will.

"But we're even. I help you with your Spanish," Will reminded Clarice.

"True. The difference is that I know what the point of Spanish is!"

"Okay. I get it! Math is so important!" He laughed.

The drive to Jade and Zhou's house was quick. Jade had arranged settings at a large table under the ramada in her backyard garden. Candles were lit in the dusky evening light, and the wine glasses were ready.

Laurent was standing in the garden admiring the lovely fall evening.

"So many stars in this desert sky," he said softly.

"Jefe," Jade called. "You and Will, please set up the buffet table and help me carry out all this food."

Zhou and Will did her bidding. Soon everyone had filled their plates with various dishes on the buffet table.

Before they began to eat, Zhou stood and raised his wine glass. "I salute Monsieur Jean-Pierre Laurent, who has been a good friend to me. I thank you again, Jean-Pierre, for arranging my release from the jail in Beijing. I wish you a long and happy life."

Laurent raised his glass along with the others.

"Merci, Zhou, merci beaucoup," Laurent thanked Zhou with a smile.

The evening was pleasant and full of light conversation. Laurent did not mention at all his desire to see Zhou return with him to France.

Finally Letty said, "We must go now. Will has a test tomorrow. Zhou and Jean-Pierre and I are meeting with the local police. Also I have a meeting with a client. Busy day tomorrow."

They all stood and said their goodbyes. As Letty departed, Laurent approached her and said, "Mademoiselle."

"Oh, you can call me Letty." She wondered later if that glass of wine had changed her mind about allowing him to call her by her first name.

"Merci," Laurent said graciously. "Would you be so kind as to have dinner with me tomorrow evening at the Arizona Inn? It will be my final evening in Tucson."

Letty hesitated. She noticed Zhou approaching.

"Yes, Jean-Pierre. I would enjoy having dinner with you."

Zhou rattled off a string of sentences in French directly at Laurent who smiled patiently the entire time Zhou was talking.

Clarice said to Letty, "What was that all about?" She and Will were walking to her car, and Letty was headed to her pickup truck which she'd left earlier at Zhou and Jade's house.

"I don't know. I don't speak French." Letty shrugged her shoulders.

"Well, I do. I spent my junior year abroad in Paris. Zhou said to Laurent that he better be good to you and not hurt you or Zhou will deal directly with him. Zhou sounded really serious. What does he mean 'hurt you?'"

"Okay," Letty sighed. "You two will be happy to know that I have a dinner date tomorrow evening with Laurent. But Zhou isn't happy about it. He thinks Laurent will break my heart."

Will cheered, "Yay, Big Sister has a date!"

Clarice added, "And Zhou should know by now that Big Sister is perfectly capable of taking care of herself."

CHAPTER 11

THE next morning, Letty met Zhou and Laurent outside the Tucson Police Department headquarters. They went in together. This time they didn't have to wait. De Luca came out almost immediately to meet them and to escort them to his office. Apparently De Luca considered an Interpol official worthy of much quicker attention than a lowly Tucson private investigator.

De Luca introduced a waiting uniformed policeman.

"This is Detective Alejandro Ramirez. He is chief of our Robbery Unit in our Violent Crimes Section." Ramirez nodded. He seemed to already know about the three of them.

"Mr. Laurent, feel free to tell us as much as you know about this jewel thief."

Laurent, his usual unruffled self, began, "The thief's name is Audrey Parker." He continued talking for a few minutes and explained in detail everything he had already told Letty and Zhou about Parker's career in Europe.

"Do you have any reason to think she's operating here?" Ramirez asked.

"I have no idea. I am only here to warn you. Have you had any jewel thefts or thefts of other small but highly valuable items in recent months?"

"Only the usual break-ins. Offices and homes are the typical targets," Ramirez responded. The thieves take whatever they think they can pawn quickly. Often that means electronic equipment, tools, family jewelry, stuff you'd find in the typical home. Also we have a fair amount of auto thefts and there are the bike thefts from around the University."

"No thefts of highly expensive jewelry from a museum, a known collector, or a jewelry establishment?" Laurent asked. "Parker most often seeks the very most expensive items. Also she is usually hired by someone on a contract basis. She takes the risk and is very well paid for delivering the goods."

"I'm not sure we have much really expensive stuff like that in Tucson," Ramirez said, "except maybe during the yearly gem and mineral show. That happens in January and February every year. Some of the vendors bring in really valuable items."

Laurent shrugged his shoulders. "Perhaps Mademoiselle Parker has actually retired."

Letty considered whether or not she should bring up the murder in the library. She decided to go ahead, if for no other reason than to see their reactions. Zhou knew about the murder because she had already told him that she was investigating. She wanted to know what De Luca was thinking.

Letty directed her comment to Laurent but watched De Luca's reaction. "We recently had a murder at one of the libraries in the University of Arizona system. The librarian thinks the murderer was planning on stealing something when he was interrupted. There are signs that he or she disturbed the stored materials, as if searching. Also he or she may have entered the library through a ventilation duct."

De Luca frowned. Letty could see that he just didn't like it that she was investigating this case. As far as De Luca was concerned, she was stepping on his toes.

"We checked that out. It does appear," De Luca said almost grudgingly to Letty, "that the thief made use of the ventilation duct system. But as you know, I cannot discuss ongoing investigations." He glowered at Letty.

Laurent noticed all this. His smile grew. "You cannot discuss this with Interpol?"

This threw De Luca off guard. "I don't mean to be rude, Mr. Laurent. I can tell you that Ms. Valdez is the one who suggested the ventilation duct as the entry way into the library. She was right about that. The person must have been small to be able to get into the duct. It is considered a large duct but still, for a person to navigate it, that person would have to be thin. Also we found a bit of blood just inside the duct opening. It may be the victim's blood or perhaps the thief cut himself or herself when opening the vent. We're getting it tested now for DNA. But this is not to be revealed at all with anyone. Got that, Valdez? You, too." He gestured at Zhou.

"Was anything stolen from the library?" Laurent asked, again smiling at Letty.

"So far the librarians haven't found anything missing," Letty said. "So far. However, the intruder appears to have done a fairly thorough search, according to the librarians."

Laurent said, "That could just mean that what the thief was looking for was not actually there."

"That's what I've been thinking," Letty said. "I'm meeting with the librarians later today to brainstorm with them. We'll try to determine if there was some valuable item expected to go into the library but not yet delivered. Also we'll talk about who might be interested in that item."

"How is the murder investigation going?" Laurent turned to De Luca.

"Not so great," De Luca said. We have few leads other than the murdered woman's boyfriend. We're hoping the DNA analysis of the blood leads us to a known local thief. But it just as easily could be the DNA from the blood of a workman who installed the duct."

"Perhaps Mademoiselle Valdez can assist you," Laurent said casually. This time he gestured toward Letty as if she were his most valued investigator.

Letty suppressed a smile. Laurent was making fun of De Luca by praising her. Zhou sat quietly, his face expressionless. She wondered what Zhou was thinking.

De Luca's face turned red.

Ramirez intervened. "We thank you, Mr. Laurent, for taking time to come to police headquarters and tell us about Parker. We'll definitely keep an eye on her."

Laurent stood and said, "Very nice to meet you, Detective Ramirez, and you, Detective De Luca. I don't want to keep you any longer. My friend Zhou is going to give me a quick tour of the city of Tucson. I've never visited this part of the world before now."

Ramirez grinned. "We have great food here. Tucson is the first U.S. city that has been designated a UNESCO World City of Gastronomy."

"Ah," Laurent said. "Impressive! Any recommendations for lunch?"

"My mother's house! She's the best cook in Tucson!" Ramirez laughed. "Actually there are too many great restaurants to make one recommendation. You'll have to return again and again."

"Perhaps I will," Laurent said, smiling and looking at Letty the entire time.

Letty was certain that De Luca was about to blow a fuse. His face was bright red.

Laurent shook hands with the two policemen, and they said their goodbyes.

Back in the parking lot, Letty said to Laurent, "You are a bad boy, Jean-Pierre. Teasing De Luca like that." She couldn't help but laugh.

"Some women like the bad boys," Laurent said seductively in his so-very-French accent.

Letty could hear Zhou mumbling to himself in Mandarin Chinese. She tried not to laugh out loud. Zhou was taking this big brother stuff very seriously.

"Okay, I'm off. Jean-Pierre, I'll see you later for dinner. Zhou, keep an eye on Jade. She doesn't have much time left. Looks to me like the baby has dropped."

At the mention of Jade, Zhou's frown disappeared. "Yes, I am watching. What do you mean 'baby has dropped'?"

"Zhou, I delivered several babies when I was in Iraq. For Iraqi women, I mean. So I can see that the baby has moved to position its head lower in preparation for birth. There's not much time left. You will soon be a father. So keep watch."

Zhou smiled broadly. "Yes, I keep watch carefully. I text Jade every thirty minutes."

"Good. You two have a great lunch! My recommendations are El Charro, La Cocina, or Café Poca Cosa. Closer to my place and just as good is this tiny restaurant called Ponchos on Speedway Boulevard. They have great burritos and chimichangas! There are even more terrific restaurants. Ramirez is right. There's too many for just one meal. You'll have to return, Jean-Pierre, just to eat."

Laurent smiled agreeably.

***

On the way to the library, Letty thought about what had just happened. Aside from Laurent's behavior, teasing De Luca and making eyes at her, she trusted his observations. Zhou told her previously that Laurent had a long and illustrious career in investigations, first with the French equivalent of the CIA, the Directorate-General for External Security, and later, with Interpol. Laurent saw immediately that what the murderer was looking for was most likely not even in the library.

That's the direction where Letty would go now.

Twenty minutes later, she was sitting with Seri and the Institute's reference librarian, Amanda Flores. Seri picked up the phone and called the main desk. "Hold my calls, and please take messages. Thanks."

"Any missing items?"

"No. We went first through the most historically-valuable documents. Everything is there," Seri said. "Amanda, feel free to comment if you have anything to add."

"Nothing missing, but I agree with Seri. Nearly every storage unit had been tampered with. For those of us who work with the materials on a daily basis, it was subtle but clear that items had been moved around. Things were put back but not necessarily as neatly as we like them to be."

"Any particular group of documents that seemed especially disturbed?"

"Well," Seri answered, "maybe the new boxes upstairs."

"Yes," Amanda said, "Looks like he or she went through those really thoroughly. The documents were not organized, but they were fairly neatly stacked in the boxes. They were not neat at all when we opened those boxes. It looked as if everything had been taken out and gone through then hastily shoved back in."

"Anything of interest there?"

Seri said, "We haven't done an inventory so I cannot say for sure. But both of us had looked through those boxes when they first came in. There did not appear to be anything special in them. In fact, Amanda and I discussed the possibility that most of the items would be going back to the families because they were of little value to us."

"What about that box that Maggie gave you? It wasn't here, was it?

"No. Maggie gave it to me quite recently and I hadn't brought it to the library yet. The plan was to read the memoir to our friends and then bring everything here. But as I said, I went through the box and most of the stuff is not especially valuable. There are a few photos from the turn of the nineteenth to twentieth centuries. The memoir will have value to historians interested in family history, immigrant history, and the ethnic Chinese population in Arizona. But frankly, I don't know why that would be of particular interest to a thief. It's the kind of historical document that adds color to a narrative, but that does not have the value of an official government document or some other legal document, or especially something from the colonial period."

"Or an original map or correspondence by a really famous person would be something really valuable. But what Seri describes is kind of like icing on the cake for an historian. Not the cake itself," Amanda said.

"Of course," Seri added, "I have not read the memoir cover-to-cover. There may be some really significant information in it that we just haven't found yet."

"Okay. Then let's take a look at who might be interested in new documents. If we can figure out who is interested, maybe we can figure out what the thief was looking for. I notice that I see familiar faces in the library every time I come here. Are any of them doing research that might explain this?" Letty asked.

Amanda handed Letty a piece of paper. "There are six names on this list. Four are professors. Two of the professors teach here at the University of Arizona. One is a visiting professor from Seattle, and one is a professor visiting from Guangzhou, China. We also have a visiting scholar from New York City. He's a researcher and writer for the China Institute. He's working on a book about the Chinese in northern Mexico and Arizona. The last one is a woman who is a post-doctoral student, also writing a book. She's from San Francisco."

"The problem, Letty, is that these scholars regularly ask for materials from our collection that they hope will support their research," Seri added.

"Okay. Have any of them mentioned the new boxes upstairs, or made any other request that you thought was out of the norm?"

"No," both women said at once. The group fell silent.

"Have you had any interactions of a more social nature with any of them?"

A long pause followed while the two librarians considered Letty's question.

"We did have a faculty party recently to welcome a new member to the history department. I didn't actually talk to the new guy except to say hi and introduce myself," Amanda said.

"Same for me," Seri added. She fell silent again. She said, "There was that interaction, very casual, when we all standing around in a circle with our wine glasses."

"That's right," Amanda said.

"Who was in the circle?"

"The names on that list plus a couple of grad students," Amanda said.

Seri added, "One of them asked me if we had anything new coming in."

"That's right. I said we had new boxes of family materials, but nothing of any great historical value," Amanda added.

"Who asked you this?"

Amanda looked perplexed. "I don't remember."

Seri said, "I think it was the visiting prof from Seattle, Dr. McIntosh. No one commented on what we said or followed up. We started talking about other things going on at the University and in town. I think the question about new materials was casual."

"Okay. I want to start by interviewing the people who are on your list and were at this faculty party. Try to remember who the grad students were, too. Are any of these folks now in the library?"

"Yes," Amanda said. "Dr. Miller is here. He's on our faculty."

"Seri, can I borrow your office for about twenty minutes? After I talk to Miller, I'd like to go upstairs and go through those new boxes myself. I'll come back later and try to interview the others."

"Sure."

"Amanda, one more question. What are you thinking about the break-in at your apartment? Do you think there's a connection to what happened here?"

"Well, I don't know what to say. Seems like it's too much of a coincidence. But there's no obvious connection. The police are treating it like an ordinary break-in. The thief took some cash, my laptop, and some of my granny's old costume jewelry from the 1940s. The jewelry might have a little value if you tried to sell it. But it's just costume jewelry."

"What about the laptop? Any work-related info on it?"

"No. I do photography for a hobby. So the laptop had a big collection of photos and some photo editing software. I have the photos backed up on an external hard drive and Google Drive, too, so nothing was lost."

"Good. Backing up is good! If either of you thinks of anything relevant, contact me. Seri, can you introduce me to the professor here now?"

Amanda went back to work. Seri and Letty went into the Institute's main reading room.

Letty noticed that nearly everyone in the reading room was watching her and Seri as they approached one of the scholars sitting at a table with a pile of books and a laptop in front of him.

"Dr. Miller, could you please take a few minutes to come into my office?"

Dr. Miller, a middle-aged man in a rumpled suit and loosened tie, looked surprised. "Certainly."

In Seri's office, Letty smiled, hoping to put the professor at ease.

"My name is Letty Valdez. I'm helping Seri look into the murder of her colleague here last week."

"I thought the police were investigating."

"They are. But we're trying to help them by determining what the murderer's motivations might have been."

"Okay. I don't think I know much but I'll try to help."

"Did you notice anything unusual in the days leading up to the murder? Did you see anyone here that you hadn't seen before?"

"No, same old crowd every day except the undergrads are sometimes different. You can identify them because half the time they are looking at their smartphones, not at their text books."

"What are you researching, Dr. Miller?"

"Not much right now, if the truth be told. Don't tell my departmental chair that. But I've been slacking off some. I published a book a few months ago and I think that's given me an excuse not to have to publish anything for a while. I come to the library because it's quiet and I don't have to explain anything to the secretary back in my department. She's likes to keep track of everyone."

"Which department are you in?"

"Political science. I just wrote a book about the emergence of new political parties in northern and central Mexico and how that has been impacted by the drug cartels."

"Interesting," Letty said. "So does this library have a lot of useful material?"

"Not really," Dr. Miller looked apologetically at Seri. "I understand that the Institute has some excellent historical materials, but it's not strong on contemporary events. I work here because I can get away from my office with its constant interruptions. I did most of my work for my book on a computer, reading research papers and news articles on my laptop. Then I went to Mexico several times to interview informants. And like I said, I'm taking a little break now so I'm not getting a lot done."

"Okay," Letty said. "You've been very helpful."

Seri showed Dr. Miller out of her office.

"Really? Helpful?"

"If he's telling the truth, his academic interests don't seem to have anything to do with most of what you have here and, in particular, what's in the recently-donated boxes."

"So this is a process of elimination, keeping in mind that things could change later."

"Exactly. Let's go upstairs now and I'll go through those boxes just to see what's there. I'll come back tomorrow and try to interview more of these folks on the list."

***

After the library, Letty stopped for a quick sandwich and went to her office. She spent the afternoon on her computer doing background checks for all the names on Amanda's list and for a certain Interpol official now visiting Tucson.

Late afternoon back at home, Clarice and Will hovered over her.

Will couldn't help himself. He teased her in a sing-song voice. "Letty has a date. Letty has a date."

"Will, you better shut up, or I'm going to practice all my new martial arts moves on you!"

"Ignore him, Letty," Clarice said. "What are you going to wear?"

"I have no idea. Maybe Army fatigues."

"Trying to be sexy, huh, Big Sister?" Will laughed.

"Let's go look through your closet," Clarice said. "Will, go do something useful. Go play with Teddy and Millie. They look lonely."

"Oh, poor sad doggies. Come on, let's go play frisbee," Will said. He headed out the door to the backyard with two happy dogs and a frisbee.

Clarice and Letty went through Letty's closet and finally found an indigo blue silk dress that had a slightly-curved neckline, short sleeves and a hem just above Letty's knees.

"This is a beautiful dress. I've never seen you wear it."

"It's been a long time," Letty said softly. She didn't want to talk about the last time she wore it. She and Chava had gone to a nice restaurant when they were on leave at the same time. They had flown to Germany on an Army transport plane. Later in their hotel room, Chava removed her blue dress and made love to her. She missed him.

After a shower, Letty got some help from Clarice, who fixed Letty's hair into a long braid that was wrapped and pinned artfully at the back of her head. Letty looked into her bathroom cabinet for makeup. She didn't have any. She'd thrown out what she'd had because it was old and she wasn't using it. The foundation never seemed to be the right color for her skin anyway. She found an old tube of red lipstick behind a tube of toothpaste. She applied the lipstick and scowled at herself in the mirror. She just wasn't accustomed to getting dressed up and certainly not accustomed to dating. Finally, she put on the blue dress and found some low heels to wear, too.

Clarice disappeared for a few minutes and came back with a pair of gold hoop earrings. "You can borrow these. They will look good with your dress."

"Thanks, Clarice. You're a sweetheart. What do you think of Laurent?"

"Smooth dude." She shrugged her shoulders.

"Whoa, Big Sister. You are a looker!" Will exclaimed when Letty walked out. Clarice took a photo.

"You two are treating me like a sixteen year-old going to her first prom!"

"Go, Letty, go and have fun," Clarice said.

"And if you don't come home tonight, that's okay with us," Will grinned.

Letty punched his shoulder. "Shut up!"

Will laughed. "Just saying!"

***

The dinner with Laurent at Arizona Inn was perfect. The elegant dining room was lovely and very quiet despite being nearly full of guests. She had a wonderful meal with Laurent, complete with three varieties of wine that he selected himself.

The conversation was light and full of humor. She found herself laughing at his descriptions of his escapades in Interpol and his life in France.

"I know it can't possibly be as much fun as you describe, Jean-Pierre. I think you're trying to convince me to join you as an agent."

"I think you would make an excellent agent. But after observing your life here, I understand why you do not want to leave this beautiful place, this Sonoran Desert."

"What about Zhou? What do you think of his situation?"

"Hopeless. Hopeless for me, that is. I had known for some time, maybe two years or more, that he was becoming restless. He was looking for a new life. I can see from the way he looks at his Jade that she is that new life. The child coming just assures the change. I believe that I have lost him forever as an Interpol agent."

Letty nodded knowingly.

"Let us go for a walk now, Mademoiselle Letty."

Laurent led her around the interior grounds and gardens of the Arizona Inn. They walked past the doors of several casitas. Finally he stopped in front of one door painted a bright blue.

"Letty, I am leaving early tomorrow." He pulled her toward him and he kissed her on the lips.

"I want you to come with me into my room," Laurent said softly. "I want to spend the night with you. I want to make passionate love to you." He kissed her again, this time a lingering kiss.

Letty smiled. She liked his kisses. It had been such a long time.

"Ah, you are so French, Jean-Pierre."

"C'est vrai," Laurent said. This is true.

"So charming."

"Yes?"

"So handsome."

"Yes?"

Letty moved closer and kissed him.

"So sexy."

"Yes?"

"And so married," Letty said regretfully. She took a step back.

"Ah," Laurent frowned and sighed.

"I'm sorry, but I must decline your invitation, Jean-Pierre. I'm going home now."

"Oh, you Americans. So puritanical."

Letty smiled. She saw that Laurent was smiling, too. No hard feelings.

"Did Zhou tell you about my wife?"

"No."

"Then how did you…Ah, you are a very good private investigator."

"I have very much enjoyed getting to know you. Have a safe trip home, mon ami."

She kissed Laurent again. Letty Valdez turned and walked away.

***

Back home, Letty phoned Zhou.

"Sorry to call so late. Is Jade okay?"

"Yes, Jade is well. Where are you?"

"I'm at home."

She could feel his approval radiating over the phone. He was pretty conservative, come to think of it.

"Zhou, remember you told me recently that you wanted to practice sprinting?"

"Yes. You jog. I sprint."

"Can you meet me at 7 a.m. tomorrow at the Rillito River Trail Swan parking lot? We met there once before. We'll go running on the trail. Okay? Also I want to tell you what I've been working on and get your ideas."

"Okay! See you tomorrow."

Despite the fact that spending the night with Laurent would have been very pleasurable, Letty knew what she wanted. One night with a married man wasn't it. At least she was awake now and noticing men. Maybe Teddy would find her a good man up in a tree somewhere. She laughed to herself at the thought. Meanwhile, she would meet her friend Zhou tomorrow and they would get some exercise together.

CHAPTER 12

LETTY was already at the trail when Zhou arrived. Her Nissan pickup was parked in the dirt parking lot off Swan Road. She stretched her legs against the metal railing that ran along the paved trail that followed the Rillito River.

"Good morning, Letty," Zhou called to her as he got out his car.

"What exactly do you have in mind, Zhou?"

"You jog at a steady pace. I follow behind you. Next I sprint to catch with you."

"Catch up, you mean. Okay. Why are we doing this?"

"I don't want to lose my skills. I may need them sometime. I must be in shape. Sprinting is work."

"Yes, a lot of work!"

They stood together on the edge of the paved trail. They could choose to go to the left, west, or to the right, east. A bicyclist passed them going east. In front of them past the metal railing was the dry and sandy Rillito River bottom. On the other side of the river to the north, the sunlight cast early-morning light and dark shadows on the Santa Catalina Mountains.

"Okay," Letty said. "I'll jog west on the trail and you decide when you want to…"

"Catch up."

"That's right." She smiled. "But what if you can't catch up with me?"

Zhou grinned. "I *will* catch up with you!"

And she knew he would. Letty had never known anyone more athletic than Zhou Liang Wei.

Letty stepped onto the trail, turned left and went into an immediate, moderately-paced jog. The trail was level for a bit. Then it dipped down to go under the Swan Road overpass. The traffic on the overpass above was loud. A second bicyclist passed Letty on her left. She was heading up the other side of the dip under the overpass when Zhou stepped onto the trail in preparation for his sprint.

Zhou watched as the trail leveled again and Letty as she continued to run forward. She had just passed a large mesquite tree and some creosote bushes on her left on the south side of the trail.

That was when Zhou saw them. His eyes grew wide.

Three men appeared suddenly from behind the mesquite and creosote bushes. They quickly moved toward Letty, coming up fast behind her. Zhou knew that she wasn't aware of them. She wouldn't be able to hear them because of the overpass traffic. Two had faces that were uncovered, and the third, the tallest of the three, had his face covered with a black ski mask. Only his eyes were visible. All three men were running directly toward Letty. Zhou knew right away that they meant no good. He also knew that she wouldn't have time to defend herself, not against three of them.

Before the three men even touched Letty, Zhou went into the fastest sprint of his life to get to her.

One of the men smashed his body with maximum force into Letty. This pushed her violently to the right and back against the metal railing on the river side of the trail. The second man threw a punch that caught her in the jaw while the first man pushed her forcibly against the railing again. Letty slammed into the metal railing for the second time. She bent backwards over the railing at the impact.

Only then did the third man step forward. He kicked Letty viciously in her exposed stomach and ribs. As she started to fall, he kicked her hard in her upper chest. Letty began to sink downward. He grabbed her braid and pulled her head up with one hand as he smashed his fist into the side of her head and jaw. The other two men began to kick her repeatedly as she fell to the trail pavement. The attack was vicious.

Zhou first encountered the two men kicking Letty. He quickly put both men out of commission, one after the other. In seconds, both men cried out in pain and moved away. The third man let go of Letty and faced Zhou. He went immediately into a classic martial arts stance.

Zhou readied himself. The two men circled each other on the trail, Zhou in Chinese wing chun stance, the other man in Japanese karate. The tall man moved first. He attempted a kick against Zhou, but he was too slow. Zhou grabbed his upraised foot and jerked forward and upward. The man fell back and Zhou snatched the ski mask off his head. Zhou got a good look at him. Letty raised her head momentarily and saw him, too. Then she fainted. Although the attacker managed to get to his feet again quickly, it was clear that he knew he couldn't defeat this gong fu master. The battle was over in fifteen seconds.

The other two men helped each other to escape up a side trail away from the river. The tall man, now unmasked, followed close behind them. When Zhou was sure they were no longer a threat, he turned to Letty.

"Letty, Letty," he bent down. "You are okay?"

"Zhou, I didn't see them coming." She felt light-headed, as if she might pass out again. She struggled to stay conscious.

Suddenly Zhou realized that another man was approaching from the west, a jogger. He was running at top speed toward them. Zhou stood, faced the man, and readied himself to protect Letty if necessary.

"I saw what happened," the man called out as he approached. "They attacked her. There were three of them. Is she okay? No, of course not. I'm a doctor. Can I help?" The string of sentences flowed out from him as he stopped forward and bent down toward Letty.

"You are a doctor? Yes, we need help," Zhou responded.

The man's eyes widened when he knelt down and looked at Letty. "What's her name?" he asked.

"Letty Valdez," Zhou said.

The man breathed in and then said her name softly, "Letty Valdez."
Zhou watched the trail to make sure the third man did not return.

"Ms. Valdez," the jogger spoke directly to Letty.

Letty looked at him. "I hurt all over," she whispered.

"I know. I'll take care of you," he said softly. The jogger turned to Zhou.

"We want to be careful of her spine and her joints, too. I'm calling 911 for an ambulance."

The jogger pulled a cell phone from a deep back pocket and dialed a number.

"This is Dr. Dan Ennis. Send an ambulance to Rillito River parking lot on the east side of Swan, just north of Fort Lowell." A pause followed. "That's right. Look for McDonald's on the west side of Swan. The turnoff to the river is just after that on your right, the east side." Another pause. "Assault. Trauma. Get here as quickly as you can." The man pocketed his phone and returned his attention to Letty.

"She needs to go to the emergency room at Tucson Medical Center. TMC is very close. I work there in the ER."

Zhou nodded. He looked at Letty. The abrasions on her face were bleeding slightly but the real damage wasn't on the surface. She groaned in pain.

Only a few minutes later, the two men could hear the ambulance siren coming toward them. Two paramedics appeared soon with a gurney. They consulted briefly with Dr. Ennis.

Letty opened her eyes.

"Ms. Valdez, can you hear me?" the doctor asked her.

Letty nodded, "Yes."

"We're taking you to the emergency room. I'll go with you in the ambulance. Do you understand?"

"Yes," she whispered.

"Where do you hurt?

"My ribs and…my chest…and my back…and jaw. My face. My hip and thighs."

The doctor shook his head and frowned. "So you hurt all over. We'll determine the extent of the injuries. Then we'll give you something for the pain. Okay?" One of the paramedics put a C-collar on her neck to protect her spine.

"Yes. Please call my brother."

The doctor turned to Zhou. "You can follow in your car. Can you call her brother?"

"Yes. I will call him."

The ambulance paramedics and Dr. Ennis lifted Letty carefully onto the gurney. She groaned and lost consciousness again for a few seconds. They loaded her into the back of the ambulance and headed toward the hospital, sirens blaring.

Zhou called Will and explained the situation.

"Clarice and I can be at the ER in just a few minutes."

The ride to the TMC emergency room was quick. Zhou stood just outside the ER in the hospital hallway. Will and Clarice showed up a short time later. Zhou pointed to the room where Letty was being examined. There they found Letty.

"Oh my god," Will said. "Letty, can you hear me?"

Letty opened her eyes, groaned again, and closed her eyes.

Dr. Ennis reappeared, this time dressed in green scrubs and green cloth cap. He had a stethoscope around his neck. He and the nurse removed the C-collar around Letty's neck. He began to examine Letty by first listening to her heart and lungs. Then he palpated her abdomen.

"Ow! That hurts!"

"Sorry," he said, "I'll be done in a just a second." He looked into Letty's eyes with a small light.

Out in the hallway, Zhou's cell phone buzzed.

"Shénme? Zhēn de ma? Wǒde mā ya!" he exclaimed. (What? Really! Oh my god!) "Okay. Sorry. Sorry, Jade. I will speak English now. I come to you. Breathe!! Okay. I am breathing, too. Why you are laughing? Never mind. You wait. I come to you now. Yes, I drive safely. Breathe! I love you."

Zhou turned to Will. "I must go. Jade has the labor pain and I must return here with her to hospital. The baby is coming! Take care of Letty. " He ran from the emergency room.

The doctor looked up and gestured for Will to come closer. "Who are you? Are you her brother?"

"Yes, I'm Letty's brother and this is my girlfriend Clarice. My name is Will Ramone. Is Letty going to be okay?"

The doctor nodded at Will, gesturing behind him. "Where's her husband going?"

Will looked at him blankly.

"That's not her husband," Clarice said. "That's Zhou. His wife has gone into labor so that's why he's leaving."

"Zhou and Letty work together sometimes and she takes martial arts class from Zhou. Letty isn't married," Will added.

The doctor nodded. He directed his attention again to Letty and said, "Ms. Valdez, we're going to do a FAST scan and we'll follow up with a CT scan. That will tell us if there's any internal bleeding or damage to your bones and organs. Do you have a headache?"

"No. My cheekbone and jaw hurt."

"Is she going to be okay?" Will was clearly anxious.

"She was conscious and responded to me at the river and she's responding here as well. That's a good sign. I saw them attack her. Three of them. They beat her up pretty badly. She's in a lot of pain. We'll do our best to take good care of her and relieve her suffering."

Letty was removed from the ER for her scans. She fought the urge to lose consciousness. She was finding it easier to stay awake now although the pain was intense. She was really, really angry, and her anger kept her awake. What the hell? She felt outrage at the attack. Three on one. Not fair. The thought flitted through her mind that this may be part of the murder investigation she was working on. The perp couldn't find anything at in the library or Amanda Flores's house. But why attack her? To stop her. Of course. To stop her investigation. Someone wanted her out of the picture. Who and why? She groaned in pain.

The attendant and nurse returned Letty to the ER examining room a few minutes later. Will and Clarice stood nearby.

Dr. Ennis reappeared after viewing the scan results. "We're going to give you something for the pain now, Ms. Valdez." He gestured to the nurse who administered the injection.

"It looks like you lucked out. Your injuries could have been a lot worse. You have a hairline fracture on your lower right number eight rib and it looks like the costal cartilage was separated from the rib. You have hematomas on your back, chest, rib cage, and left jaw. You will have a black eye, too. But there's no sign of internal bleeding and no cranial trauma.

He glanced up at her. "Your color is better." He paused. "In fact, your face is quite red."

The doctor removed his stethoscope from his neck and listened again to her heart. "You heart rate is up. What's going on?"

"I'm really pissed off," Letty growled.

"That's my Big Sister," Will said in a low voice.

"I'm going to go get those pendejos!" Letty gritted her teeth.

"Pendejo? What does that mean?" the doctor asked.

The nurse laughed. "It's a bad word, Dr. Ennis. She's cursing in Mexican Spanish."

Will and Clarice were grinning now. Letty was acting like herself, which was a great relief to them both.

"Okay, Ms. Valdez," Dr. Ennis said in a stern voice. "You need to calm down now. You need to give yourself a chance to heal before you go beat up anyone. You should know, too, that your friend took care of two of them. One had a complete break in both his left radius and ulna. His lower arm was flopping around. The other one had a very seriously dislocated shoulder. I saw them myself. The damage was quite obvious."

"Good. I can count on Zhou. What about that tall, skinny guy with the blue eyes?"

"He got away. Your friend knocked him around and he ran off. Now I'm serious. I want you to think about getting better, not beating up, what was the word, 'pendejo'?"

"Very good, Doctor Ennis. You're learning Spanish," the nurse laughed.

"Don't give me any opioids!" Letty demanded.

"No, ma'am. No opioids," Dr. Ennis had an amused smile on his face. He turned to Will. "She's accustomed to giving orders?"

"My sister is the alpha in our pack. Clarice and me and the dogs and my brother and sister."

Clarice nodded her head in agreement. "She's the head of our family. But she's usually more polite than this."

The pain killer was starting to work. Letty's eyelids began to droop and her head bobbed.

"We're going to admit you for one night just for observation, and …."

"No!" Letty's head jerked up. "I can't stay in the hospital!" She struggled with all her strength to pull herself into a sitting position. She winced in pain and grabbed Dr. Ennis's forearms with her hands.

"I was a medic in Iraq. I can't stay in the hospital." She looked directly into the doctor's eyes. "Please. Please don't make me stay in the hospital. Please." She slumped against him.

Dr. Ennis gently returned her to a lying position, her head and neck cradled by his right hand.

"Is she afraid of hospitals?" he asked Will.

"We don't know," Will said in a frustrated voice. "Something happened in Iraq. Something terrible. Or a bunch of terrible things happened. She won't talk about it. But she has these dreams. We hear her calling out and crying in her sleep. She says Arabic words and bomb words like RPG and IED and things like 'femoral artery' and Kiowa something. I think Kiowa is a helicopter. Often she just says, 'I can't find him' over and over. Sometimes she calls for 'Chava.' Clarice looked it up. 'Chava' is a nickname for 'Salvador.' After these nights, she looks exhausted the next morning."

"Sounds like PTSD to me." The doctor shook his head and frowned. "Iraq was bad and so was Afghanistan. A lot of us came home wounded in ways that can't be seen."

"We think she needs to relax and have some fun," said Clarice.

"Yeah, she never has any fun. She works all the time," Will added.

Dr. Ennis look sharply at them. "So do you two think you can take care of her?"

"Yes!" Will and Clarice said at the same time.

"Here's what we'll do. You can take her home in your car. Do you have a backseat where she can lie down?"

"Yes. I do," said Clarice.

"At least one of you will need to be with her for the rest of today and tomorrow, too. If she's doing okay, then on the day after, you can let her stay by herself and just sleep. I'll come by your house this evening and give her another injection so she can sleep through the night. Starting tomorrow, you will be responsible for giving her the meds. Don't leave that to her. She could get dopey and forget that she's taken them. She might take too many. You will monitor meds and make sure she's getting the right amount at the right time. And don't listen if she tries to order you around."

"What should we feed her?" Will asked.

"She needs to stay hydrated so make sure she has water. Give her something easy to swallow with no chewing. Her jaw is going to hurt. Try a smoothie with fruit, orange juice and a little yogurt. Add protein powder if you have any. Do you know how to make a smoothie?"

"Yes," they both said.

"She's going to be in a lot of pain for a day or two. The meds will help. The pain will slowly start to ease off. She needs to give herself three weeks at least with no jogging, no martial arts, no beating up pendejos. Better would be six weeks. And if there's any change that you feel uncomfortable about, you must call me immediately. Change in respiration, color, any bleeding, anything out of the ordinary. I'll give you my personal mobile number."

"Okay. We'll follow your instructions to the letter," Clarice said.

Dr. Ennis turned to the nurse again. "Let's get one of the attendants to help move her to the car."

Will and Clarice took Letty home. Will half-guided and half-carried Letty to her bedroom. Clarice helped her change into cotton pajamas and put her in bed. The dogs, Teddy and Millie, seemed to understand that something was wrong. They stood back quietly and watched. They made no attempt to approach Letty.

Early in the evening Zhou called to ask about Letty.

Will explained what happened, about the extent of her injuries, and what the doctor ordered. "She's asleep now. You can come and see her in a couple of days."

"I have a surprise for Letty."

"Yeah? What's that?"

"Jade and I are parents now. We have a little boy. His name is Ben Ben."

To Will's ear, it sounded like Bun Bun.

"Congratulations!"

Clarice pulled the phone from his hand.

"Oh, Zhou! How wonderful! How is Jade?"

"She is quite well. Very happy. She is very brave."

Clarice laughed. "Yeah, you dudes don't know how hard it is giving birth until you see it for yourself!"

"True. Very true. I admire Jade greatly for her bravery. She is beautiful and strong and she is a very good mother. She is the best mother in the world."

An hour later, Dr. Ennis showed up at Letty's house. He was dressed casually in a shirt, light-weight sport coat and blue jeans rather than his hospital scrubs. Clarice thought he looked more like a young entrepreneur from some high-tech start-up than a doctor. She decided that he wasn't much older than Letty. Maybe thirty-five years old at most? Clarice and Will led Dr. Ennis to Letty's bedroom.

The doctor woke Letty and asked her how she felt.

"I'm tired. Leave me alone." She closed her eyes.

"Please sit up, Ms. Valdez."

"Don't be so pinche demanding! Go away!" She closed her eyes again.

"Pinche? Is that another Spanish curse word?" the doctor asked, smiling.

Clarice and Will stifled their laughter.

"Yeah," said Will, grinning.

"Ms. Valdez, I need to listen to your heart and lungs." He carefully pulled Letty to a sitting position. She groaned softly.

Dr. Ennis tilted Letty forward, lifted her pajama top and looked at her back. Next he listened with his stethoscope. He gently pushed her down and lifted her top in the front just enough to see her rib cage and abdomen. Letty was black and blue front and back. Ennis listened again with his stethoscope at various points on her chest.

"Look at me," he said to Letty in a firm voice.

Letty frowned. She opened her eyes.

"Now look straight ahead." He looked closely in her eyes with a small light. "Any blurred vision or light sensitivity or a headache?"

"No! no! and no! Can I go to sleep now?" She closed her eyes again.

"Yes, go to sleep."

He turned to Clarice and Will.

"She looks and sounds good. Did she eat?"

"About half the smoothie."

"I'm giving her another injection. This will get her through the night."

Letty flinched when the doctor inserted the needle into her arm.

"Hey!" she glared at him.

"I'm going to leave you alone now, Corporal. Go back to sleep. That's an order."

"Yes, sir. Thank you, sir."

Letty sighed and closed her eyes.

Dr. Ennis chuckled. "Well, that worked."

Ennis turned to Will and Clarice. "Here are her meds." He handed a bottle of tablets to Clarice. "Remember what I said earlier. You are in control. Don't let her order you around in English or in Spanish. Maybe the day after tomorrow, she needs to get up and start moving around. Nothing strenuous."

Clarice nodded.

Will and Dr. Ennis traded cell phone numbers. "Don't hesitate to call if you need me."

"Why are you giving Letty all this special attention?" Will asked.

"I'm a vet, too. One tour in Iraq. One in Afghanistan. Vets get priority as far as I'm concerned."

Clarice asked, "Was Letty a corporal?"

"I don't know. I just guessed."

"What was your rank?"

"Captain," the doctor said. "I outrank her." He grinned.

On his way out, Dr. Ennis bent down to pet the dogs. "And these dogs are part of the Letty Valdez pack?"

Both dogs wagged their tails. Millie licked his hand and Teddy tried to lean against his legs.

"The black lab is Teddy and this is Millie. She's a pit bull. Letty found her dying in the desert and we adopted her. Both dogs love Letty. She's their alpha."

Dr. Ennis smiled and nodded. He said good night.

Will and Clarice put their arms around each other.

"Let's take good care of Big Sister," Will said.

"Just like she takes good care of us," Clarice responded.

Chapter 13

Letty woke early the next morning. She struggled against the pain that radiated out from every inch of her body. She managed to get out of bed and go to the bathroom on her own. When she came out, she found Clarice standing in the doorway of her bedroom. Letty went back to bed.

"I'll get you some breakfast, Letty," Clarice said. "I have some pain medication for you that the doctor left with me. I'll be here all morning. Will is taking off work and he'll be here this afternoon. You can call on us if you want anything."

"Thank you, Clarice."

After another smoothie for breakfast, Letty went back to sleep. In the afternoon, she was awake a bit longer. When Clarice returned in late afternoon, she helped Letty take a shower and change into some loose, comfortable clothing. Letty joined them at the kitchen table for supper. Will and Clarice gave Letty some chicken vegetable soup that Will had run through the blender to make it easy for Letty to swallow without chewing.

"I'm a lot better," Letty told them. She noticed how worried they both looked.

"The doc says you have to take it easy," Will insisted.

"Yes. Dr. Ennis said you can start moving around tomorrow. You shouldn't stay in bed all day. That's what he said."

"I don't remember any doctor. Did I see a doctor?" Letty said.

"You don't remember the emergency room?" Will asked.

"No. I just remember those men coming at me and punching me," she paused. "Zhou was there and this other jogger. I sort of remember being in an ambulance."

"They gave you some pain meds," Clarice added, "Your pain was bad. You passed out, too. That's why you can't remember anything."

Letty sighed. "Have I missed anything?"

"Oh my god!" Clarice slapped her forehead. "I forgot to tell you. Jade had the baby! He's a little boy."

"All went well?"

"Yes, Jade is fine. She's over-the-moon happy. Zhou managed to survive somehow. He was a nervous wreck," Will laughed. "He told us that Jade was very brave. They named the baby Bun Bun."

"No," Clarice said. "Sounds like that when Zhou says it but really it's Ben Ben."

"Whatever. Ben or Bun. American or Chinese. Baby and Jade are doing fine and Zhou is okay, although I think he thought the whole experience was traumatic," Will said. "They will come to visit soon so you can admire their baby."

"And the dogs? Have they been good?"

"I took Teddy with me on a jog," Clarice said. "He's such a gentleman. He ran right with me and he didn't try to pull on the leash at all," Clarice said. "Someone trained him well."

"Millie and I have been playing frisbee and fetch-the-tennis ball," Will added. "She goes after the ball but she doesn't always remember to bring it back to me. She just drops it and wags her tail."

Letty nodded approvingly. "Okay. I'm going back to bed."

Clarice gave Letty her medication, and Letty dropped into a dreamless sleep almost immediately.

Before Will and Clarice went to bed, Clarice said, "I wish Dr. Ennis would come back. He was cute."

"Cute?" Will made a face. "Cuter than me?"

"You're not cute."

"I'm not cute?" Will sounded hurt.

"No, you are drop-dead gorgeous."

Will grinned. "I love you, baby." He kissed Clarice.

"I love you, too. You are the handsomest man in the whole world."

"If I'm so handsome, why do you want the doctor to come back?"

"So Letty can look at a cute guy. Maybe she'll get ideas."

"I like the way you think, girl," Will laughed.

***

Letty woke at her regular early hour the next morning. She dressed slowly and joined Clarice and Will at the kitchen table again.

"The doc said you can be on your own today if you feel up to it," Clarice said.

"I'm doing well," Letty reassured her. "I'm still sore all over but the pain is not as bad as it was. It seems to help if I walk around some."

"That's exactly what the doc said you should do. But nothing strenuous! I'm serious. He said nothing strenuous."

"Got it."

Just then the front door bell rang. Will went to answer it.

Seri Durand appeared with a cardboard box in her hands.

"I heard about what happened to you. How are you, Letty? You don't look too great."

Letty grimaced. "Gosh, thanks, Seri. Actually I'm doing well. I feel like a truck ran over me, but I'm better today than I was yesterday. Tomorrow should be even better."

Seri frowned. Letty's black eye and bruised jaw looked terrible. She could imagine the bruises elsewhere on her body.

"That's good to hear," Seri said. "I brought you something to keep you occupied. I've been thinking about it. I have concluded that someone wants you off this case. I think someone was looking for something at the Institute, didn't find it, was surprised by Stacey and killed her, broke into Amanda's apartment looking for something and didn't find it, and attacked you to take you out of the picture. Then they tried to break into my condo."

"What! Your condo? When did that happen?"

"Right after I left for work this morning. I have an advanced security system. I got a call from the security company and they sent a guy out. Whoever it was couldn't get past my system."

"I've been thinking along the same lines. Someone wants me off this case because...."

Seri interrupted. "Because they think you will discover what they are looking for and even worse for them, you will discover who is doing the looking."

"Is this the box you had at Zhou and Jade's house?"

"Yes. You can go through it. I suggest you read the rest of the memoir. I can always take it over to Jade's next weekend and read the rest of the story to everyone else. I'm hoping that you'll find something relevant in the memoir."

Seri paused. "At this point, we don't have much to go on. The materials in this box are the only items that have never been housed at the Institute. I can't be sure, but it's logical to conclude that there's something in Peter Arianos's memoir that the murderer wants to know, or he already knows and wants to keep whatever it is under wraps. Either way, he wants to get control of it."

Letty nodded in agreement. "Okay. I'll read it today. Seri, watch your back. Make sure no one is in your car when you get in and make sure no one is following you."

"Will do. Call me if you find anything. I have to get to the library now. Time to get to work."

***

Will and Clarice took off on their bikes soon after. They traveled together along the bike route on Third Street then parted. Clarice went to the University of Arizona campus, and Will traveled on to the downtown campus of Pima Community College.

Letty called Maggie. After assuring Maggie that she was fine and chatting a bit about the new baby, Letty got down to business.

"Maggie, Seri and I think maybe there's something in your great-granduncle's memoir or his box that someone wants. This is all we have to go on at this point. I'm calling to ask you if you have any more papers that belonged to Pete Arianos."

"No, my mother gave this box to me. Someone in the family had given it to her mother and I ended up with it."

"Remember that Arianos wrote in the memoir about some documents belonging to his stepdad Drago?"

"Yes, but I've never seen any papers like that. They weren't in the box when I received it."

"Could you call around and ask your family members if they know of any more papers?"

"Sure. Wouldn't that be great? To find something written by Drago? I wonder if he wrote about his love for Rosa. Oh, how romantic."

Letty smiled to herself. Jade and Maggie. Both hopeless romantics.

"Maybe. But somehow I doubt that this is about their love affair. There's got to be something else going on. Call me back if you find anything."

"I will. I'll call my mother and my granny, too. I'll let you know what I find."

***

Despite her intention to start reading, Letty found that by mid-morning she was sleepy again. She called the dogs in from the backyard and took them with her to her bedroom. She figured if the dogs were taking a morning nap at the same time as she was sleeping, they would be less likely to wake her up.

Both dogs settled onto their beds, placed next to each other on the floor and off to the side of Letty's bed.

Less than an hour later, Letty was startled awake. She sat up in bed.

Both Millie and Teddy were up, alert, and facing her bedroom door. The fur on their necks and along the ridge of their backbones was standing up erect. Both dogs were very tense and staring at the bedroom door with full attention.

Letty's heart began to pound. She couldn't hear anything but she knew there had to be an intruder. The dogs would not behave this way if Will or Clarice were on the other side of the door.

Millie growled.

Teddy growled, too, a low rumbling growl from deep in his chest. Teddy's lips curled up sharply, exposing his teeth. Letty remembered that someone had told her once the correct term for dog lips was "flews" but right now, lips was all Letty could think of. Teddy's lips were pulled back showing his bare fangs. His pink tongue flicked in and out of his mouth. Teddy looked ready to attack and to tear someone apart with those fangs. He growled again.

Millie was ready, too. She stared at the door and growled a second time. She showed her fangs, too.

Letty felt like she almost couldn't breathe. A paralyzing combination of fear and fury immobilized her. She was too banged up to be able to fight anyone. And whoever was on the other side of the door couldn't be a welcome visitor. Letty realized that beyond a doubt, she had become a target.

The knob on the door began to turn slowly as if someone were trying to quietly enter the room.

At the sight and sound of that turning knob, Millie barked a short warning bark. Teddy followed with a deep woofing sound. Don't even try it, they communicated to the intruder.

The door knob returned to its original position. Both dogs continued to stare intently at the door.

Letty knew that the person on the other side of the door knew now that there were two dogs in her room and those dogs were not happy.

Letty quietly got up from her bed and went to her closet. She pulled down a box from the top shelf, retrieved her Glock, and quickly assembled it. Just as quietly, she loaded the gun.

Letty moved toward the bedroom door, listening intently. She didn't hear anything. She opened the door, gun in hand aimed and ready to shoot.

Both dogs bolted through the door past her and ran through the house. They were following the scent of the intruder. The backdoor was open. Letty did a quick check of every room in the house, gun ready. Nothing. The intruder had fled. Letty followed the dogs out the back door and into the backyard. Teddy did a quick survey of the backyard and Millie stood at attention close to Letty. Whoever had been there was gone now.

Letty returned to the house. She found the dog biscuits and gave one to each dog. "Good Millie. Good Teddy," she said. She patted their heads. Both dogs were relaxed now and wagging their tales. They were happy to receive the praise of their alpha.

This wouldn't do, Letty thought. She didn't want Will and Clarice to be in any danger. The old house was entirely too easy to break into. She found her mobile phone and called a security company. She made an appointment for a representative to come over and give her an estimate for installing a good security system. This was long overdue, Letty thought. She should have taken care of this earlier. She would get the security system installed as soon as possible, starting with new front and back doors with a deadbolt lock and a locked heavy metal screen.

Next Letty called Alejandro Ramirez, the Tucson detective in charge of the Robbery Section at the Tucson Police Department.

"Hello, Detective Ramirez, I hope you'll remember me. My name is Letty Valdez. You were at a meeting with Detective De Luca and me."

"Of course I remember you. How can I help you?"

"I'm calling you because I think De Luca doesn't like me and isn't interested in cooperating. I hope you will be more open-minded and work with me."

Ramirez laughed. "I think he's scared of you. A six-foot-tall brown-skinned Chicana-Native American freaks him out. You are too Wild, Wild West for him. Probably thinks you're going to scalp him or something."

Letty chuckled. "I tried to be nice to him."

"Like I said, he doesn't know what to do with the likes of you. I don't think he's going to last here much longer anyway. He's a New York City boy through and through. He only came out here to help his aging parents who retired to sunny Arizona. But they both died in the last six months. He'll probably go home soon enough. By the way, you can call me Alejandro."

"Thanks. You are a lot friendlier than De Luca."

"You come well recommended. You're good friends with my cousin Adelita García. Really she's more like my sister. We grew up together. Our mothers are sisters. Adelita and I got into quite a bit of trouble together when we were kids."

"Oh, yeah! I remember Adelita talking about you. She said you two had a lot of fun. She said your mothers were certain you'd both end up in juvenile detention." Letty chuckled. "And instead you both became cops. How did that happen?"

"Guess we both chose the easier path." He laughed again.

They chatted for a few minutes about family connections.

"So what can I do for you?" Ramirez asked.

"I have an update on what I told De Luca. The story ends with an intruder coming into my house this morning." Letty told him about her investigation and her sense that the murderer was actually bent on stealing something at Seri's library and had been surprised. That's what led to the murder. She reminded him of the break-in at the apartment of librarian Amanda Flores. She told him about getting attacked and beaten at the Rillito River, the attempted break-in at Seri's condo, and now an intrusion into her own house that very morning. She added that her dogs were what stopped any further violence toward her.

"So you see, Alejandro, I think you have a role to play in these attempted robberies and the assault on me, too. It's not just De Luca's territory. I feel certain this person is looking for something and will steal it if he can find it."

"That's quite a story. I'm glad you are okay. I have an update for you, too, but one not so exciting," Alejandro continued. Your friend Monsieur Laurent gave us that tip about the jewel thief, Audrey Parker. We've been keeping an eye on her. She's a social butterfly involved in all sorts of things at her gated community like dance lessons, golf lessons, and bridge club, and all that. She's also changed her appearance a lot. Laurent gave us photos of her when she lived in Europe and she's not the same person she was before."

"What? Dyed her hair or something?"

"No, let's just say that she has been enjoying her taquitos and guacamole and plenty of cerveza since she returned to Arizona."

"Put on a few pounds, huh?

"Ain't no way Miss Gordita could get through that ventilation duct in the library."

Letty chuckled. She liked Alejandro.

"We're keeping an eye on her because there's always the possibility that she might have an accomplice or be training someone in the way of thievery. So far no likely person has shown up. And there haven't been any major thefts reported either. It really does look like she retired from the business."

"That's good to eliminate her. When I was attacked at the river, there were three men. Two were Mexican-American. The third, the leader, was a tall, very thin white guy with narrow shoulders. He's a possibility for getting through the ventilation duct. It would be a tight squeeze but I think he could do it. Zhou ripped off his ski mask. I could see very blond eyebrows and lashes, almost white. His skin was pale, too. And he had these icy-blue, sort of dead-looking eyes."

"Good to know. I'll see if I can find anyone in our database that fits that description."

"Okay. I'm going now. Let's stay in touch. And say hi to Adelita if you hear from her. She's still on her honeymoon as far as I know."

"Yes, they went to Mexico. His family has a home in Mérida. I think they are making it their home base and exploring the Yucatán."

"I hear she's pregnant. Think she'll return to being a cop again?"

"Hard to say. The last time I talked to her, she told me she was thinking about going to law school."

"Adelita would make a great attorney."

They said their goodbyes. Alejandro's last words to Letty were, "Watch your back. Ten cuidado." (Be careful)

Letty ended the call. Excellent. Alejandro Ramirez was a man she would be able to work with easily. She thought for a moment what it would be like to be an attorney. Would she have to get dressed up and work in an office all day? She could never wear those really pointy-toed high heels like Jessica Cameron wore. Way too uncomfortable, she thought, and you can't run in them. Nah, she thought to herself.

Letty called the dogs in. They all found a comfortable spot in the living room. Letty sat in a cushioned chair and began reading the next chapter in Pete Arianos's memoir.

CHAPTER 14

LETTY found the passage where Drago and Rosa were married in St. Augustine Cathedral. She liked Pete's insistence that fireworks at Chinese New Year were the best thing ever, much better than a wedding or any other holiday. Typical little boy, Letty thought. Very charming. She remembered her siblings when they were young with a combination of affection and sadness. She wished she could have been with them throughout their childhoods. Life didn't turn out that way for her.

Letty continued to the next chapter.

***

As I mentioned earlier, Drago and my mama had big plans. Drago moved in with us and started working on the plans right away. He began restoring the rooms in the crumbling part of our old adobe structure. Drago hired a young Chinese man to tend his garden on the other side of the river. The young man's name was Chung. Mama continued her baking and lunch business. Sometimes Chung came to eat with us but he didn't say much. He couldn't speak much English so he talked mainly to Drago. Most of the old customers continued to come for lunch. William House didn't come to eat lunch at Mama's little restaurant any more at all.

I could tell that Mama and Drago were happy being near each other all day. She watched him work while she kneaded her bread loaves. He watched her work while he built new walls and put a new roof on the new rooms. I helped both of them when I wasn't in school.

About six months later, we moved into the new rooms. A new grocery store took over the rooms we had been living in: the bedroom that I had lived in most of my life, the bedroom that Drago and Mama shared, plus a small living room with a door to the outside street. These rooms were all converted into Drago's new market. This meant that Drago shifted his attention from growing vegetables and rebuilding our adobe house to becoming a merchant. He put a big sign over the door that said Shaw Market. We had a fiesta to open the store and we invited everyone in the barrio. Drago and Mama made a feast for everyone and gave candy to the children.

In the smallest room of the new grocery store, Drago stocked some items that were mainly of interest to the Chinese in Tucson. They were special kinds of vinegar and something called jiàngyóu imported all the way from China in pretty glass and pottery vessels. Later I found out that jiàngyóu was what we call soy sauce. But most of the store was given over to Mexican food items. The store carried delicacies that Drago had ordered from towns in the interior of Mexico. Drago also offered items from local producers. That included vegetables from the Chinese gardeners and fresh cuts of meat from the Mexicans. He also sold chorizo pork sausage so beloved by the Mexicans. Buying from local producers made Drago well-regarded. He helped everyone prosper.

Back then, most of the people in Tucson were Mexican, although eventually the Anglos came to outnumber everyone. At first the Anglos didn't come to the store. But when word got out about the fresh meat, fresh eggs, Mama's pastries, and those strawberries and other fresh vegetables and fruits, the Anglos became customers, too. There was something for everyone at Shaw Market. Our little grocery market became quite successful. The store also was a place where everyone came together for a little while to talk.

I haven't mentioned the Papago Indians. That's what we called them then. Their real name is Tohono O'odham, People of the Desert. I read in the newspaper that the tribe is talking about ditching the word 'papago.' They want to call themselves by their true name. We'll see what they do. But back then, we called them Papago. They got the short end of every stick. They were rarely included in anything good, and they were often mistreated. But Drago found a place for them as well. I'm talking about the ones who lived in Tucson or nearby. Most of them lived out west of town in the desert on their ancestral lands. Drago hired some of them to do work for him and he often fed them, especially the kids. He sometimes hired the Papago kids to run errands for him. He paid them in food and coins. The Papago called Drago Ali Cu:kcug which meant Chinaman in their language.

Things were going great. Then Mama announced one day that a baby was coming in a few months. Drago wasn't all that surprised but it was clear that he was very happy to hear this news. He made Mama stop working so hard. She protested, but he insisted that she cut back on both her little lunch restaurant and her bakery. He hired a couple of Mexican girls to do most of the work. Mama's job was to give them instructions and to watch over their work. Drago was firm, and as she grew in size, Mama complied. She got so big that it was hard for her to move around much.

Mama and the little Papago kids weren't the only ones that Drago cared for. When Drago lived on his little farm west of the Santa Cruz and before he married Mama, he became friends with an old man named Bernardo Dominguez who lived nearby. Dominguez came from an old family that had been landowners there on the west side long before Arizona became a territory. The Dominguez family had been there even before Mexico had revolted against French control. I don't know why but Dominguez never had the prejudice against the Chinese that most of the Anglos and many of the rich, old Mexican families had. Or maybe Dominguez was just lonely and he really liked Drago. His wife and children had died years earlier in a cholera epidemic, and he had been left alone. He and Drago became friends. They drank tea and played chess together.

Dominguez was not well and his health deteriorated over time. Drago hired a couple of the Papago boys to take Señor Dominguez some food every day so he wouldn't have to cook. Drago also hired them to fill Señor Dominguez's water tanks so he wouldn't have to haul water. After Drago and Mama married, Mama got involved, *too. She would make soups and bread and Drago took them to Señor Dominguez himself. Sometimes Mama would go along. She would sing to the old man, too.*

Then in 1900 at the beginning of a new century, Mama took to her bed. The midwife came and so did Maria de los Angeles Gonzalez, my mother's best friend. Drago paced up and down in the courtyard for hours. He said nothing, just paced back and forth. I went to school like usual. When I came home, Drago was still pacing. In the early evening, we heard Mama cry out. Drago looked like his heart had been pierced by a knife when he heard her wail in pain. We heard a baby crying. Then a second baby! Two babies! Mama had given birth to twins! Two little boys. I was a brother! A big brother! Drago had tears in his eyes when he went in to see Mama. I went with him, holding his hand. Honestly, my mama looked like the Madonna in her bed holding the two little baby boys. For the second time in his life, Drago couldn't speak because his emotions were so strong.

Later my two little brothers were baptized in St. Augustine Cathedral. They were given the names Leonardo Yu Shaw and Matteo Long Shaw. But we called them Leo and Matt. They turned out to be a lot of fun when they got a little older. I enjoyed being their big brother. They loved me, too, but I think they loved my dog Mancha best of all. All the kids loved Mancha best.

Mama recovered pretty fast. But she didn't go back to working all the time like she had for years. Drago insisted that such hard physical work wasn't good for her. He made it clear that he expected her to care for his new sons. He also expected her to help him in the grocery store. He made compelling arguments that she was needed more now to help him keep up with inventory and orders and the accounts. They could always hire someone to do the hard physical work. He reminded her that she had more education that the average woman in Tucson. She was needed for her intelligence and organizational skills. My mama found this very flattering, which was exactly what Drago intended. So she agreed to help him in the store. And, he reminded her occasionally that they had agreed to have a big family. There would be more babies coming. He was right about that. Drago and my mama would eventually bring into the world three sisters and another brother to join Leo and Matt and me. I was dàgē, Drago said. Big brother to them all.

The twins were born in the early summer not long before the monsoon rains began. In the fall after the summer rains were gone, one of the Papago boys came into the store and approached Drago. He whispered to Drago that Señor Dominguez had fallen ill. Immediately Drago closed the store. On the way out, he called me first. Then he gave that little Papago boy a reward for being a messenger. He gave the boy a bag of corn meal and a small bag of sugar to take to the boy's mother. For the boy himself, Drago gave him a package of Mexican candy and a coin. Then Drago and I went to Señor Dominguez's house on the west side.

When we got there, we found Señor Dominguez in his bed, pale and breathing heavily. Drago gave him some water and said, "We'll get the doctor."

"No, Señor Drago. Too late for the doctor. Better to call the padre."

Drago sent me off to find Father Rodrigo. We returned in about thirty minutes.

Meanwhile, Drago told me later, Señor Dominguez spoke to Drago in a low voice. Drago had to sit close to the old man's bedside to even hear him.

"You are a good man," Dominguez said to Drago. "You do not deserve the bad things that have happened to you. I want to give you a gift."

Drago told me that he reassured Señor Dominguez, "No gift is expected. I have enjoyed our friendship. You are an honorable man, and you play chess well. You have challenged my chess game and provided me with enjoyable hours of conversation. I am grateful to you."

Later, because I heard about this, I asked Drago to teach me chess. He did, and he also taught me a similar game that the Chinese play. The pieces were round and flat on the top with Chinese characters painted on them. I got pretty good at both games. But I was never as good as Drago.

Drago told me that Señor Dominguez directed him to retrieve a metal box from a high shelf in the old man's room. Drago brought him the box.

Señor Dominguez said to Drago, "You take the box and keep it safe. After I am gone, take this to that new lawyer in Tucson. He is a young man. His name is Jack Murphy. I went to his office after your sons were born. I paid him already. He has been instructed to help you. And you will need the help."

Drago told me that he had no idea what Señor Dominguez was talking about until later when he looked in the box. So he put the metal box in his pack and he sat quietly with Señor Dominguez until the padre arrived. Drago told me that the old man whispered stories about his wife and children who had been dead for many years, and how he would be so happy to see them again in the afterlife.

When I returned with the padre, Drago and I went outside and waited. Father Rodrigo gave Señor Dominguez his last rites. Not long after, the old man breathed his final breath and departed this earth forever. The padre came out and told us that he would arrange for transport to the cathedral, preparation for burial, and for the final Mass in celebration of the old man's life.

Everything got more complicated after that.

***

On the evening after the Mass for Señor Dominguez, Drago and Mama and I sat at the kitchen table. My baby brothers were asleep in their cribs. Drago turned the lantern up and opened the box left to him by Señor Dominguez. He removed three papers and a small box. Still in the big box was the old gentleman's chess set.

The first paper was a letter. It was written in Spanish followed by an English translation. Drago read the English out loud to us.

Dear Señor Drago,

If you are reading this letter, I have gone on to my heavenly home to be with the angels and my beloved wife and children.

I want to thank you and your wife Rosa for your kindness to me. Playing chess and that Chinese game with you gave me hours of entertainment. You will find my chess set in this box. Please continue to enjoy it.

Even more than chess, I appreciated our conversations. I learned a lot from you, Señor Drago, about many interesting things. I hope the Mexicans and the Chinese will always be friends. I also want to thank you sincerely for the help you provided me as my health declined.

To your wife Rosa, please tell her I say thank you for her delicious foods and most of all, I thank her for her songs. She has the voice of an angel. Please find a cameo necklace in the small box. This necklace belonged to my beloved wife Paloma.

In recent years, I have watched many of the newcomers in this territory take land away from the Mexican residents. I refer to the Anglos, the white Americans. The lands they took had been in Mexican families for many, many years but the families usually had no formal proof of ownership. The Anglos used money and knowledge of American law to steal the land from the rightful owners.

My family lived on a ranch south of Tucson for generations. But we also have this small parcel of land west of the Santa Cruz River where I live now. Thanks to my father's foresight, I have a legitimate, legal deed to this land.

In this box you will find my last will and testament. In the will, I leave to your two newborn sons, Leo Shaw and Matt Shaw, this small parcel of land on the west side of the Santa Cruz River. You will also find the deed to the land in my name in this box.

I choose to leave this land to your sons because I believe it is more likely that they, both born in Arizona Territory, will have a better chance of proving ownership. If I left it to you, Señor Drago, I believe that they would not allow a Chinaman to keep the land. They would find a way to steal it from you. Your sons will have a better chance of keeping what is rightfully theirs.

Please visit my attorney and he will tell you how to claim your sons' inheritance and how to make this small parcel theirs. The land has little value now. But I foresee a time in which this pueblo will became a great city. My hope for you is that the land will have value in the future.

Dios te bendiga y a tu familia. God bless you and your family.

Bernardo Dominguez

Drago removed the cameo necklace and gave it to Mama. She had tears in her eyes as she put it around her neck. Drago removed the other papers. As Señor Dominguez had said, Drago found a last will and testament and a deed to the land. We said very little after that. What could we say? The old man expressed his gratitude in the best way he knew how. In the process, he tied Drago and our family to this beautiful desert forever.

***

The next morning Drago and I went to see the lawyer. He was a young man who had only recently come to Arizona Territory. He and Drago eventually became friends. He told Drago that he was the grandson of Irish immigrants. They and their children had been treated badly back in Boston. His parents had sacrificed everything so their son could go to college and become a lawyer. Jack Murphy figured that his chances of overcoming prejudice against the Irish would be better in the Arizona Territory. He was right about that. He became a prominent attorney and civic leader in our town. He was my inspiration for going into the law. Also he married my favorite teacher in elementary school, Miss Flinders. They were good people.

At that first meeting, Murphy took the deed and the will and said he would begin the process of making my little brothers the rightful owners of the Dominguez land.

However, when it all came down in the end, Jack Murphy couldn't help Drago and my family. Murphy told Drago that the will and the deed were legal and Drago's claim on behalf of his sons for the land should hold up in court with no problem. But Jack Murphy didn't count on the vile actions of William House, who had never forgiven Drago for taking Mama away from him. House never seemed to accept the fact that Mama didn't like him at all. He blamed Drago.

A couple of days after we visited Mr. Murphy, William House came to Shaw Market. It was his first and last visit to the market. One of the Papago boys told me that he took Drago aside and spoke to Drago. Mama was in her kitchen and didn't see this. The boy told me that House had an angry, hateful look on his face. But when he spoke, his voice was barely above a whisper. No one could hear what he was saying. The boy told me that Drago had no expression at all on his face. Drago said nothing. House left immediately after their short interaction.

Drago was silent for the remainder of the day. On the following day, he put a big "Closed" sign on the door of the market, and he disappeared. Mama was frantic with worry. Drago returned late that night. He remained silent.

Very early the next morning before dawn, he woke me.

"Come with me, Xiao Pete. We go to watch the sun rise."

We walked west, crossed the river and hiked up to the top of Sentinel Peak. The early light from the rising sun was just then reaching the Santa Catalina Mountains across the valley. Some of the saguaros were lit up like candles by the rays of early sunlight. We sat in silence for a while.

Drago said to me, "Xiao Pete, I am going to see the lawyer Murphy today. I am going to withdraw the claim on Señor Dominguez's land."

"Why, Drago?" I was genuinely surprised and confused.

"William House came to me and threatened our family if we go ahead with this claim."

"What do you mean he threated our family?"

Drago was silent for a while. Finally he spoke to me.

"You are twelve years old now. You are old enough to understand what I am going to tell you. I want you to agree not to discuss this with your mother or any other person. This is man-to-man. Agree?"

"Yes, I agree." The gravity of the moment did not escape me.

"House threatened to kill me. But first he said he would bring a gang of men with him and they would all take turns violating your mother. I would be forced to watch before they killed me. Do you understand?"

"Yes, Drago," I could barely speak.

"Your mother would be left without a husband to protect her. House said he would make her his plaything for as long and as often as he wished. You and your brothers would have no father."

I was shocked. "That bastard." Immediately I was glad that Mama wasn't there to hear me talk like that.

Drago nodded. "Do you remember when he and his men beat me? He was never punished for that."

"I will shoot him if he comes near Mama."

"No, killing a man is not a good way for you to start your life. Better is to find a way to take care of your family and protect those who need protection. Best is to live an honorable life."

He was right, of course. If Drago killed House, Drago the Chinaman would be hanged. If I killed him, I might get away with it because I was so young, but I would be changed forever.

Later that day, Drago went to the lawyer's office and told Murphy that he was not going to claim the land willed to his sons. He explained in enough detail that Murphy got the picture. Jack Murphy didn't like it but he understood. He had known enough prejudice in his own life to realize that Drago had little power against a man like House. Murphy returned the will and the deed to Drago. I don't know what Drago said to Mama but she accepted his decision.

That early morning on Sentinel Peak was a turning point for me. I vowed to myself to do just as Drago suggested. I became an attorney and I did everything I could in my life to protect the vulnerable and to fight for justice. I wanted to do honor to our family.

Drago had been forced to abandon his Chinese family and his home-land because of his revolutionary activities. He sought refuge in a strange land. He had made a new life in a new place with Mama and me and my little brothers and sisters. As the sun rose above the horizon, it became clear to me that Drago had a vision for his life in America.

He said to me that morning, "I decide that ownership of this land is not necessary for our family to have a good life. We will work together. We will love each other. Our family will be respected by all, and we will prosper. That will be my revenge."

CHAPTER 15

"Seri, you were right about the memoir. I think I found what we're looking for."

"You finished reading the memoir? What did you find?"

"Yes." Letty gave Seri an overview of the relationship between Señor Dominguez and Drago, the letter, the will, and the deed to the land. She told Seri about William House and the theft of land that should have gone to Drago's family. "I'm going to talk to Jessica Cameron about the possibility that Maggie's family could get some compensation."

"But this doesn't help us to know who is out to get you."

"True. Targeting me suggests that someone has a big stake in this. So we'll follow the money, as they say. We have to figure out who stands to lose or benefit if we can find the original documents."

"I'm going to work on things on this end. I have your list of people. If it's okay with you, I'll see what I can find out about each one. I know you intended to interview them all but Dr. Miller was the only one here that day. I'd like to help with this, especially considering how injured you are now."

"Be my guest. I need all the help I can get. I don't think I could have a better co-investigator than you. I've always thought you missed your calling. You'd make a great detective."

Seri laughed. "Being a librarian is usually safer than being a private investigator or a police detective. Let's hope it stays that way. I don't fancy being beat up or shot at. I always figured Mycroft had the best job because he never had to leave home. Jade had it right when she pegged me as being Mycroft to your Sherlock."

Next Letty called Jessica Cameron at her law office in downtown Tucson.

"Hi, Letty." Jessica said. "How are you doing? I talked to your brother when they brought you home from the hospital. I'd sure like to find those thugs and throw the book at them. They deserve a long stay in jail. Are you feeling better?"

"Yes, thanks. Much better."

"I have an update for you. That goon who attacked you made bail. His boss, Roy Lewis, bailed him out. But he'll be back in court soon. I think it's very likely that he'll get a jail sentence for assaulting you. He has priors on assault and that's not going to help his case."

"Good. Actually I'm calling because I'd like to give you a hypothetical scenario and you tell me what you think from a lawyer's perspective."

"Okay. This should be interesting."

"Imagine it's 1900 in Tucson, Arizona Territory. An old man, a Mexican man, dies and leaves a small acreage of land to a couple of twin baby boys. He leaves the land to the babies because he fears if he leaves it to their father, a Chinese immigrant, then the Chinese man won't be allowed to claim it."

"Yes, that was very possible. There was a lot of prejudice and some clearly racist laws back then discriminating against the Chinese. The babies born here would have had a better chance at obtaining legitimate ownership."

"But according to a memoir written by a family member in the 1970s, the Chinese man and his Italian wife were both threatened by a local ruffian. So to protect his family, the Chinese man withdrew the claim. I'd like to know if you think the Chinese man's family still has a claim to the land even though more than one hundred years have passed."

"Very possibly. The claim would be much stronger if you found the original will. Also you'd have to prove that the deceased actually was the legitimate owner and could legally pass it on in his will. Is there a deed proving the deceased owned the land?"

"I have the memoir that describes these documents. I'm looking for the will and the deed now."

"You will probably have to hire a documents expert to prove that the original will and deed are legitimate. Another issue is the ownership of the land in the intervening years. If the legitimate inheritors didn't get ownership, who did? It may mean proving that whoever ended up with it back then didn't actually have a legal right to it. That might also require a documents expert if the person used fraudulent documents to claim ownership."

"That fake deed might be easier to find, right? It would have been filed so that the new owner could take possession."

"Possibly. Also another issue is ownership in intervening years. Has the land been sold? Or sold more than once? And what has the land been used for in the past one hundred years? If there are big condos or a bank or shopping center on the land, some kind of financial settlement is more reasonable to expect rather than to have the land and everything on it returned to the legitimate owner."

Letty was taking notes on Jessica's commentary.

"Another option might be for the legitimate owners to sell the land to the ones currently claiming ownership. Or the land could be sold by the legitimate owners to another entity. That could be a substantial amount of money."

"That would great for Maggie's family."

"Ah, so this isn't entirely hypothetical?"

"No. I've been reading the memoir. It's pretty clear that I have to find that original will and deed before anything can come of this."

"Yes, and I bet you're going to tell me now that those morons who beat you up have something to do with this."

"Not a hundred percent sure, but my friend Seri and I think everything is connected. There are too many coincidences. We think whoever is behind this wants me off the case so that I won't be the first to find what they are looking for. Based on my reading of the memoir, my best guess is that they are looking for the will and deed. They'd like to get their hands on the memoir, too."

"They hope to destroy any documents that prove the Chinese man and his descendants have a claim to it?"

"That's my best guess."

"Where is this land?"

"I haven't verified this yet. I know for sure it's on the west side and I think it's very close to El Mercado just south of Congress. It's not that much land, no more than five acres, maybe fewer."

"Wow! Yes, that little patch of dirt will be worth a lot, maybe a million dollars or more."

"Yes. I think it has to be worth a lot. There's a lot of development over there."

"Well, I'm available. Maggie will need me to argue her case. Tell her there's no charge for her to hire me. I'll get my cut when I win the case."

Letty smiled, "I like your confidence!"

"Thanks, Letty. Now you take care of yourself. You have too many people trying to knock you around. Be safe."

They said their goodbyes.

There was a knock on the door. Letty found the home security representative at her front door. They did a tour of the inside and outside and came to a quick agreement.

"I can fix the doors right now with deadbolt locks. I'll send someone out this afternoon to put the metal screens on the windows and a metal screen door on both your front and back doors. Your home will be much safer," the security rep said.

"Great!" Letty responded. "Let's do it." They shook hands and the security man started working on the front door and back door locks.

The phone rang. It was Maggie.

"I called my granny, and she called her sister, and then they called some cousins who live out in California. Not really cousins. You know that side of the family is by marriage, not by blood. Anyway to make a long story short, when Pete Arianos died, none of his direct descendants still lived in Tucson. That side of the family went to California to make their fortune. And apparently they've done quite well for themselves. I heard stories about the high-tech industry and investments in a company that came to be known as Google. A couple of them were in the movie business in Hollywood, too. That means several of them have lots of money."

"When Pete died, some of them came back for the funeral. But none of them wanted to hassle with taking care of his personal items. That would have taken too much of their valuable time. They were going to hire an estate sales rep to auction everything off. But one of Pete's grandchildren reminded them that Pete Arianos had this O'odham man who had worked for him for nearly forty years and that it would be a good idea to reward him for his service. The O'odham man's name was Tomás Navarro. Over time Tomás and Pete became good friends. So the family decided to give the contents of Pete's house to the Navarro family. One of those California cousins invited the O'odham man's family to go in and take whatever they wanted from Pete's house before Pete's family put the house on the market."

Letty chuckled. "That was big of them."

"Yeah, that's what I thought, too. But it turned out to be a good deal for the Navarro family because Pete owned a lot of valuable Native American art from several Southwestern tribes. Navajo silver jewelry, O'odham basketry, Zuni kachinas. No one in the Arianos family even bothered to check on what was there inside the house. So Navarro's family got all that art and more."

"Good for them. Any leads on the documents?"

"Not directly. Your best bet now is to track down the Navarro family and see if there's anything left from the Arianos estate."

"Will do. Thanks, Maggie. One more thing. Please call Jessica Cameron and make an agreement with her to represent you." Letty gave Maggie a brief summary of what she'd found in the memoir. "It's a long shot, but if we find anything to support the claim on the land by your family, Jessica would like to represent you."

"Okay," Maggie responded. "I'll call her right away."

Letty was enjoying herself. She liked tracking down clues like this. Solving a mystery was like solving a puzzle and she liked puzzles. Even better, no one was beating her up or breaking into her house.

Next she called her Uncle Armando Antone, who lived with his wife Valerina on the O'odham reservation. Uncle Mando's sister was Rhonda Antone Ramone, the mother of Letty and her siblings, who had run off with a Navajo cowboy when they were all kids.

"Yes," Uncle Mando assured Letty. "I know the Navarro family. Some live in Tucson but many still live out east of Topawa. Their family has three houses fairly close together about thirty minutes by horseback from my house. You can drive there on a dirt road."

"Do you have time to contact them and see if we can come by tomorrow maybe and ask them about the Arianos estate?"

"Sure. Let's make it a family thing. I'll get your brother Eduardo, his girl Esperanza, and your grandmother. You bring Will. Why don't you come this afternoon? We'll have dinner together and then go see the Navarro family tomorrow morning. Bring that girlfriend of Will's. What's her name?"

"Clarice. Okay, that sounds like a good idea. See you later."

Letty called Seri a second time.

"Want to dog-sit this evening? We're going out to the rez and I need you to babysit these two dogs."

"My pleasure!" Seri responded. "I love your dogs."

"And they love you. Why don't get your own dog?"

"I travel too much. Borrowing your doggies works well for me."

"And for me. By the way, I have a home-security guy here now. By the end of the day, this place will be far more secure than it ever has been."

"Good. I also have my taser gun and the dogs can alert me if there's a problem."

"Good idea. I think you'll be okay. As for me, I'm carrying my handgun until I'm not an easy target anymore."

"Makes sense to me.

"Okay. See you late afternoon. By the way, I'm leaving the memoir with you. Maybe you can read the last chapter to Zhou and Jade and Maggie tomorrow morning."

"Will do!"

***

Not long after Seri arrived to take care of the dogs, Clarice, Will, and Letty piled into Clarice's hatchback and off they went. Letty scanned her street to see if there were any cars or trucks she didn't recognize. Everything looked normal. The neighborhood was quiet.

On the way west to the little town of Sells, Will coached Clarice on some O'odham phrases.

"Okay, so when you meet our grandmother, you can say "S-ke:g huduñig. Bañ ce:gig.'"

"Oh, I'm so excited. What does that mean?" Clarice grasped her hands in front of her.

"It means, 'Your grandson Will is a genius and incredibly sexy.'"

Letty shook her head and clicked her tongue. "Will, she wants to learn. Help her out."

Will chuckled, "Okay, okay. Actually 'S-ke:g huduñig' means 'Good evening,' and 'Bañ ce:gig' means 'My name is...' So you just say, 'Bañ ce:gig Clarice."

Clarice stumbled over the strange syllables. "This is difficult."

"Not really."

"Not really?" Clarice punched him on the arm. "Not difficult for you! You grew up speaking this language!"

"Whatever. Your French isn't so easy! Also Grandma might say 'Hebai 'ab 'amijed'? That means "Where are you from?" and you can say 'Boston.' But Grandma isn't going to know where Boston is. Maybe you should just say Tucson."

Clarice practiced her phrases for several miles until Will got tired of her and started chatting with Letty in English.

They arrived at Mando and Valerina's house southwest of Topawa just in time for a big meal. Letty put her arm around her grandmother's shoulders and gave her a loving greeting. Next she greeted her little brother Eduardo and his soon-to-be wife Esperanza, a teenage Mexican girl rescued by Eduardo in the desert nearly a year earlier. She had come north to find a job when she got lost in the desert and ran out of water.

When Clarice met Grandmother Antone, she practiced her O'odham phrases and said them well enough that Grandma understood her. Will helped her. Grandma Antone took Clarice's hands in hers and smiled at her in a very affectionate manner. Clarice was thrilled.

Letty felt her heart fill with a great love for her grandmother. When she came home from Iraq, Letty was very ill. She had a spirit sickness that could only be cured by living in the desert and following the desert ways. During the months she lived with Grandma Antone, she rarely spoke at all. The nights were taken over by dreams of violence, bombs going off, and people dying. Sometimes the dreams came suddenly upon her when she was awake, too.

Grandma Antone asked Letty no questions and made no demands on her. She simply took Letty with her everywhere. They went into the desert to collect the fibers to make 'hoh,' the traditional O'odham basket. They walked for miles early in the morning and cut bear grass and yucca. They put the fibers in a basket on their backs. Sometimes they found the dried devil's claw seedpods and those also went into the baskets. Then they trekked back home again.

Grandma never asked Letty if she wanted to learn how to make a traditional basket. She just put the materials in Letty's hands and began guiding her. Grandma was a wonderful basket maker. She occasionally sold her baskets to supplement her family's income. The quiet of the desert, the concentration on the basket weaving, the sunrise and sunset, the night sky, the old ways, Letty knew that this is what saved her. The old ways started her on a path away from the spirit sickness and toward wholeness. She wasn't entirely there yet, but she knew that someday the demons of Iraq would be gone and the serenity of the desert would overcome everything bad that had happened to her and turn it into good.

Grandma Antone was getting old now. Letty noticed that she seemed to have shrunk in height. She moved more slowly than ever. He face had more wrinkles, too. Other things had not changed. Her long gray hair was twisted into a bun at the back of her head. She continued to look at her grandchildren with enormous love.

Letty turned her attention again to her family eating at the large table on Mando and Valerina's large front porch.

"Did you learn anything helpful, Mando?" she asked.

"I talked to a couple of members of the Navarro family. One of them said that Tómas Navarro lived in an old adobe a few miles off the road east of Topawa. The generations that followed him built houses close to each other and closer to the main paved road. Tómas's great-grandson Trick Navarro is coming tomorrow morning to show us where it is."

"Hey, I know Trick. He and I went to Baboquivari High School before Letty took me with her to live in Tucson."

"How did he get that name 'Trick'?" Clarice asked.

"When he was a kid, he was an ornery little fellow. He liked to play tricks on people and joke around. We started calling him 'Trick.' Later when we played basketball together, his tricks were useful. He would distract the other team's defense, and then he'd go for the basket. He usually made some points by doing that."

Mando continued, "He'll be on horseback. I thought maybe Eduardo and Will and I could join him and go over by horseback."

"Clarice has volunteered to drive me. I don't think I've recuperated enough to be riding a horse. Next time, though, we'll join you. Clarice knows how to ride." Letty couldn't remember the first time she'd been on a horse, certainly before she even started elementary school.

Letty was exhausted after dinner. She found a quiet spot under the ramada and sank down onto a cot that Will and Eduardo put there for her. Esperanza brought her a pillow and some blankets. For a while, Letty watched the millions of stars in the dark desert night sky. Then she slept. No Iraq dreams tormented her.

***

After breakfast, Letty and Clarice watched the Ramone brothers and Uncle Mando saddle up and lead their horses out of Mando's corral. A few minutes later, they were joined by a young man on horseback. Trick Navarro was almost as tall as Will and had the O'odham rusty brown skin. He had short, black hair, and a thin, longish beard and a moustache. Will and Trick greeted each other warmly.

"Introduce me to your girlfriend," Trick gestured toward Clarice, smiling.

Will put his arm around Clarice. "This is Clarice and she's *my* girlfriend. Don't forget that."

Trick laughed and winked at Clarice.

Letty noticed right away that Mando, Eduardo and Trick, too, had long gun scabbards with .22 rifles in them attached to their saddles.

"What's with the rifles?" Letty asked. Her own handgun was in a holster on her hip.

Mando replied, "We've been getting reports, some from Border Patrol agents, that a gang of so-called "hunters" has been seen wandering around out here. They claimed to be hunting deer, which they aren't supposed to be doing on the reservation anyway. But we're getting reports that what they are really doing is hunting and stealing from undocumented workers coming across the line. There are reports that they've raped a number of undocumented women, too. These guys are very well armed. Needless to say, they aren't supposed to be here at all and certainly not if they are raping and killing. The last thing we need on the rez is a bunch of vigilantes."

"And there's always the odd rabid skunk or coyote or a rattlesnake in the wrong place. A week or so ago, we had a mountain lion sighted not too far from my parents' place. But he left on his own," Trick added.

Trick Navarro gave Letty explicit instructions on how to find his great-grandfather's old adobe house. The men took off on their horses at a trot. Letty and Clarice went back inside to help Esperanza and Grandma clean up after breakfast. The men had about a fifteen-minute head start when Letty and Clarice got into Clarice's car and drove back to the paved highway.

They drove north almost to Topawa on the paved road then Clarice turned east onto a hard-packed dirt road toward the Baboquivari Mountains. Soon they passed a cluster of three houses belonging to the Navarro clan. The dirt road got a lot rougher after that. It narrowed and began to climb uphill slightly. It passed through thick groves of old velvet mesquite trees. Clarice had to slow down and navigate the numerous potholes and ridges in the road. They found the old adobe house only a couple of miles from the Navarro family homes, but those miles were arduous.

Only ten minutes or so had passed when the men on horseback appeared among the mesquite trees.

"Clarice, if you decide to go inside the house, pay attention. There may be rattlesnakes in there. I know we don't usually see them this time of year, but we don't want to take any chances. It's been very warm lately so we might see one. Have you ever heard a rattlesnake's rattle?"

"No, but Will told me all about them, and he showed me a video on YouTube of them rattling. Maybe I'll just stay out here with Will and the horses."

Mando and Trick went inside first and Letty followed. The adobe house was very run down with one wall completely slumped over. Only half the interior space was covered by a roof and what was left of it had patches of daylight showing through. Mice scurried out of the way but no rattlesnakes appeared. They didn't hear any warning rattles.

The three of them went through what looked like junk still left in the house. There were old pieces of furniture, broken dishes, and some rough looking cardboard boxes that had pieces of metal and other discarded items in them.

In the corner, Letty spied an old wooden trunk. Trick pulled it out to the center of the floor and opened it. On top were some old newspapers damaged by water. Clearly the roof had not protected the contents from monsoon rains. Letty sighed. She may find the documents but if the rains had ruined them, they wouldn't be readable.

Under the newspapers, Trick found a metal box. He brought it out of the trunk, put it on the rough wooden table and opened it.

Letty pulled out a tightly-wound paper scroll. The paper, once thick and sturdy, was now a stained, darker color and appeared to be quite fragile. She opened it just enough to see that it was filled top to bottom with rows of Chinese characters. Oh my god, she thought to herself, Drago wrote this!

She carefully set the scroll aside. Next she pulled out a handful of papers, also fragile-looking. She began opening them one by one.

Within a few minutes, Letty had in her hand the original deed written in Spanish proving that Bernardo Dominguez was the owner of the parcel of land just west of the Santa Cruz River and the Old Presidio of Tucson. Next came the will, the original, handwritten will in both Spanish and English. The will clearly confirmed that Leonardo Shaw and Matteo Shaw would become the owners of the parcel upon the death of Bernardo Dominguez.

She wasn't sure why, but Letty suddenly felt very moved. She held in her hand a scroll that had been written by Drago. She held in her hand documents that Dominguez had held and signed. She held in her hand the old man's desire to gift Drago and Rosa's children with his land.

Letty had everything now – the memoir, the will, and the deed. She would turn these over to lawyer Jessica Cameron. She would have felt more elated, but she still didn't know who was after her. Now she hoped to put her full attention on finding the one who wanted to do her harm.

CHAPTER 16

L ETTY came out of the adobe house and held up the box with the documents for Will and Clarice to see. Her elation showed on her face.

"Found 'em!"

"Awesome!" Will and Clarice echoed each other.

Letty put the metal box with all the documents in it on the back-seat floor of Clarice's car.

"I'm going to take these directly to Jessica Cameron," she said to Clarice. "Maggie is hiring Jessica as her lawyer. I'll give Jessica the memoir, too, as soon as Seri returns it. Jessica will have everything she needs for a lawsuit. We'll prove that Maggie and her family own that land on the west side."

"So you are heading back to Tucson now?" Uncle Mando asked Letty.

"Hey, can we go by Baboquivari High School?" Will asked. "I'd like to show Clarice where I went to school."

"We can go to the O'odham community college, too," Trick added. "Eduardo is a student there and so I am. But that means a ride in the car because it's a little farther away."

"Sure," Letty said. "Then it's back to Tucson. I'd like to pass these on to Jessica before the day is over."

Uncle Mando, Eduardo, Will and Trick mounted their horses again.

"I think we'll wait a bit before we follow you," Uncle Mando said to Letty. "We don't want to eat your dust."

Letty and Clarice drove away from the old adobe house. The four men on horseback waited patiently for the dust on the dirt road to settle.

Five minutes later, Eduardo said, "What was that? Did you hear that?"

"Yeah, I heard something. Sounded like a gunshot," said Uncle Mando. Will and Trick nodded their heads in agreement.

All four fell silent and listened.

The unmistakable sound of a second shot rang out.

"Yeah. The first one was a rifle. This last one sounded more like a handgun," said Trick.

"Shit!" Will said. "Someone is after Letty again." He started forward.

"Wait just a minute," Uncle Mando said. "We don't want to ride into a gun battle and get shot. Follow me."

Mando led the three young men through the mesquite trees uphill from where they heard the shots coming and toward the sounds.

Another shot from a rifle sounded.

Mando pointed to where it was coming from.

"Look!" said Will.

Ahead a short distance and below them on the hillside, they could see Clarice's car half-way off the road. The front windshield had a bullet hole in it and cracks in the glass radiated outward from the hole. Both doors on the passenger side were open. The men could see Letty and Clarice crouched low on the ground. Clarice was shielded by a back tire and Letty was shielded by a front tire.

Just at that moment, Letty carefully crept upward to take a look. Another shot rang out and a bullet sped past her head. Letty responded immediately. She shot toward the direction where the bullets seemed to be coming. She ducked back behind the car door.

Letty's heart was hammering in her chest. She knew she was going to have to get a better idea of where the shooter was hiding if she had any chance of hitting him. She would run out of ammo with no results if she couldn't isolate and target the person shooting at her. What really scared her was knowing that the shooter could circle around to where he would have an open shot. She and Clarice would be sitting ducks. She had to put an end to this. But how?

"Here's what we're going to do," Mando said. "Eduardo, you and I will move around on foot above Letty. Will, you and Trick dismount and tie the horses someplace safe and out of sight. We don't want them getting spooked and running off, or worse, getting shot. Both of you! Stay low!"

Mando and Eduardo dismounted, retrieved their .22 rifles, and handed their reins to Will. "Follow me," Mando said to Eduardo.

The two carefully moved through the mesquite grove, one tree at a time for cover, until Mando said, "Stay here, Eduardo. You are just above the car now. Watch over there through the trees and see if you can see exactly where the shots are coming from. If he fires again, shoot in his direction. I'll do the same. That way he'll know there's more than one of us. We can distract him from going after Letty."

Mando crawled on the ground past Eduardo's hiding place to find cover about twenty feet away behind a big mesquite tree. Both men waited.

Another shot ran out. This time the bullet hit the roof of Clarice's car.

"Now!" Mando called out to Eduardo.

Both men shouldered their rifles and fired toward where the bullet had come from.

Letty jerked her head up. She could see both her uncle Mando and her brother Eduardo slipping back behind their hiding places again. Her heart was still hammering. This wasn't over. But the odds had turned in her favor.

Letty glanced at Clarice. The young woman was pale. "Clarice, stay down," she said in a low voice. Letty couldn't let anything happen to Clarice, not only for her sake but for Will's.

Neither Letty nor Clarice could see Will.

Will was uphill out of sight helping Trick tie the horses to mesquite trees. Will turned to Trick and said, "I'd like to borrow your .22 if I could."

"Sure." Trick pulled the rifle from its scabbard and handed it to Will.

"Is it loaded?"

"Yep, ready to shoot," was the response.

Will moved forward to where he could see Letty and Clarice. He dropped to the ground and began crawling toward them.

"Letty, I can see Will. He's coming to us."

"Oh my god. Why is he doing that? He doesn't have enough cover."

Clarice was fighting tears. She waved her hands and shook her head toward Will and silently mouthed, "No!" He ignored her.

Will pulled himself into a crouch with the rifle ready to shoot. He carefully scanned the trees beyond Letty and Clarice. Another shot rang out. Will directed his gaze to a particular mesquite tree. He paused. The rifle rested comfortably against his right shoulder. Will pulled the trigger. His bullet hit the mesquite tree trunk. Bark flew off. The bullet was too close for comfort for the shooter who was hiding behind the tree. For a brief moment, a man dressed in dark clothes became visible. He ran toward the shelter of another tree trunk. He was visible just long enough for Letty to get a look at him. He disappeared again.

Letty had a sinking feeling. It was a man, the same man who had attacked her at the river. Tall and thin, very blond hair, very pale.

After finding another tree trunk to hide behind, the shooter fired his gun again. This time the bullet was aimed at Will. It hit the ground only three feet from his body. Will ducked down even lower and rolled back behind a big creosote bush and a pile of brush under it.

Immediately Eduardo and Uncle Mando fired again toward the shooter. At the same time, Letty rose halfway from behind the car and fired. This time she had a much better idea of where the shooter was hiding because Will had drawn him out.

Suddenly they heard Will yelp. They looked his way and saw him rolling on the ground quickly to his left. A big rattlesnake struck at the same instant. Its head and fangs landed in the dirt exactly where

Will had been three seconds earlier. Will scurried on his belly to hide behind a downed mesquite tree trunk.

"Oh god, I can't take much more of this," Clarice whispered.

Another shot rang out. This time it was Mando. His bullet smashed into the snake's head before it could coil and strike at Will a second time.

Everything suddenly became very quiet.

Letty realized that the gunman had stopped shooting. She heard an engine roar. She couldn't see a vehicle because of all the mesquite foliage but a cloud of dust appeared on the road below. Whoever had been shooting at them realized that four against one shooting at him from different directions was too much to overcome. He fled.

Uncle Mando was the first to come out from behind his tree.

"Letty, you two okay?"

"Yeah, we're okay."

By this time Will was running toward Clarice. She held her arms open and he scooped her up.

"Will! Will! Will!" she cried, clinging to him.

"It's okay. Everything is okay." He tried to comfort her.

"You scared the shit out of us," Letty said to Will. "Do you know how close that bullet got to you? And that rattlesnake?"

"Yeah, pretty close. The rattler was under that brush. I didn't mean to disturb him."

Clarice looked at Will with tears in her eyes. "Will, you could have been killed twice! A bullet and a snake bite!"

Will grinned. "I can't be killed twice. Usually people can only be killed once."

Clarice was stifling sobs. "I don't know what I would do if I saw you die in front of me."

Will pulled her closer.

"Will, you did a good job of bringing the shooter out in the open. You are a very good shot," Letty said. "Next time I'd like to see you take better cover. Okay?"

Will nodded seriously.

"Good shot, Uncle Mando," Letty called out. "You nailed that rattler."

Letty felt a profound sense of relief. She had so much adrenaline in her that she felt light-headed and much to her surprise, no pain at all. Impulsive Will and his old-fashioned, very serious, very circumspect brother Eduardo were just about complete opposites. She loved them both, but she was quite sure that Will was the one who could make her crazy. She realized suddenly that she was hurting now all over, especially in her rib cage.

Trick Navarro had appeared now with the horses. He had a big grin on his face.

"The Antones and the Ramones really know how to put on a show. This is the most excitement I've had in ages. Who the hell was that shooting at you?"

"I don't know," Letty said. "But I'm going to find out. I'm tired of this. Getting beat up and having my home invaded and now getting shot at is not okay."

"Did anyone see the vehicle?" Eduardo asked.

"No, but whoever it is will go right past my mom's house. Let's go ask her if she saw anyone."

The men mounted their horses and Letty and Clarice started down the hillside again, going very slowly. This time the men on horseback went first.

"Sorry, Clarice, about your car getting shot up. I'll pay for a new windshield and any other damages."

"Letty, don't worry about the car. Right now, I just want you to catch that piece of shit and put him away. That's all I can think about." Clarice stared at the road and drove carefully. "And I want Will to be more careful. Less impulsive, I mean. Seriously. I mean *seriously.*"

Letty smiled. "Good luck with that."

Clarice was frowning but when she looked at Letty, she had to smile "Your brother is so charming. He's irresistible. Do you suppose he'll ever grow up?"

"Probably not," said Letty. "We'll just have to try to keep him more or less corralled and hope for the best."

Clarice nodded solemnly.

They were quiet for a bit and then Letty said, "If your parents find out about this this, if they knew you were caught in the middle of a shootout on an Indian reservation in Arizona, they'd pull you out of here and force you to go home to Boston so fast your head would spin."

"Hmmmm…." Clarice frowned. "They can try that, but it's not going to work. They don't need to know about this. It will just worry them for nothing. And 'home' is here for me. I won't leave. I won't leave Will and I won't leave southern Arizona." Her lips were pressed into a thin line.

When they came to the Navarro homes, Trick tied his horse to a fence and went inside one of the houses. He came out soon after.

"Mom says a man in a dark red pickup came by driving pretty fast. She thinks maybe the truck was a Toyota. She said he was a white guy, fairly young. Maybe in his late twenties or early thirties. She can't come out now because she's taking care of my sister's baby and it's feeding time."

"That's the man who beat me up at the river," Letty said. She turned to the others. "Can we postpone more activities here? I'm worn out and my rib is starting to hurt. I think I need to go home and rest." She turned to Trick Navarro. "Thank you so much. We'll keep you informed."

"Please do, Letty. Will always told me that his big sister is someone to be reckoned with. I believe it now. I'd like to know how all this turns out. As for me, I'll say goodbye to you all. I'm going to visit with my mom for a while and maybe play with my baby nephew."

Trick Navarro turned to Will. "Hey, Ramone, how about if that pretty girlfriend of yours gives me a goodbye kiss?"

Will just shook his head no and pulled Clarice closer.

Trick laughed uproariously.

They said their goodbyes and headed for the paved road to Sells. Letty got out of the car and patted the shoulders of Mando and Eduardo.

"Sorry I can't hug you," Letty told them. "My rib is hurting again. But I want to say thank you. You both made a big difference today. That man could very well have killed me and Clarice if you hadn't been there. My only advice to you both, especially you, Uncle Mando, is this. Don't let the U.S. Army know about that rattler. The Army will try to recruit you as a sniper."

Mando nodded. "We'll keep it to ourselves. Take care of yourself, Letty."

"Yeah, Letty. Be careful. Please be careful. I want you to come to our wedding when Esperanza and I get married," Eduardo added.

***

"Clarice, will you please drive us home? I need to make a call, too." Clarice took the wheel, Letty sat in the passenger seat and Will stretched out in the backseat.

Letty dialed Jessica Cameron.

"Hey, are you in your office? I've got two important documents for you. A will and a deed."

"Oh my god!" Jessica came close to squealing. "Oh, you found them! I've been thinking about this. I think this is going to be a super fun case to work on. If we win, and I do believe we have a chance, the settlement will be a big one. I'll get creds with my boss, too."

"But mostly you like it because you think it will be fun, right?" Letty chucked.

"Okay. I admit it. I love these cases that have some real fight in them. I can be competitive."

"Oh, is that right? I had no idea."

Both women laughed.

"Just lucky for those guys on the NBA teams that you aren't six feet nine and know how to shoot a basketball. You'd be all over those big guys."

"True. I love basketball. I'd take on Serena, too, if I knew how to play tennis. But law is what I do. By the way, Maggie called. We made a verbal agreement, then a written one. I'm officially her attorney now. I will represent her in the lawsuit to prove that she is the owner of that land."

"We'll be at your office within the hour."

On the way back to Tucson, Will fell asleep in the back seat.

"Letty, I want to talk to you about Will."

"Okay. What's up?"

"He's in school but he doesn't seem to know what he wants to major in."

"Isn't that true for you, too?"

"Not exactly. I've been thinking about becoming an investigative journalist. I like to write and I'm good at it. I write fast, too. God knows these days we need journalists to dig out the real facts. I'm thinking about specializing in environmental issues. I like my science courses. I think people need to know what's going on with a number of environmental topics, like water resources, disappearing wildlife and climate change."

"You'll be great at that." And she would, Letty thought to herself. Smart, persistent and charming. Clarice would succeed at anything she chose to do.

"About Will, a week or so ago a bunch of little kids came in the bike shop. The teacher was showing them different kinds of work you can go into. The kids were all minority kids, mainly Pasqua Yaqui, Tohono O'odham, Chicano, and a few black kids. The black kids were from Somali refugee families."

"So Will was the resident Indian working at the bike shop?"

"Yeah, something like that. The teacher wants the kids to know they have options other than a day laborer or dealing drugs."

Letty nodded. Lack of options was always a problem for poor, dark-skinned kids.

"Will showed them around, showed them how he repairs bikes, told them how he likes to race bikes, how he's a college student, and all that stuff. They loved him. They asked a lot of questions. They were all over him, too. Some of them were literally climbing on him."

"That must have been funny to watch. How did Will react?"

"He loved it!! I mean *loved* it! He loved them. He was beaming when they left."

"So what are you thinking?"

"Elementary education. He'd make a great elementary school teacher. What do you think?"

"I think you're on to something. Talk to him about it. He could do some volunteer work with kids, too. Go into the schools and do some demos."

"Great idea about visiting the schools. Will is going to love that."

They fell silent.

Letty marveled at her brother and his girlfriend. It had been only an hour or so earlier that they'd all been ducking bullets. Now Will was snoozing and Clarice was cooking up a plan for Will to spend time with elementary students. Letty, on the other hand, was trying her best to push away an unwelcomed memory of a sniper on the roof of an Iraqi house who had shot at her and the others soldiers in her unit. The fear returned in a flash. She imagined she could smell the cordite from the bomb explosion that had rocked the neighborhood only a few minutes earlier. She forced herself back to the present. She began studying the landscape as their car neared Tucson.

By the time they entered the western outskirts of the city, late afternoon light cast shadows on the Santa Catalina Mountains to the north. Letty directed Clarice to the multistory building downtown that housed Jessica's law offices.

"I think we'd better come with you," Clarice said as she parked her car in the parking garage. "Will, wake up. We're going be Letty's bodyguards." She had noticed that Letty was scanning the parked cars looking for a dark red pickup.

"I'm awake. That's awesome. I've never been a bodyguard before."

The three went up the elevator to the twenty-first floor. Jessica came out to meet them. Letty introduced Will and Clarice.

Letty handed the box of documents to Jessica, who was clearly elated.

"Oh, I am so excited about this!" She held the box close to her chest. "This goes in the locked vault right away."

"I'll get the memoir to you tomorrow. We've had a difficult afternoon and I'm worn out." Letty explained briefly about the gun battle they'd been engaged in on the reservation.

"Outrageous!" Jessica said. "Letty, now I'm going to be really worried about you. This man sounds like a psychopath."

"I recognize that this guy is out to get me. I'm dealing with it. So don't worry. See you tomorrow."

Letty, Clarice and Will headed home.

CHAPTER 17

SERI was sitting in the backyard with the dogs when they arrived home. Millie and Teddy greeted Letty, Clarice and Will enthusiastically, as if the humans had been gone for months. They both ran around in little circles wagging their tails and crying with joy.

"Good doggies! Happy to see you, too." Letty said, petting both dogs.

Letty sank into a chair next to Seri.

"I have a story to tell you." She recounted the events of the afternoon, of finding the documents, the gun battle and sighting of the white-haired young man driving a dark red pickup.

Seri shook her head from side to side, frowning.

"I'm sorry I ever called you, Letty. I had no idea your life would be put in danger. I should have just let the cops handle this. My curiosity got the better of me."

Letty smiled. "That's what I like about you, Seri. Your curiosity makes you a lot like me. You're my good friend. On top of all that, don't forget you're going to pay me!"

"It would be great for Maggie's family to get something out of this, but not if you end up hurt or dead." Seri couldn't shake her feelings of guilt and worry.

"Stop it, Seri. Everything is going to be okay."

Seri sighed. "Okay. Okay. Well, I guess we're going to have to play this out. What do you suggest we do next?"

"I'll come to your library tomorrow and we'll interview more of the people on your list. Did you get a chance to finish the last chapter of the memoir?"

Letty didn't tell Seri that she didn't want Seri keeping the memoir overnight. Letty was concerned that Seri's condo might be successfully broken into and that Seri would be attacked. If that happened, Seri would be on her own with no protection. Letty had Will, Clarice and two very alert dogs that considered it their job to take care of their alpha.

"Yes, I finished it. Fascinating story. This man Drago was amazing. I wish I could meet a man like that. I wish I could hear Rosa sing."

By this time, Clarice and Will had prepared a quick meal. All four of them ate together. Then Seri said her goodbyes and left for home.

"See you in the morning, PI Letty Valdez."

"See you in the morning, Dr. Seri Durand. And stop worrying about me. I'll be okay. If that man tries anything again, I'll just put a couple of bullets in his knee caps. That should slow him down."

Seri snorted and shut the door behind her.

"What will we do about your car, Clarice?"

"You've got enough to worry about, Letty. I'll take care of it. I'm thinking about renting a car while my car is being repaired. How about a Jaguar, Will? Want to go driving around town in a Jag?"

"Definitely!" Will kissed her. "You have awesome ideas."

Letty said good night to them and went to her room. She decided to retrieve her email first before getting some well-deserved rest. There was an email from Detective Ramirez at the Tucson Police Department. The email read: "How about this dude, Letty? His name is Nathaniel Johnson. He has a long arrest record, mainly assault and battery. Some drug dealing, too. He's been in and out of jail. Let me know if he is your pendejo. We could get him on aggravated assault, which has at least a fifteen-year mandatory jail sentence."

Letty opened the attachment. It was a color mug shot of the tall, thin, white-haired man who had assaulted her at the river and who had shot at her on the reservation. His icy blue, dead-looking eyes stared back at her. She guessed him to be in his early or mid-thirties.

She immediately forwarded the email and mug shot to Seri and to Jessica with a brief explanatory note. Next, she responded to Ramirez. She told him about the gun battle on the reservation earlier in the day and the documents she found there. She ended her email with, "Thanks so much, Alejandro. This is definitely my pendejo. Keep an eye out for him. He's up to no good."

To the mug shot on her computer screen, Letty said, "Very good. Nice to meet you, Mr. Johnson. Better watch out. I'm coming for you now."

Letty collapsed into bed.

***

The next morning, Letty asked Clarice for some pain meds to carry her through the day. She had given up arguing with Clarice about managing her meds herself. Some doctor had convinced Clarice that she was in charge of pill distribution. Letty decided not to make an issue of it. Clarice did so much for her family and she clearly loved Will with all her heart. Clarice had everyone's best interest at heart. If Clarice wanted to be the Queen of Pills, Letty was willing to go along with her, for a while anyway.

"Don't give me anything that will make me dopey. I need to be able to think well. Maybe just some Ibuprofen."

"The doctor gave you some prescription-strength ibuprofen. It shouldn't affect your cognition at all. Consider eating something and then taking the pills if you think your stomach will get upset."

Letty ate a banana, took her pills and then headed downtown to Jessica's office. Again, she scanned parked cars to make sure there was no dark red pickup anywhere nearby. She continued to have her gun in a holster around her waist.

Once in the law offices, Letty handed the memoir over to Jessica, who had a big grin on her face.

"You should read it. It's actually quite interesting."

"Oh, you better believe I'll read it. Today, in fact. I'm doing some research now on the legal context in this time period, 1890s and

1900. Arizona was still a territory, not a state yet. That will help me figure out how those people got away with taking ownership of the land."

"I think you'll find it to be pretty simple. This man William House just stole it."

"I'm really looking forward to working on this, Letty. Thank you for bringing me into the loop. The cases you bring me are always legally challenging and a lot of fun."

"Sure. By the way, what happened with that guy you asked me to do a background check on?"

"We went out to dinner. He's pleasant enough to be around, but he's pretty full of himself. He has a lot of money, a lot of women chasing him, and he's used to getting what he wants. Now he wants me."

"Wants you? You mean sexually?"

"Yeah, that. He made a kind of not-very-subtle proposition. You know? The "come up to my place and look at my etchings" old-fashioned way of saying it? Also, he wants me to sign an exclusive contract with him. I told him that a contract with my firm is the way we do things, but he wants it to be personal between the two of us. I'm not sure why. I think there's something else going on."

"I could look into it, but right now I'm too tied up just trying to stay alive. I need to catch this guy Johnson first and put him out of business."

"Yes, your priorities are right. I can put Bill West off for a while. No problem."

They parted company and Letty headed to the University of Arizona campus.

Seri greeted her and took Letty to her office.

"We're lucky because several of the people on your list are in the library today. Also, I printed out that mug shot you sent me of Nathaniel Johnson. I thought we could ask if anyone knows him."

"Okay. Who shall we call first?"

"Let's try Dr. McIntosh. He's been here the longest this morning so he's most likely to leave first for a break."

They asked the professor to come to Seri's office.

After some preliminary chitchat designed to make the professor feel more comfortable, Letty asked, "What kind of research are you doing, professor?"

"I'm interested in the Native American tribes and the gaming industry in this part of Arizona. I put in time on the Navajo reservation. Here, I've spent part of my time at your library and part of my time at the Pasqua Yaqui headquarters or in Sells out at the Tohono O'odham reservation. And I've put time in at the casinos and other gaming establishments. I'm interested specifically in the economic impact that the gaming industry has had on the tribes. What, if any, have been the benefits of the industry? Who benefits the most? What about any negative outcomes, like increased crime? Or drug use? Once I finish here, I'll be going up to the Phoenix area. I'll be there longer because there's more going on in the gaming industry due to the higher population. I hope to leave by spring and go home before it gets too hot in Phoenix."

"Have you found anything useful in our collection?" Seri asked.

"Yes, some useful documents, primarily on the economic development of the tribes. But there's not that much available. Actually that's very good for me because when I publish, I'll be one of the very few researching and writing on this subject."

"Have you heard any rumors about new documents in the collection that might be of interest to you?"

Dr. McIntosh's eyebrows went up. "No. Are there new documents? I'd certainly like to know about them if you have something new."

Seri responded reassuringly, "Not in your area. We're just trying to track down some rumors about nineteenth-century historical events."

"Oh, well. That doesn't apply to me at all. I'm a mid-to-late twentieth-century guy. Too bad."

Just before he left her office, Seri handed the full-page mug shot photo to McIntosh. "Have you ever seen this man?"

McIntosh shook his head. "Nope. Never seen him before."

Letty and Seri thanked him and he left.

"I believe him," said Seri.

"Me, too. I also don't think he recognized the man in the photo. It's often possible to tell if someone is lying by subtle changes in the face and eyes. I didn't see any sign of that in McIntosh."

"I agree."

"Next up?"

Seri called in Wu Ming Ju, a researcher from Shanghai. As the case with so many Chinese citizens, she read and wrote English quite well. But her listening comprehension and conversational abilities needed some work. They were able to determine that she was working on the history of the Chinese in northern Mexico and the southwestern United States, but primarily in the mid-nineteenth century before the Chinese Exclusion Act of 1882. She also did not recognize the man in the mug shot.

A researcher from the China Institute in New York City, Kenneth Yang, was next. He also was researching the Chinese in Sonora and Arizona, as was Ms. Wu. He said they knew each other and shared information. Yang was an American child of Chinese immigrants. He was bilingual in English and Mandarin so he was able to easily communicate both with Ms. Wu and his fellow Americans. His interest had an economic focus because the nineteenth-century Chinese involvement in the mining industry and the railroad was emphasized. He had not heard of any rumors about new materials. He did not know the man in the mug shot.

For the rest of the morning, they spoke with several graduate students. Seri and Letty took a lunch break and went to one of the Student Union restaurants to eat. Letty's jaw was hurting a lot less, but she still stuck to soft foods. She considered that overall that she was feeling much better. The pain was not as intense and seemed to be mainly focused in the area of her lower right rib.

"Are you getting frustrated?" Seri asked Letty.

"Yes. We don't seem to be getting anywhere. We know the name and a bit about the man who attacked me. But we don't know if he was the intruder in the library who killed your colleague, why he would be here, or what he was looking for. We don't know for sure that the attacks on me have anything to do with this murder. We need to know more about him. I'll start researching and see what I can find. You do the same."

Seri nodded her head.

"After that shootout on the rez, it's pretty clear he's after me," Letty continued. I don't want anyone to get hurt. I have to stop him before he attacks again."

They returned to the library and began to interview students. This time they asked undergraduate students who were not on their list but who came into the library frequently. They showed the photo to everyone, but no one knew the man.

At mid-afternoon, Letty began thinking they had run out of options when Dr. Miller came into the library. He was the first professor that Letty and Seri had interviewed a few days earlier.

"Dr. Miller, you graciously talked to us the other day, but I was wondering if you have time to look at a photo," Seri asked as he was unpacking his briefcase.

"Sure."

"Want to come into my office for just a minute?"

Seri turned and both Letty and Dr. Miller followed her into her office.

Seri handed him the mug shot and Letty watched his reaction closely.

Dr. Miller's eyes widened. "Has he been here?"

"You know this man?" Seri asked.

"Yeah. This is Dr. Alexander Kent's son. Kent is a full professor in our department specializing in Arizona history, especially Tucson's history."

Letty felt her heart begin to beat faster. Finally a connection!

Seri closed the door of her office so that no one in the reading room could hear them talking to each other.

"This man's name is Nathanial Johnson," she said. "This is a police mug shot."

"I don't know about that. I can't explain why he has a different surname. But he's definitely Kent's son. He's something of a troublemaker."

Seri prompted him, "Tell us as much as you can."

"He's an adult, maybe around thirty years old. Grew up in Tucson. I've just heard talk about him, mainly from the department staff members. Really, I mean the secretaries. I met him at a dinner a few years ago but I didn't really interact with him. We just exchanged greetings when introduced. But you can't forget him. He has very distinctive pale coloring and these penetrating blue eyes. Apparently he started getting into trouble as early as middle school. Then came minor offenses like fighting, drunk driving and small-scale drug dealing. I don't know what all. Dr. Kent sent him off to those rich-kid "adjustment" camps and special schools and to a series of therapists. Nothing worked. The boy had an attraction to crime. He's something of a sociopath apparently. I heard that Kent and his son finally parted ways. The son refused to have anything to do with his dad any more when his dad stopped paying all the bills. I heard that the son left Tucson. I haven't seen or heard of him for at least a couple of years. It's sad really. Kent's wife died a few years ago. Nathaniel is his only child. Now Kent is aging and on his own. In fact, he went into hospice just recently. He has terminal cancer and isn't expected to live much longer."

"Anything else?"

"No, that's all. Is Nathaniel the one that police think broke in here and killed the other librarian?"

"No, no. We're not saying that at all! So please don't spread that around. We just got this photo in connection with another matter, an assault to be specific," Seri explained.

"That's right," Letty added. "He assaulted a woman we both know and we're trying to help the police catch him so that he doesn't go after her again." Letty didn't look at Seri. She was afraid both of them would start laughing at the 'woman we both know' description.

Miller shook his head in agreement. "Assault sounds like something he would do. I won't mention this. But keep me informed. Okay? I'm curious about what is going on here."

"Certainly," said Letty. No way, she thought to herself. Her guess was that Miller liked to gossip in the department's front office with the secretaries more than the average guy. She didn't want to take any chance that word would get back to Johnson of their interest in him.

"We really appreciate your input, Dr. Miller," said Seri as she moved to open the office door.

Miller left. Seri and Letty exchanged big smiles. They both felt a real sense of elation. Finally a clue and a connection.

"I'm going home now," Letty said. "I'm going to go online and see what I can find out about this guy Johnson and his father."

"I'll do the same here. Talk to you soon."

***

Letty rested at home briefly but did not fall asleep. She wanted to be able to sleep at night and a late afternoon nap might disturb that. Also, she was just too excited. If she and Seri could figure out where Nathaniel Johnson was hiding out, they could tell the police and get him arrested. He had, after all, assaulted her at the river and she had been taken to the hospital. Assault charges alone would put him out of commission for a while. But that would only be the first step. Maybe next, they could figure out if he was the one who intruded in the library and why. And she hoped, learn if he was the one who murdered Stacey Frederick.

She spent a couple of hours tracking Johnson down on every database open to her. She found a long list of arrests and convictions. He had no apparent reason to find something in the library. If he had been there, perhaps he had been hired by someone to find a particular item. If so, who was that someone and what was he or she looking for?

She also spent some time looking at Professor Kent's personal history. He had quite a few publications, primarily in nineteenth-century Tucson history. He seemed to be very well-regarded.

In the late evening, Letty called Seri just to make sure she was safe.

"Everything is fine, Letty. My security system is state of the art. I did find additional photos of the Kent family with father, mother and son Nathaniel. But he was just a boy then. He had this angry, pouting look on his face in every photo. Looks to me like he grew into an angry and violent person."

"Yes, if I can figure out where he is, my first step will be to call Detective Ramirez and get him arrested. I'll call you tomorrow, Seri."

"Take care, Letty. I think we may be coming to the end here."

"Yes. I certainly hope so."

They said goodnight.

***

Letty slept well that night. She didn't miss at all what she had come to think of as her "Iraq Dreams." She wondered if those pills Clarice was giving her had something to do with that, but Clarice insisted she was getting only extra-strength generic pain killers. Maybe the lack of dreams was linked to the demands of the case she was working on and the possibility that she was coming close to finding a man who was trying to kill her.

Early the next morning, she checked her phone and found a voice message from Seri.

"Hi, Letty. I'm going to the library to open up. I'll be there a little before eight. Come by and I'll take you out to breakfast. We can talk strategy."

Letty called her back but there was no answer.

A few minutes later, her phone buzzed.

"Hello."

"Miss Valdez, the private investigator?"

"That's right. I'm Letty Valdez."

"I have your friend Seri Durand. Seri who works at the library."

Letty's body went rigid.

"Who is this?"

"You've got something I need."

"What?"

"You have a memoir, a deed, and a will. I want them. All of them."

Letty was scarcely able to breath.

"I don't have them."

"You better have them or your friend Seri is going to be in a world of trouble."

Letty thought fast.

"So you want to trade those documents for my friend?"

"That's right."

"I have to know she's safe before I hand over anything."

"Of course. That would only be fair."

Letty didn't believe him for a second. She knew who the man was on the other end of the connection. Tall, thin, almost white hair, pale skin, cold blue eyes, and now a voice high and reedy and full of the willingness to do violence. She would have to figure out how to get Seri away from him before he could enjoy hurting her.

"I want to talk to her."

"You'll get your chance. For now, I want you to bring the papers to an old abandoned house off Alamo Wash just south of the Rillito River. I'll send GPS coordinates. Meet me there at one this afternoon. Don't be late. And if you bring the cops with you, you won't see your friend again." He ended the call.

Oh my god. Letty sank into a chair and tried to think. She had until the early afternoon to come up with a plan.

CHAPTER 18

LETTY felt sick to her stomach. The aching in her back and jaw had returned. The pain in the cracked rib and separated cartilage had never left. She had been attacked by this low life less than a week ago. She was still recuperating from the injuries. Then he followed her out to the reservation and shot at her, her brothers and uncle, and Clarice, too. He was a madman determined to get those documents and willing to kill anyone who got in the way. Now he had her friend Seri Durand who only wanted to know why there had been a trespasser in her library and why a colleague had been murdered.

Letty knew she wasn't in any shape to fight this guy. Despite what she said to Will and Clarice, the pain still came and went. She wasn't even sure she was thinking straight. It was early morning and already she felt like taking a nap. And she had no bargaining chips. The documents – the memoir, the will, and the deed – were all locked up in a vault in Jessica Cameron's law office.

Letty called Zhou. "I'm coming over to your house," she said before he could say anything more than hello.

When she arrived, Zhou led her to the backyard where Jade was sitting in a rocking chair nursing the new baby boy. Now Letty knew what people were talking about when they said a woman "glowed." Letty had never seen anyone look as happy as Jade. Except maybe Zhou. He glowed, too.

"Jade, he's beautiful. He looks like both of you. I'd like to hold him sometime but I can tell he's busy right now. Filling his tummy comes first. Plus I'm still getting over that beating I had a few days ago."

"Not to worry, Letty. We'll be here when you are ready to hold Ben Ben. Would you like some coffee? I think Jefe will be happy to get you some."

"Actually I'm here to talk to Zhou. I want to get his ideas about a case I'm working on."

Zhou's eyebrows went up in surprise. "Come with me, Letty. We go to the kitchen. I will make coffee for you." Letty followed him to the kitchen.

"Zhou, I need your advice. But first I want to make clear that I am not asking you to go with me to solve this problem or to get involved in any way at all. Okay?"

"Okay. What is the problem?"

"Remember that tall, skinny guy at the river? The one you chased off?"

Zhou nodded his head. "His gong fu not so good."

"He tried to kill me. I mean he tried to shoot me with his gun."

Zhou breathed in sharply and frowned.

Letty reviewed the events that happened on the reservation, her retrieval of the documents, the shootout, and her uncle and her brothers with their .22 rifles.

"Good. Good uncle. Good brothers," he said.

"Now he has abducted our friend Seri."

"No! Our Seri, the librarian who reads to us?"

"Yes, and he wants me to bring the documents to him. He claims he will let her go if I do that. I don't believe him. But I'm in no shape to fight him or to sneak up on him or anything else."

"You need help. I help you."

"No! You must stay with your family now. I can't call on you every time there's a dangerous situation. That's not fair to you or Jade or your new son. Anyway, that wouldn't work. Don't forget. He knows you. He'll recognize you. He told me to not bring any cops. He said if I call the cops, we'll never see Seri again. What will he do if he sees you? I'm sure he considers you more dangerous than any cop. No, you can't get involved."

Zhou fell silent and stared into space.

Finally he looked at Letty and said firmly, "You must call the police."

Letty sighed. "They are unpredictable."

"They are trained. And you have no other choice. You are correct that he will know me. That will cause a problem. Police are your best choice now."

"Okay. I came to the same conclusion but I just wanted to run this by you first to make sure I'm doing the right thing. I'm going to call Detective Ramirez and see if he can help me. I can't do this by myself. Especially now. I can't protect myself much less Seri. I'm still hurting too much." She rose and put the coffee cup down. "Say goodbye to Jade. I'll call you later when this is resolved."

"Who is Detective Ramirez?"

"Alejandro Ramirez, head of the robbery section at TPD. He and I have been cooperating. I'm going to go home now and call him."

"Be careful, Letty."

"I will. I'll call you when this is all over."

***

Back home, Letty called Detective Ramirez. He answered immediately.

"Is someone shooting at you today? I got this great image in my head of the boys in your family riding around on horseback and shooting their rifles at gringo cowboys. It would make a great movie. The Indians would win for a change!" He laughed uproariously.

"I don't have anybody shooting at me right this minute, but very possibly I will this afternoon."

"Well, that doesn't sound too good. What's happening?"

"I need help." Letty first told Ramirez how she and Seri had identified Nathaniel Johnson as the son of a University of Arizona professor and a descendant of William House, the man who had stolen the land that should have belonged to Drago and Rosa. She reminded him that Johnson was the one who attacked and beat her at the river and also the man seen shooting at her near Topawa on the reservation.

"And don't forget he's a murder suspect, too. We want to bring him in for questioning," Ramirez reminded her.

"Everything got worse this morning. Johnson called me early and told me he abducted Seri. He wants me to bring the documents I found. He says if I call the cops, I'll never see her again. My bet is that he'll try to eliminate me, too, once he gets what he wants. He sounded desperate. Arrogant and desperate."

"You did the right thing calling me. We've dealt with situations like this before. I'll start putting together a team. Did he tell you where to go and when?"

"Johnson wants me to meet him at an abandoned house just off Alamo Wash. I have the GPS coordinates. I'll send them to you. I'll go first to the Rillito River then walk up Alamo Wash until I find the trail to the old house."

"I have a general idea of where that is. Our team can blend in fairly easily there. We'll just become joggers and dog walkers. Yeah, I'll call the K-9 team and have one of them bring over a dog to walk. The only difference is that this dog will be perfectly capable of ripping off Johnson's arm." He chuckled. "You may be disappointed to know that your best friend De Luca won't be there."

"No?"

"He's taken a vacation. Gone home to New York City. My guess is that he'll try to get his old job back while he's there."

"Oh, I'm so disappointed not to see him again."

Ramirez laughed.

Letty became serious. "What should I do? I'm not in very good shape. I'm still hurting all over from when those guys beat me up."

"You will go up the trail carrying something like a backpack or whatever that supposedly has the documents in it. If he's watching you, you don't want to alert him to the fact that there are cops there. In other words, don't stare at the people you pass or try to figure out if they are police officers. Just act like you are worried and you are trying to get to the rendezvous point as soon as possible."

"I *am* worried."

"Of course you are," Ramirez said comfortingly. "But you are not handling this alone. Let us do our job. We'll be there for you. If I let anything bad happen to you, I'll have to answer to my cousin Adelita."

***

Letty retrieved the metal box that she had found in the old adobe house on the reservation, the box that had originally held the will and deed and some of Drago's writings. She removed the Chinese scrolls and then stuffed the metal box into a backpack. Then she sat on the back porch and worried. Millie and Teddy sat quietly and watched her. She decided that they both had an amazing ability to know what she was feeling. Man's best friend, she thought. Woman's best friend, too. She found their presence comforting.

Around twelve thirty, Letty headed for the Rillito River. She parked her car and went out onto the dirt trail that would lead away from the river and up Alamo Wash.

A light breeze brought in thick clouds that covered the normally sunny skies of southern Arizona. Along with the clouds came the threat of a late-autumn rain. Now and later in the winter, the rainfall would be what the Navajos called a "female rain." Soft, slow, soaking, nurturing rain, not the wild and violent 'male rains' of the summer monsoon.

Letty considered the clouds to be a good sign. It meant the temperature had dropped, maybe as low as into the upper fifties. That meant that the police officers would be wearing jackets or fleece hoodies. It would be easier to hide a gun and harder to see that gun. Letty put on a loose jacket herself. Her handgun was in its holster at the small of her back.

She headed along the dirt trail and came to where a bridge crossed the river. Then she turned right to go up the narrow, hard-packed dirt trail that followed Alamo Wash. Both on the main paved biking-walking trail and on the dirt-packed trail, she saw plenty of walkers, joggers, and bicyclists. Some of them were very likely cops. There were two men in particular who had on gray-colored hoodies. They walked together at a moderate pace, saying almost nothing to each other. She made an effort not to stare at them. But she could see that one of them was Alejandro Ramirez.

Letty passed a woman with a dog on a leash. The dog was a Malinois, sometimes called a Belgian shepherd. This breed was often chosen for K-9 units. The dog was big, a male dog. He eyed her curiously as they passed each other. The woman didn't look at Letty.

Then there was that lone man, also in a fleece jacket and wearing an Arizona Wildcats baseball cap. He had on sunglasses, too. He would have been impossible for most people to identify. But Letty knew the man was Zhou. She didn't know how she knew but she knew. He was following her at a distance. Good grief, Letty thought to herself. He thinks he's my big brother. He's here to protect me. She desperately hoped that nothing bad happened to him.

She came to the place where the trail ended. She noticed a man and woman, both dressed in thick sweaters and big straw hats, sitting on a concrete bench where the trail ended. They were drinking coffee from paper cups. Both glanced at her but said nothing. Alamo Wash continued on but without a trail to follow it further. A bridge and road crossed the wash at that point. She turned left and went to the other side of Alamo Wash and walked back down the wash for a short way. Then she turned onto a very narrow trail that led up away from the wash.

Ahead Letty could see an old bungalow-style home with a pitched roof and a covered porch that went all the way around the house. It was designed to increase air ventilation and to prevent direct sun and accompanying heat from entering the house. She guessed that it was at least a hundred years old, maybe more. The house appeared to be in poor condition and without inhabitants. She glanced into the wooded area around the house with its mesquite and blue palo verde trees, creosote brushes and other undergrowth. She couldn't see anyone but she felt certain there was someone there. She hoped it was Ramirez and his pals.

Letty went onto the porch and approached the door. She stopped and listened. The door was open only a crack. She pushed the door open and waited. A voice came out of the dim interior.

"Come in, Miss Valdez. I've been waiting for you."

Letty entered and saw Nathaniel Johnson leaning against a wall out of sight of the windows.

"Where's Seri?"

"She's safe. For the time being, anyway. Did you bring my papers?"

"I'm not sure what you are looking for. Are you the man who broke into the library and killed the librarian?"

"I didn't break in. I found a better route to gain entrance. As far as Stacey, that was her fault."

"You are blaming her for your stabbing her to death?"

"She wouldn't shut up. She was going to call the cops."

"How do you know her name?"

"I used to play in a band with Stacey's boyfriend Axel. She was always such a tight ass. Finding her in the library early that morning made me realize she hadn't changed at all. She wouldn't help me find what I was looking for."

"What exactly were you looking for?"

"Stacey happened to mention to Axel that the library was supposed to get some new boxes of donations. That included a memoir from someone my family knew who lived a long time ago."

"Why do you want this memoir?"

"You ask a lot of questions."

"Look. You attacked me and beat me up at the river. Then you were out there on the reservation hiding behind a tree and shooting at me."

"I didn't know you were going to have a posse with you." He was close to whining.

"You were trying to kill me. Why?"

"I tagged you at the river to get rid of you. I was afraid you would find the papers first. Then it occurred to me that it would be easier on me if you found the papers for me."

"Why are these papers so important to you? When I looked at them, they were in Chinese."

"Now, come on, Valdez. You know what I want. There's a deed and a will that leaves the land to that chink and the dago woman. My grandpa told me all about it."

Letty realized that Nathaniel Johnson was very proud of himself. He thought he was very clever and wanted everyone in the world to think the same, especially private investigator Letty Valdez.

"Your grandpa?" Letty wanted him to keep talking. Maybe she could get him to tell her where Seri was.

"Yes, he told me all about how those invaders came into Arizona. They didn't belong here. The Chinese should have been banned forever from this country. That dago bitch. The dagos brought the Mafia to Tucson."

Letty would have laughed but she knew her laughter would infuriate his racist rant. Mafia in Tucson? Los Zetas or Sinoloa Cartel maybe, but not the Mafia. She thought about the dignified Chinese man from Suzhou who read T'ang dynasty poetry to his beloved, his beloved who sang in the cathedral with the voice of an angel.

"I don't understand. What did your grandpa tell you?"

He sighed impatiently. "You really don't know what this is about?"

"Tell me. I'd like to know why I got beat up."

Johnson snorted. "You deserved it. You get way above yourself, bitch."

Why above myself? Letty asked herself. Too Mexican, too Indian? Too female?

"Your grandpa?"

"He told me that the land was supposed to go to the chink and his family. But my great-great-grandpa fixed everything. He made sure that that our family got the land. That was as it should be. The Americans are the ones who made this country great. Not the Mexicans and certainly not those invaders."

"So everyone in your family has known about the land deal all this time?"

"Yes, and we knew that there might be papers out there some-where that would cause trouble."

"You mean that might prove your family didn't own the land at all?"

Johnson frowned with annoyance. "It should have been ours. It *is* ours," he said vehemently.

"You all knew about it and no one in your family did anything about this all these years?"

"Why should we? My dad is the only one who felt guilty about it. He considered it a kind of theft. But he always felt guilty about everything. And he didn't do anything about it, either."

"So why now?"

"Stacey told me that a memoir had surfaced that was written by Pete Arianos. Everyone in my family knew about Arianos. That's why I went to the library, to get the memoir and see if it had anything in it that would have a bad impact on my deal."

"Your deal?"

Johnson stood up straight and stuck his chest out.

"I have a buyer. My dad is going to die soon. I'm the only one left and when he's gone, I'll inherit everything. I already have someone ready to pay me big bucks for that land. As soon as I inherit it, I'll sell it to him immediately. Then I'm out of here."

Something was off, Letty thought. Johnson didn't really need the deed and will. He could just sell the land to the buyer as is. Let the buyer deal with the consequences if the will and deed ever surfaced and if a lawsuit was filed. But what if the buyer knew about the land's history? He may have demanded of Johnson that the will and deed and the memoir, too, be secured before the deal could go through.

"Who is your buyer?"

"None of your business. Hand over those papers!"

"I want Seri."

"She's not here."

"You don't get the papers then."

Johnson pulled a gun from his jacket and pointed it at her. "You don't understand what's going on here. You have no choice. Hand over the papers."

He was too far away from her to try to disarm him. Letty wasn't sure she could do that anyway, considering the beat-up shape she was in. She pulled her backpack off her back and unzipped it. She removed the metal box from the backpack. Then she rose and threw the box at Johnson with as much force as she could manage.

He stepped back to avoid the box hitting him. The gun wobbled in his hand.

Letty dropped to the floor and pulled her handgun from its holster at the back of her waist.

At that instant, Alejandro Ramirez and another cop burst through the door and ran into the room. Both had their guns pointed at Johnson.

"Drop the gun!" they both yelled at once.

Johnson lifted his gun and got off one shot that went wild. The cops were faster. Ramirez shot Johnson in the shoulder. Blood spurted out just as Johnson's gun went skittering across the floor. He fell back, groaning in pain.

"Good shot, Alejandro!" Letty pulled herself up.

"You okay?"

"Yeah. Thank you for saving my life. When Johnson figured out that I really didn't have anything for him, I'm certain he would have shot me."

"Yes, you would have been of no use to him then. He would have gone elsewhere and figured out pretty quickly that the lawyer had all the documents. We couldn't take a chance on Johnson simply deciding that you had become an obstacle." Alejandro grinned at her. "I sent a man out here right after I talked to you and before Johnson arrived. My guy set up a video camera so we've got everything on tape." He pointed to a camera up high on the wall in a dark corner.

"I'm glad you didn't kill him. I'm hoping he'll tell us where Seri is."

"We'll get him medical care and then question him. I sent an officer to his dad's house but we didn't find anyone there."

"Need anything from me?"

"Not right now."

"Then I'm going to try to find Seri."

CHAPTER 19

Letty walked out of the old house and stood on the porch. She focused on the sandy wash below, but her thoughts were on Seri. Zhou came to stand beside Letty.

"Zhou, I thought I saw you on the trail. What are you doing here?"

"Yes, I passed you on the trail. I came to assist you. When it is crime, we are partners. In family matters, you are my xiao mèimei. My little sister."

Letty smiled briefly then said in a low voice. "Zhou, I don't know how to find Seri."

"I will help you."

"Did you hear what Johnson said?"

"Yes, I was in the police van watching the video."

"I think there's something else going on."

"Yes. I suspect the buyer knows about this situation and is using Johnson to do his…"

"…do his dirty work. I agree. If it comes out that the land was originally obtained in a fraudulent manner, then the new buyer won't have clear ownership. It's highly likely that the buyer is already committed to some kind of real estate development planned for that piece of land. He's probably afraid of losing money if this doesn't go through."

"Buyer stays in the shadow. No one knows who he is. Johnson does the dirty work and finds the documents. But Johnson is stupid and makes many mistakes."

"Like killing a woman in the library."

"Yes, and beating and trying to shoot and kill Letty Valdez. Big mistake."

"Let's go visit Johnson's father, the professor. He's in hospice. Maybe he can tell us something."

"I will go with you. Also, I now have a communication channel with the Tucson police. I had a conversation with your friend Ramirez while we were waiting to take our places near here. I told him about my work as a Beijing Detective Inspector and then work for Interpol. He has invited me to do some gong fu demonstrations for his police officers. I will enjoy this, I think."

"That's good. And this will be a safe thing for you to do. Jade and Ben Ben need you now."

"Let's walk to the bench where the bridge crosses the road. You sit. I will bring your pickup."

"Okay." It took the two of them only about five minutes to get to the bench at the head of the Alamo Wash trail. She couldn't help but notice that Zhou was watching her carefully, ready to catch her if she fell. He was acting like the Big Brother that he claimed to be. She was profoundly grateful for his friendship.

While she waited for Zhou to bring her pickup, Letty started thinking about what Johnson might have done with Seri. She admitted to herself that she was really scared. Johnson had already demonstrated a willingness to kill. Seri could already be dead, her body dumped in the desert somewhere. But Letty held out hope that he had hidden Seri to use as leverage against her so he could get those documents.

Zhou returned in about ten minutes. "Can you drive me to my car then drive yourself home? You are not in too much pain?"

"No. I'm okay. I can drive. Zhou, if I were Johnson, I think I would have tied her up and hidden her somewhere that it wouldn't be really easy to find her, somewhere that her calls for help wouldn't be heard. I want to go to my house and get Teddy. That dog is trained to sniff out people buried in rubble after an earthquake. If we can figure out places he might have taken her, maybe Teddy can sniff her out."

"Good idea."

Letty paused and said, "Thank you, Zhou. You're a stand-up guy."

"Meiyou wenti."

"Your words sound like 'mayo win-tee.' Is that something to eat with mayonnaise on it?"

He grinned. "No, 'meiyou wenti' means 'no problem' in Mandarin. Jade says 'meiyou wenti' often now. I think it is her favorite saying. I am her Mandarin teacher. She is my Spanish teacher. Your thoughts of mayonnaise may suggest you are hungry?"

"Yes. I was so upset about Seri that I forgot to eat this morning. I'll get something at my house. But first…"

She pulled out her phone and called Ramirez. "Did your officers find Seri at Kent's house?" There was a pause. "Okay. Zhou and I are going to look for her." She disconnected before Ramirez could say anything.

"Okay, Zhou. Let's go find Seri."

***

Letty went to her house and Zhou followed her there. After greeting the dogs, Letty made sandwiches and coffee for both of them. They ate and Letty took more pain pills.

"Oh, that feels better. I needed to eat. Now I'm going to see if I can find the hospice where Johnson's father is located."

Letty made a couple of calls and found Professor Kent fairly quickly. She made a final call and asked for an appointment to see the professor.

"I drive my car. You ride with me and rest," Zhou said.

Twenty minutes later, they arrived at a hospice care center on the far east side of Tucson. Saguaros were scattered around the neighborhood and along the ridges of the looming Rincon Mountains a short distance to the east. There was little traffic and the early afternoon was quiet.

Letty and Zhou found Professor Kent sitting in a wheel chair near a large window. He had a book in his hands. He smiled when she approached.

"Hello, Professor. My name is Letty Valdez. This is my friend Zhou LiangWei."

"Nice to meet you, young lady, and you, too, sir. I don't get too many visitors these days."

"Professor, I'm a private investigator looking for a friend of mine, Seri Durand. I'm not going to sugarcoat this. Your son abducted her. He's been arrested but he won't tell us where she is. I'm hoping you can give me some ideas of where to find her."

Professor Kent groaned and shook his head. "That boy. He was trouble from the day he was born. I honestly think he's wired together all wrong. No moral compass. I tried everything I could to put him on a straight path, but he wouldn't have it. After his mother died, he took her name and disappeared. I didn't hear from him again until he needed help getting out of a Texas jail."

"So that's how Nathaniel got the name Johnson?"

"Yes, that's his mother's maiden name. What's this all about?"

Letty sighed, not knowing where to begin.

Zhou spoke softly, "Your son attempts to sell your land to someone."

"But there's a cloud over the ownership of the land," Letty added.

"Oh, you mean that acreage over on the west side of the Santa Cruz. It's been a burden to me all my life. I never knew what to do about it. If the family stories are correct, my great-grandfather essentially stole it from some immigrants. There was a lot of that going on back then. The Mexicans often didn't have proof of ownership that would be accepted by American courts. As far as that acreage is concerned, we were never sure who owned it originally, who inherited it, or any certainty about my great-grandfather's role. So what has happened? Did you find ownership documents?"

"Yes, I have the original deed indicating that Señor Bernardo Dominguez had legal ownership. I also now have his will passing the land on to the twin sons of two immigrants, Drago Shaw and his wife Rosa Arianos Shaw. I also have the memoir that Pete Arianos wrote explaining how the land was stolen by William House."

"My grandfather Nate House explained all this to me when I was young, and later, I told my son about it. So now there is proof that the stories were true."

"You son took it upon himself to find a buyer for the land. But the buyer insisted that Nathaniel acquire the documents first and give them to the buyer to destroy. Otherwise, the buyer refused to complete the deal or to give your son any money."

Zhou added, "We do not know how the buyer knows about the history of the land and why he made these demands on your son. Why not just buy the land from your son?"

"That's because of me. West approached me first and made an offer to buy the land. I told West about the land's history and how there could potentially be a lawsuit contesting his ownership if those documents were ever found."

"West?" Letty tried to mask the surprise in her voice.

"Yes, Bill West. He's from the Seattle area."

Letty thought immediately of her lawyer friend Jessica Cameron. She took a deep breath. West wasn't interested in Jessica personally. He probably knew about her connection to Letty. He wanted to tie Jessica up to work for him in case a lawsuit was filed contesting his ownership of the land. He likely didn't know that Jessica had already agreed to represent Maggie and her family as the descendants of Drago and Rosa.

"I was hired by Seri Durand to investigate this case. Your son attempted to intimidate me off the case when he realized that I had found the documents proving your family does not own the land. He abducted Seri to force me to give him the documents." Letty left out the part about how Nathaniel Johnson had tried to kill her or that he was man who killed Stacey Frederick. She had no desire to distress this sick old man even more.

"I'm so sorry. So very sorry. After his mother died, I just sort of gave up on Nathaniel."

"We're hoping you might have some ideas about where Nathaniel may have hidden my friend Seri."

The old professor sighed. "Well, there are places on my property where he could have hidden her. The house itself has a lot of nooks and crannies. There's an old barn at the back of the property where we had a couple of horses when my wife was alive. It's not visible from the house or the road. You just follow a trail from the east side of the house over a little hill and you'll find it quickly enough. There's a shed next to the barn as well."

"Where is your property?"

"Up in the Foothills of the Santa Catalina Mountains. Go all the way north on Swan up and up and up. Turn east onto Palacio and go past the homes on this road. They will all be big estate-like places. Go past all that. Eventually you'll find a very rough dirt road that leads back to my place. My wife and I lived closer to the university when I was teaching, but after I retired, we moved up there. It's very isolated and quiet. Wonderful views of the Santa Rita Mountains to the south. The sunsets to the west are stunning."

Letty stood. "Professor, thank you so much. I think you've helped us a lot. I'm sorry to bring you such sad news about your son."

"It's okay, young lady. I'm accustomed to it now. The news about Nathaniel has always been bad. I'm just glad his mother isn't here to learn how far he has gone down the wrong path."

Zhou reached out and shook the man's hand. "I hope you find peace in your life."

"Thank you for your kind words."

Letty and Zhou said their goodbyes.

"Zhou, let's find something of Seri's that will have her scent, and then we'll take Teddy and search for her."

***

Zhou called Jade and asked her if Seri had left anything at their house. Jade searched and found nothing.

So Letty and Zhou went to her house.

"Seri spent the night here and took care of the dogs when we went out to the reservation," Letty explained to Zhou. "Maybe we'll find something."

And they did. Behind the living room couch, Letty found a cash-mere sweater that Seri often wore while at work in the library which was, according to Seri, excessively air conditioned. The soft, blue sweater had been worn many times and, no doubt, had absorbed Seri's scent. The sweater should be a good item to get a sniffer dog going.

"This is enough?" Zhou asked.

"Dogs have a sense of smell that is up to one hundred thousand times better than a human's."

"Wah!"

"We have six million smell receptors and the dogs have three hundred million. On top of that, Teddy has been trained to sniff out people so he'll know what we want. Even if we can't find her, Teddy will be able to find her – if she's there. My greatest fear, Zhou, is that Johnson may have killed her and dumped her body in the desert." That was the first time Letty had expressed out loud what she feared the most, that Seri was already dead.

She called Teddy and he came, tail wagging. "Come on, big boy. Let's go find our friend."

Letty left a note on the kitchen table telling Will and Clarice that she had Teddy and to please give Millie a little extra attention. Letty, Zhou and Teddy the black lab piled into Zhou's sedan. Teddy sat in the back seat.

The trip up into the Foothills took about twenty minutes. They climbed and climbed until the houses became fewer and the saguaros increased in number. They turned onto the street mentioned by Professor Kent. He was right. The word "estate" was a better de-scription for the huge houses on acreages, complete with swimming pools and decks of solar panels on the roofs.

Finally they passed the last house and came to a barely-detectable, very rough dirt road that went higher up the mountain. Letty knew that the road would be impassable during monsoon storms, but Kent and his wife likely hadn't cared. They were there for the solitude, not a daily commute.

Zhou parked in front of Kent's house.

C.J. SHANE

"Let's see if we can find that barn," Letty said. "Alejandro said they had already searched the house. If we don't find her in the barn, we can look in the house for hidden rooms or passageways that the cops may have missed."

Letty put Teddy on a leash and the three started walking up the rise. Around them, the desert dominated. They were high enough to be in a different ecosystem. From the lower Sonoran Desert floor, they had passed into upper Sonoran oak woodland and chaparral. There were more native oaks and the manzanita, a small tree with a deep red trunk and branches. Bird life abounded. It must have been a wonderful place to live, Letty thought to herself. So peaceful.

The old barn came into sight. Letty and Zhou walked into its interior. Broken planks in the walls and a roof with multiple openings let in plenty of light. There appeared to be no loft.

Letty pulled Seri's sweater from her backpack. She unleashed Teddy.

"Sit, Teddy."

Teddy sat and looked at Letty expectantly.

She held the sweater to his nose. He sniffed it repeatedly. His whiskers twitched as he breathed in.

"Find, Teddy. Find!"

Teddy took off to his right, making a detailed olfactory investigation of everything he encountered. He circled from the right toward the back of the barn then around to the left. He sniffed his way into and out of the horse stalls.

Teddy then disappeared into a narrow space next to the outer wall of the barn and behind a rough pile of old hay. He reappeared momentarily and looked at Letty. Then he sat facing the narrow space behind the hay pile. He looked into the space then he looked at Letty again.

"That's his alert!" Letty ran toward the pile and squeezed behind it. Zhou was right behind her. Her heart was pounding. Seri was her best friend. She couldn't bear thinking of Seri gone forever.

There appeared to be nothing but with Teddy alert behind her, Letty knew there had to be something there. She quickly spotted the edges of a trap door in the floor next to the wall. She brushed away hay and pulled open the door to find a small space with dirt walls below the surface of the barn floor. The room appeared to be lined with old wooden shelving units. The trap door would have been very easy to miss were it not for Teddy.

Letty lowered herself and peered into the carved-out room.

There was Seri in the shadows! Her arms and legs were bound and she was tied by a rope around her waist to a large metal ring in the wall. Her mouth was duct taped. She looked up at Letty. She squirmed and made muffled sounds. Her eyes held a combined look of intense relief and absolute fury.

Letty bent down. "Seri, the best way to remove this duct tape is really fast. Okay?"

Seri nodded, and Letty ripped the duct tape from her face in one quick movement.

"That mother fucking son of a bitch," Seri spit her words. "I'm going to kill him right now. Where the fuck is he?"

Zhou's eyebrows went up. Never had he heard Seri the librarian speak like this.

"Sorry, Seri. You can't kill him now. He was arrested this afternoon and at this moment, he's in the Pima County Jail."

"Well, all right!" Seri huffed as Letty unbound her arms and legs and took the rope from her waist.

"Are you okay?"

"Yes," Seri said in a voice best described as cosmically annoyed. "He knocked me around a little but didn't hurt me all that much. He talked constantly, bragging about himself the whole time. He's the one who killed Stacey. He hates you, Letty. He thinks you are in his way and preventing him from doing some kind of big deal that will make him a lot of money."

"Well, the cops have him and he's not going anywhere. What do you need right now, Seri?"

"I need to pee super bad and I could use some water."

"Zhou, do you mind going back to the car and getting one of those bottles of water for Seri?"

Zhou nodded and headed for the car. Seri took the opportunity to pee in the hay.

"Should we take you to the hospital?"

"No, I'm not hurt really. I'm just really pissed off." She paused. "Actually, the best thing I could do now is to go home and take a hot shower, eat something and then take a nap."

"We can arrange that," Letty said. She was so relieved that Seri was unhurt.

Zhou returned with a large bottle of water. Seri grabbed it and guzzled it down.

"Thanks!" she said, wiping her mouth.

Letty turned to the black lab standing next to her. "As for you, Teddy Boy," Letty said with affection. "You get a big dog biscuit when we get back to the car, and you'll get some cooked chicken meat with no bones for supper this evening."

Teddy wagged his tail. The Alpha was happy so that meant Teddy was happy.

***

When she arrived home after dropping Seri off, Letty called Jessica Cameron.

"I suggest you call Bill West and invite him to meet with you, me and Seri Durand. Tell him to come at nine. Seri and I will be there at 8:30 a.m. and we'll fill you in."

The three women met as scheduled at Jessica's office the next morning.

Letty and Seri told Jessica what they had learned. They also told her about Nathaniel Johnson's arrest. Then Letty told Jessica about Bill West.

"That son-of-a-bitch," was Jessica's response.

Letty felt strong sympathy for Jessica. West had indicated a personal interest in her. What a disappointment. His intentions most certainly were not honorable.

West showed up a few minutes later. He seemed surprised to find Letty and Seri there. Letty had the strong feeling that he knew who they were even before Jessica introduced them.

"Look, Bill. This is what we've found out," Jessica said in a harsh and irritated voice. "I've learned that you have a real estate deal going on the west side with a large development group. Your part was to secure the ownership of a five-acre plot of land for which you were to get a substantial fee and a share of the income on the real estate investment. So you approached the owner, Professor Kent, and made him an offer. He told you then about the land ownership's murky past and that a time might come in which the land would revert to the legitimate owners. That means the deed wasn't really clear, and you potentially could lose a lot of money. Am I right so far?"

"I always want to make sure the land I purchase has a clear title," West said noncommittally.

"So you bypassed Kent and went to his psycho son. Nathaniel Johnson told us that his job was to get the documents that would verify the Dominguez-then-Shaw legal ownership. He said he was supposed to give those documents to you. He told us that your plan was to destroy those documents."

"You can't prove that."

"No, we don't know exactly what your agreement was with him, but we know what he told us. It appears that you were willing to commit a felony."

"You can't prove that."

"Furthermore, you tried to compromise me in both a professional and personal way. Professionally, you wanted me to represent you if all this came out in court. And if I chose to represent the true owner of the land, Maggie Graham, then my position would be undermined if it came out that I was sleeping with you at the same time I was representing her. Isn't that right?"

West shrugged his shoulders. "You don't have anything on me." He stood. "I'm leaving. You can call my lawyer in Seattle if need be. You and I won't have any further contact."

"Don't bet on that, Bill West. Before you go," Jessica said firmly, "be informed that I am, indeed, formally representing Maggie Graham and her family. She is the direct descendant of Drago Shaw and Rosa Arianos Shaw. I have the memoir, the deed, and the will to prove her claim to ownership. You and I will definitely see each other again – in court."

She turned away. West looked at her, consternation on his face. He said nothing and walked out.

All three women sat quietly, not speaking, for long minutes. Finally, Jessica broke the silence.

"I wish I could find a man like Drago."

"Me, too," Seri sighed. "Highly intelligent, dignified, honorable, brave, compassionate and caring."

"I bet he was really sexy, too." Jessica sighed.

"Yep, sexy as hell," Seri sighed, too.

Letty chuckled. "Maybe you two need to hire me to find you two very handsome Chinese mandarin revolutionaries. Maybe twin brothers?"

"You're hired!" Jessica and Seri said at the same time.

CHAPTER 20

NOVEMBER came. Now it was time for El Tour de Tucson, one of the biggest bicycling events in America. This year nearly ten thousand bicyclists had registered to participate in the race. For days, Letty was very careful driving around in the city because the streets had so many more bicyclists enjoying the late autumn sun and dry weather.

Participants could choose different length tours. The longest was 106 miles, and that's the tour that Clarice and Will chose. They registered for El Tour. For two weeks in advance, that's all they could talk about.

Letty went out to stand along the tour route and cheer them on. She considered bicycling a lifesaver for her brother. When she returned from Iraq and started her new career in private investigation, she discovered that her baby brother was involved with a gang on the reservation. Also his health had deteriorated and he was getting perilously close to becoming a diabetic. He wasn't doing his school work, and he had a major attitude problem.

So Letty brought Will home to live with her in Tucson. For a while, he would barely speak to her. On a whim, she took him to watch El Tour. That's all it took. A few weeks later, he had his own bike, a part-time job in a bike shop, progress toward a healthier body, and an improved attitude at school and with Letty. Then he met Clarice who was into biking, too. It was bicycling and young love all the way after that. Will became the happy person that Letty knew he was born to be.

December came, then the new year approached. Letty went out to the reservation to stay with her grandmother over the New Year's holiday weekend. The quiet of the desert was far preferable to an Iraq War vet like Letty than all the fireworks going off in the urban areas. She considered herself almost completely recovered from the beating that she had received at the hands of Nathaniel Johnson and his hired thugs. It had taken weeks, though. She scoffed at all those television programs that made getting beat up look like no big deal. The hero always jumped up and went back to his cop job or investigator's job the very next day. No way, she thought. The beating she received was not something that a person could get over in a few hours or a few days. Sometimes her cracked rib still hurt. She went back to work and tried to make sure that her jobs did not involve getting beat up or shot at. She did a lot of computer work as a result.

After El Tour, the next big sporting event was a weekend martial arts expo and competition. Jade encouraged Zhou to enter.

Zhou resisted. "I do gong fu for a serious purpose, not to win contests."

"People will see how good you are, and they will want to take your classes. You are new here and no one knows you. This will be a great chance to market yourself."

He frowned and wrinkled his nose at the idea of "marketing" himself, but he went along with Jade and signed up.

Jade set up a table at the entrance to the downtown indoor arena where the competition was held. Baby Ben Ben was strapped to her chest as she busied herself. She prepared flyers to hand out about Zhou and about his classes, starting from after-school martial arts for boys and girls, up to and including advanced classes for those who had been practicing for some time.

The key event came when Zhou was pitted against another Chinese man named Li Wei. Li was thirty years old and had come to Tucson to do postdoctoral research in astronomy. Gong fu was his serious hobby, the competition program said. Li was associated with a different martial arts school in Tucson. The organizers of the contest decided to pit Zhou and Li against each other.

The two men appeared at first to be more or less evenly matched in their competition. That meant that gong fu was much more than a hobby for Li. He was really good at it. The show-stopper came when Li began a move that involved jumping high into the air and then kicking the opponent in the face. Zhou saw this coming. He anticipated the high jump. Just as Li began his jump, Zhou took a few running steps and then fell onto his knees and slid across the floor. When Li had reached the highest point of his jump, Zhou leaned backwards and slid right under him. Li came down and turned to face Zhou who by this time was on his feet and back into fighting position. But Li, instead of continuing the fight, changed everything by a simple gesture. He put his right fist into his left palm. He bowed at the waist and said, "Laoshi." (Teacher). Li had recognized Zhou's superior abilities with that simple gesture.

At this display of gong fu mastery and Li's deference to Zhou, the crowd went wild. A standing ovation! Letty and Jade were in the crowd cheering along with everyone else.

"Oh, my god," Jade suddenly said to Letty. "I have to go back to my table. Everyone is going to want a flyer about Zhou and his school." Jade was right. She handed out all the flyers that evening. She hired Will and Clarice to develop a website for Zhou's school. In the coming weeks, Zhou acquired many new students. He acquired a friend in Li Wei as well. Jade was especially happy about that.

"Poor Zhou, surrounded by women all the time. He needs a guy friend. He should get a chance to speak his mother tongue, too."

Zhou smiled, "Perhaps I like being surrounded by women." Jade stuck her tongue out at him which made him laugh out loud.

Zhou and Li started meeting regularly in Zhou and Jade's backyard. They drank beer and conversed in Mandarin. Later when the class load became too heavy, Zhou hired Li to teach some of the classes. Li especially liked working with the elementary-age kids after school.

Letty eased back into physical activity slowly. Jogging was the easiest for her. Zhou encouraged her participation in his tai ji class and she did some yoga on her own. But Zhou said no to his advanced gong fu class.

"I am your teacher. I will tell you when you are ready. You are not ready. Your qi is not completely in balance."

Letty didn't argue with him. He had years of experience on her. Zhou told her once that he had been beaten so badly that he spent two weeks in the hospital in Glasgow. It was hard for Letty to imagine someone besting him like that. Zhou would know when she was ready to spar again. So she went to his advanced class and watched. She also figured there was no point in going up against five thousand years of Chinese culture. Qi? The word sounded like "chee" to Letty's ears. Whatever qi was, Zhou said hers was still not in balance. She would wait until he gave her the go-ahead.

Jessica Cameron's lawsuit against the Kent-House family on behalf of Maggie Graham was making its way through the courts. Given that Jessica had all the documentation, winning the suit was virtually assured. Then the real estate company, La Cienega Development Corporation, approached Jessica and suggested that Maggie sell the land directly to La Cienega, for a substantial fee, of course, as soon as she had clear title to the land.

Jessica explained the options to Maggie and her husband Brian. "The land currently has some old buildings on it. Most are empty. There are a few being rented out with only six-month leases. You can consider continuing to own the land and continuing to be a landlord. Or you can develop it yourself by getting a big loan to build on it. Or you can sell it outright to La Cienega. The developer is very eager to buy the land because they are losing money every day due to the delay in starting construction. The sooner they come to an agreement with you, the better off they are financially. They will pay even better if we can expedite the sale. I can help you set up a college fund for your children and a foundation if you want to fund good works."

Maggie said, "It's going to be *that* much money?"

Jessica smiled and nodded. "Yes. *That* much money."

Maggie and Brian chose to sell to La Cienega. "Kind of ironic, don't you think?" Maggie said. "Uncle Pete had some sweet memories about the original cienega along the Santa Cruz River. Those days are all gone."

Thanks to Jessica, Bill West had gone home to Seattle in shame. His willingness to bend the law in Tucson meant more than just the loss of a one-time deal. A stellar reputation was important in his business and he'd lost that.

Alejandro Ramirez called Letty and told her that the blood on the vent in the library was a DNA match with Nathaniel Johnson's blood. That, plus his inadvertent video confession meant that Nathaniel would be enjoying the hospitality of the Arizona Department of Corrections for a long, long time.

In the intervening months, Letty had gone to visit Professor Kent quite frequently. His heart was in the right place, Letty decided, and he didn't deserve to be so alone at the end of his life. She usually took a book for him to read. Clarice often made recommendations. Sometimes she would take Clarice along, too. While she was there, the professor asked Letty questions about her life, what it was like to be a Chicana-Native American, what Iraq was like, what her family was like, and what it was like to be a private investigator. She told him it was hard to talk about herself, and especially about Iraq, but she did the best she could.

Seri made a photocopy of Pete Arianos's memoir and Letty took it to Professor Kent. When Letty gave it to him, she said, "Dr. Durand suggests that you read the memoir as a historian, not as a member of the House family. She and I think you'll find it fascinating." Later, after Kent had read it, his only comment was, "The dragon got his much-deserved revenge."

Just a few days before he died, Letty took Maggie with her to visit the professor. Maggie told him about her family and her work as a teacher. She told him that her attorney Jessica Cameron was setting up a foundation from the sale of the land that the House family had stolen from her family over one hundred years earlier. Maggie told him that the money would go to fund programs for children all over the city. An arts program for kids from all ethnic and racial backgrounds and from all parts of the city, poor and rich, was on the agenda. Another project was to take kids out into the desert and into the Ponderosa pine forest on Mount Lemmon to learn about the natural world and to encourage an interest in the sciences.

Maggie said to the professor, "I want to thank you personally, Dr. Kent. You were the only honest person through the generations who was willing to recognize and speak the truth about the ownership of the land. You are the one who gets credit for all these kids' programs. You made it happen." Professor Kent's eyes filled with tears. Maggie hugged him goodbye at the end of their visit.

Ten days later, Letty attended Professor Kent's memorial service.

***

One morning in January, Letty leashed Teddy to go for a run. It was a cool morning so she wore a red fleece sweatshirt with an Arizona Wildcats logo on it. After about a half an hour of steady jogging, Letty and Teddy came to a quiet, tree-lined street that ended in a cul-de-sac. Around the circle were several office buildings. It was still early in the morning and there were no cars at all on the street or in the parking lots.

Letty decided to take a break when she heard her cell phone buzz. She unleased Teddy so he could have some time to run around and sniff things. Sniffing was every dog's favorite activity. She sat down on a bench and looked at an incoming text. What do you want for breakfast? Clarice asked in the text.

Letty glanced around to see what Teddy was doing. About twenty feet away, he was sitting and staring up into a eucalyptus tree. He looked back at Letty then up into the tree again.

Suddenly a cat scurried down the tree and ran off into the hedge next to a building. Teddy didn't move. He continued to look up into the tree then at Letty.

This was Teddy's alert signal.

Letty went to his side and looked up, too.

There was a man sitting on a thick branch about twelve feet off the ground.

Letty's mouth fell open. She looked down at Teddy. He was standing now, looking at the man, and wagging his tail.

"I came up here because this cat was howling and I thought it needed to be rescued," the man said sheepishly.

Letty closed her mouth.

"Yes, I saw it run off."

"Guess it didn't need rescuing after all." He had an engaging sort of lop-sided grin. He was good-looking. Letty noticed this right away.

"I'm coming down."

"Okay."

Well, she thought to herself, this should be interesting.

The man scrambled down the tree and came to stand in front of Letty. She could see that he was about her height and age, maybe a little older. Dark brown hair, a long straight nose, deep blue-green eyes, tanned, too, but definitely a white dude. Very inviting smile. Yes, quite an attractive man, Letty thought. He was dressed in jogging pants and a long-sleeve t-shirt. Teddy approached him and he leaned over to pet the dog.

"So….," the man said hesitantly, "How are you?"

"I'm fine."

"No, I mean really. How are you? How's your rib?"

"How do you know about my rib?"

"You don't remember me, do you?" He was smiling again. "Gosh, and I thought all this time that I was unforgettable."

Letty smiled at his joking, and then she frowned. "Sorry. Do I know you?"

"Try this," the man said. He pulled an Arizona Wildcats baseball hat from his back pocket, put some sunglasses on, and said, "Imagine me in jogging shorts."

Letty cocked her head. He did look familiar.

"Oh! I remember you! You were that jogger at the Rillito River who helped Zhou when I got beat up."

His grin widened as he pulled off the sunglasses. "That's right. So I *am* unforgettable. What a relief!"

Letty thought of Jean-Pierre Laurent. This guy was every bit as charming as Laurent but his self-deprecating humor made him seem a lot less arrogant and a lot more approachable.

"I think you went with me in the ambulance."

"Right again."

"Thank you very much. That was very kind of you."

"No problem. Do you remember the emergency room?"

Letty frowned again. "There's a lot I don't remember about that day. Did I go to the ER?"

"Yes. So you don't remember your attending physician?"

"No," Letty shook her head. She wished she could remember. "I just remember hurting and I passed out a couple of times. I was really muddled and I couldn't think straight at all. Then they gave me some pain meds and I got really sleepy after that. Why is the attending physician important?"

"I was your physician."

"Really? You're a doctor?"

"Dr. Dan Ennis. Or Dan Ennis, M.D. Or Doc Ennis. Or you can just call me Dan."

Definitely a charmer.

Letty's cell phone buzzed.

"Excuse me a minute. It's Clarice, my brother Will's girlfriend."

"How are Will and Clarice?" Dan Ennis asked.

Oh god. He's knows my brother and Clarice! What else does he know? Letty wondered.

She answered the call.

"Hi Clarice. Yes. Scrambled eggs and bacon sounds fine. And fruit. Will made biscuits? He's turning into a real cook." There was a pause then Letty said, "There's a man here who says he knows you. His name is Dr. Dan Ennis."

Clarice's squeal was so loud that it was audible to Ennis as well as to Letty.

"Oh, Dr. Ennis. He's so cool! Invite him to breakfast!"

"Okay. See you in a bit." Letty disconnected and turned to Dan Ennis. "They want you to come to breakfast at my house."

"Is that okay with you?"

"Yes. But don't mention that Teddy found you up in a tree. It's kind of a family joke. They will tease me unmercifully."

"Whatever you say. Let's go eat!"

Thank you from the Author:

Hello Reader! Thank you for reading *Dragon's Revenge*. I hope you enjoyed accompanying Letty Valdez and her friends and family on all their adventures. Please leave a review of this book on your favorite book vendor website. By leaving a review for others to read, you can make it much easier for mystery readers everywhere to find Letty. A new Letty Valdez Mystery is being written now. To learn more, go to www.cjshane.com, sign up for the newsletter, and feel free to email me with comments or questions.

About the Author:

C.J. Shane is a writer and visual artist based in Tucson, Arizona, U.S.A. She has traveled widely and lived and worked in Mexico, the People's Republic of China, and in the U.S. She has worked as a newspaper reporter, freelance writer, academic reference librarian, and ESL teacher. She is the author of eight nonfiction books. *Desert Jade: A Letty Valdez Mystery* (2017) was her first work of fiction. *Dragon's Revenge: A Letty Valdez Mystery* (2018) is her tenth book. See more at www.cjshane.com

CPSIA information can be obtained
at www.ICGtesting.com
Printed in the USA
FFHW010224171218
49890421-54489FF

9 780999 387443